REVOLT OF THE LAMEBREN

THE SUPER-DOME CHRONICLES

MANJIRI PRABHU

Readomania

Readomania Publishing
A division of Kurious Kind Media Private Limited
466, DDA SFS Apartments, Pocket 1, Sector 22, Dwarka,
New Delhi – 110077
books.readomania.com
email: support@readomania.com
Facebook: facebook.com/iamreadomania
Twitter: twitter.com/iamreadomania

First Published in 2018 by Readomania

ISBN: 978-93-858546-5-1

Typeset in Palatino Linotype by Shine Graphics

Printed in India by Thomson Press India Ltd.

Readomania

India has traditionally been the land of storytellers and a lot of us have an inherent skill of creating good plots, good stories and good narrations. With a little encouragement and support, many more authors will be widely read and attain a place in the sun. This is the essence of *Readomania*—an initiative that nurtures emerging stars of the literary world.

It would not be an exaggeration to say that *Readomania* is the talent hunt in fiction. It goes a step beyond by not just identifying the talent but also nurturing it and showcasing it to the world. In the process, we have created a powerhouse of content.

Readomania has four principle interest areas – traditional print publishing, online library of short stories and poetry, literary events and products.

The print publishing works towards delivering good quality content to the readers. We publish good authors in meaningful anthologies, novels and works of narrative non-fiction. Our books stand out for their perspectives, the plots, the language and most importantly their ability to enrich lives.

Take a break, read something nice, write something beautiful. Read our books or visit us at www.readomania.com and enjoy a whole new world of literature.

Dedicated to my sister Sonia Prabhu,
for her inherent strength, love and support...

Prologue

If I don't write it down, it could all get lost. I don't have a Memory Porter like the Altklugs that would accumulate memories in digital capsules, for generations to refer to. All I have is a pen and some paper, a very limited stock mind you, but still it has to suffice to create a record. Frankly, it isn't entirely my story to tell and I don't even know where to begin.... With a background of the Altklugs and the way they function? With a description of their Ace-world you have to see to believe? With the Altklugs themselves who are miniature representations of us, but with the brain power of hundreds of us? Or quite simply, a sketch of the deep Snarl, where I am right now, struggling with the imagery and the sheer existence of untouched wilderness, in abundance all around me?

I think I'll begin by sharing with you an extract from an article by Preceptor Amadeus, which appeared in the Altklug Thermiodical:

> It couldn't be called the end of civilisation yet, but if this continued, it soon could. I know that I may be penalised for saying this, or even sent to the Dissolution Crypt, but I will speak out. I am a Thinker and it is my duty to tell the world of Altklugs—to change their way of thinking.
>
> I was right there, in front of the Dissolution Crypt yesterday when the current batch of lamebren was sent in. To some they may look like over-sized, gangling creatures. But to me, they looked like frightened lamebren, pitiable, unaware of their fate and more of a danger to themselves than to the Altklugs. When the siren announced their departure, I was startled. I had no idea that the scene would stir such strong emotions within me. In bare minimum words: it felt wrong.
>
> Why can't the Governor approach this problem differently? In today's advanced age, when we have total control over

> emotions, maturity, nature, knowledge and technology, why should Age Progression be such a threat? Why should the lamebren be such a threat to our existence? Can't we experiment? And by that I do NOT mean using the lamebren in the labs to experiment on, as is the latest hot topic of debate! I mean, why can't we give the lamebren a chance?
>
> Please, this is my appeal to all the Altklugs—those with political clout and power as well as those with the civil consensus—please, awaken from your rigid models of mechanism and give nature a chance.

The day this article appeared in the Thermiodical, Preceptor Amadeus received a legal Thermiotice. He was accused of disrupting the peace of the Altklug Super-Dome and threatened with dire consequences if he continued such practices. I have no idea if Preceptor Amadeus paid heed to the warnings or showed any caution, however, I do know that while he was trying to create awareness of an important issue that could save many lives, there was someone else, just awakening to the need of self-preservation.

She was No. G23 and though known by that tag for all purposes, her name was Zinnia. A lamebirl in an Altklug world, Zinnia is unlike any other lamebirl I know. She is incomparable and in many ways remarkable. This is as much her story as that of every lamebren. I have gathered it all together, in bits and pieces. Sometimes I was a witness to the events while at most times I wasn't, but in all essence, this is definitely Zinnia's brave struggle for justice and survival of lamebren.

Map of the Altklug Super-Dome

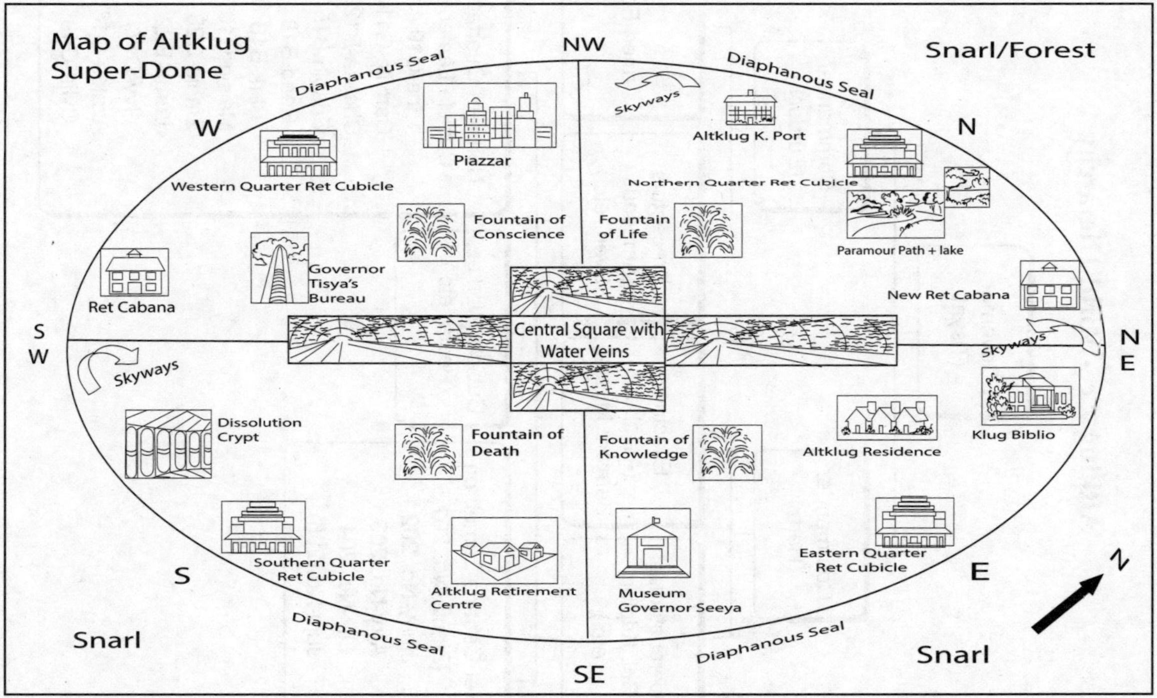

Altklug Ace-World Hierarchy

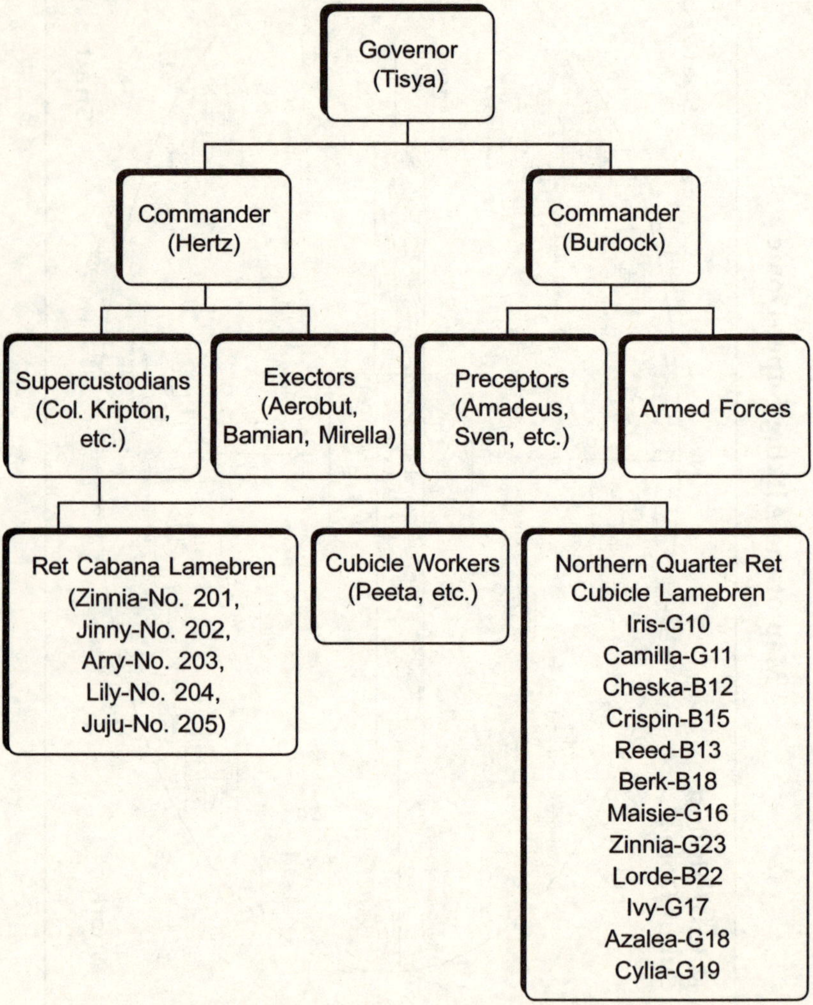

1

First, it was the siren just as the snowflakes began to fall uncharacteristically outside the window. And then later, it was the kiss.

The siren wailed and moaned, creeping into the tiniest slits of the Altklug Super-Dome, like a living, breathing entity. It swept into the Dome Piazzars, into the Job Galleries, into the Labs, through the Governor's Central Quarters and even through the Paramour Paths. Like a snake that had escaped from the Zoelter, slithering between the tiny snowflakes which had no business falling at that hour of the day and through the conscience. For some precious moments, the Altklugs paused in their work, fleetingly disturbed into a hush. Then they resumed their tasks, their minds already occupied with more pressing matters.

Inside the Ret Cabana, Zinnia couldn't bear it. The siren continued for a whole minute and it pierced her head like a painful laser beam. She clapped her hands over her ears to block the torturous sound but it filtered through her small fingers and wrapped around her brain, squeezing out all tolerance. A scream rose from her heart and she wanted to beg for the siren to be stopped. But it mourned obstinately, sucking at her insides, till the tears streamed down her cheeks.

When it finally ended, the echoes of the siren refused to ebb from her head. Outside, the snowflakes hugged the ground like a smooth, fluffy carpet, the fall concluding its journey as unpredictably as it had been activated.

Later in the day, it was the kiss. Zinnia felt as if she was swirled in mid-air and slammed into a dark pit of thorns.

She had felt dizzy, shaken and mentally bruised. And that was when she realised something was really wrong with her…with everything…

They were in Aerobut's class. It was a small room, white-washed and uncluttered, except for the glass cabinets which lined the front wall from top to bottom and the high-tech toys and miniature spinners that sat at the other end of the room. The latter were the favourites of the younger lamebren but Zinnia didn't quite fancy them. She was rather fascinated by the glass cabinets which stocked all kinds of amazing information in hundreds of tiny capsules. It was a thrilling world filled with answers to questions she couldn't even dream of. She longed to open them and pour over them, but they had been sternly requested to stay away from the cabinets. This wasn't because the capsules were for exclusive access of the Altklugs. But mainly because the lamebren were considered too ill-equipped to even operate them, let alone browse through them.

Aerobut referred to none of these capsules when he taught them. He interacted with them through the mini-K. Sensors attached to their desks. Even with the little lamebroy No. 205 or Juju as Zinnia liked to call him, who was quick to learn stuff. Zinnia was particularly good with her poems and recited them one after the other. Aerobut, sturdy-looking with a beard which Zinnia thought looked bizarre on such a short person, appeared pleased.

'Well done No. 201. You have a sharp mind for a lamebirl.'

'Thank you,' Zinnia replied, primly.

She was in awe of Aerobut because he was so exceptionally clever. He devoured capsule after capsule from the K. Bank and his face shone with all the information crammed in his head. Zinnia felt like a naïve fool at times.

He was only eleven, a year older than her and yet there wasn't anything he did not know.

'Sir…can I ask you something?' she ventured.

'Yes. But make it quick.'

'Sir, what was that sound we heard this morning? The creepy sound…'

'Oh that—that was the Siren of Departure,' the tutor replied, briefly.

'What is the Siren of Departure?'

Aerobut threw a quick look at the other lamebren bent over their mini-K. Sensors.

'It is a sign of termination. It is for the knowledge of the Altklugs that there have been some…departures from the Super-Dome,' Aerobut explained calmly.

'So, every time someone dies, the siren rings?'

Aerobut hesitated for the briefest moment. 'No, the siren rings only at the death of the lamebren.'

Zinnia stared at him, struggling with incomprehension. The others glanced up curiously.

'But…'

'That's quite enough No. 201. Now, please feed in the numbers up to ten thousand and rhyme the following words,' Aerobut continued, staring at the rest of the students.

The three lamebirls and the lone lamebroy hastily bent their heads over their K. Sensors and jotted down the dictation. In their black demi-legos and demi-sleevers, they looked earnest. Zinnia felt a rush of affection for them. They all tried so hard and yet she knew that they were not up to mark. That was the reason they were specially tutored and did not attend a proper K. Port like the rest of the Altklugs. She was aware of this, but there was so much more that was obscure and beyond her comprehension. Aerobut was very patient with them and

Zinnia was grateful for this. Unlike their Supercustodian, who regarded them with a strange scorn—as if they were creatures from another Super-Dome.

The Siren of Departure, even the name sounded ominous…

'Lamebirl No. 201, kindly report in my bureau at once,' a voice ordered in the air startling Zinnia out of her reverie. That was the Supercustodian, asking for her. Never had any lamebren been called away from the class before. What could it be? She rose uncertainly and glanced at Aerobut for permission.

'Sounds urgent…I think you had better go,' he said. A frown marred his face.

Zinnia knew that he was wondering too.

Although the voice had been amplified throughout the Ret Cabana, she couldn't gauge the direction of the sound. She never could. She had searched for long hours trying to figure out where the Sounders were placed but had come up with nothing. Asking her Cabana mates was totally useless as they were a bunch of frightened kids, much younger than her, who barely uttered a word. Finally, out of sheer curiosity, she had asked the Supercustodian, who had shaken her head at her curiosity and told her briefly that they were 'embedded in the walls' of the Ret Cabana and Zinnia had to be content with that.

The Supercustodian was seated in her revolving, glass chair and table, with a Thermionic paper in her hand. She was talking to the multi-D screen on the wall opposite her, 'Channel 24 and volume to 14'.

Instantly, channel 24 detached from the TV and appeared in multi-D before the Supercustodian. It was the news in a minute. The screen filled with several options: *Debate over the Paramour Path; Governor Tisya's new policies; Change in the day schedules of the Altklugs; Discussion of the outdated system of Cloning and its reintroduction and relevance in the present day; The miracles of a four-month Altklug and his ability to do brain-mapping…*

'Excuse me, Ma'am,' Zinnia interrupted hesitantly

'Lamebirl No. 201?' Supercustodian confirmed without glancing at her and still staring at the multi-D screen.

'Yes.' Zinnia nodded and thought to herself, *as if she didn't know. There were only five of them at the Ret Cabana.*

'Get your things together, you're leaving.'

'Leaving?' Zinnia was confused.

The warden, who was the same height as her but thrice her size, threw a sharp look in her direction, through her rim-less glasses.

'The spinner will be here at 1700 hours. You have sixty minutes to pack your belongings.'

'But, where am I going? And when will I return?'

'You're not coming back. And lamebirls don't ask questions. They just follow orders.'

'Not coming back? I don't understand…I don't want to leave. I…I can't dream of living anywhere else!' Zinnia exclaimed.

The Supercustodian passed her a stony look as if she was spouting expletives and not her concern.

'Dream? What do you mean? What kind of a word is that?'

Zinnia faltered. Dream…how had she come up with that word? How could she explain it to the Supercustodian? But mercifully, she didn't have to. Supercustodian had returned her gaze to the screen.

'Play me Governor Tisya's new policies!' she barked.

Instantly the image flickered and the Presenter made an appearance. She was so real, that Zinnia felt she could lean over and touch her physically. But of course it was only an image.

The presenter began pleasantly, 'Good Afternoon, this hour's news: This morning Governor Tisya had a meeting with her core group, Commander Hertz was also a part of this group. The Governor introduced her set of new policies in the meeting…'

Zinnia knew she was dismissed. It was useless asking the Supercustodian anything, anyway. She had always been a tight-lipped woman who had nothing to say to her.

With her heart thumping with anxiety, Zinnia returned to the classroom.

Aerobut glanced up at her, 'Well, what was so urgent?' he asked.

'I have been asked to pack. I…' she couldn't say more.

For a moment, Aerobut looked surprised. Then the look was replaced by a frown.

'Oh, I see. It's your turn perhaps. You should go and pack then.' His matter-of-fact tone was so dry, that for a moment Zinnia was perplexed.

'My turn? For what? Where am I going?' she asked, but her heart was beginning to slam in her chest.

'Well, you'll find out soon enough,' the Exector replied, airily.

All the four Cabana mates were now staring at Zinnia with wide eyes.

'But Sir…'

'Lamebirl No. 201, I don't think you should waste any time. Time is of utmost essence in the world. You may not understand it right now, but you will one day. I advise you to hasten to your room and get ready.'

'I will, Sir.'

Aerobut nodded and returned his attention to his palmtop. Zinnia threw a last look at the classroom. She felt snubbed—not even a goodbye from Aerobut or a mention of her hard work, or the fact that he would miss her in class. After all she had been a good student, hadn't she? But his indifference pinched some corner of her heart. She was just another lamebirl to him, whatever that meant.

On an impulse, she turned to him. 'Sir, one day, when I *do* understand, will you sit down and listen to me? Will you ask me what I felt when I left the Ret Cabana forever?'

Aerobut raised startled eyes to her, 'Certainly.'

'Thank you and...goodbye.'

She climbed the staircase to the room she had shared with the others. A bag had been placed on her bed for her belongings, not that there was much—a set of clothes that was given to her every year and a furry dog, a stuffed toy that had been with her all her life. It had been a parting gift from her parents.

The other lamebren entered the room one by one.

'Aerobut gave us an off,' Lamebirl No. 202 informed.

'Are you going somewhere?' No. 203, a six-year old lamebirl, asked shyly.

Zinnia nodded. She had named the two lamebirls Jinny and Arry. In fact, she had a name for each one of the four lamebren, which had instantly added a sense of familial belonging between them.

'Where?' Jinny asked.

'Wish I knew,' replied Zinnia with a sigh.

Arry appeared worried. 'You *are* coming back, aren't you?'

Zinnia turned to face her and the other three kids. 'I don't know.'

'But this is your home!' Jinny exclaimed.

It was true that this was the only home she remembered, this small, box-like white house, with a circular garden and no flowers, where every room seemed like a replica of the other to her befuddled mind. She was three years old then but surprisingly, she still remembered parts of that tearful parting with her mother. The puzzlement, the fear and the sense of insecurity she had experienced when she had been dragged away from her Altklug parents still sparked and clouded her memory. And although, over the years, the intensity of the feelings had reduced, the bafflement had continued and perhaps even augmented and only now begun to be replaced by flashes of vague understanding. Since then she had met her parents only twice every year and this year they hadn't visited at all. Was it perhaps because of her candid observation on their last visit?

Zinnia had jumped with happiness when they had appeared and she had shouted joyfully, 'Look mama, I am taller than you!'

Something changed in that instant. Her father, Radley, had withdrawn visibly and her mother, Vera, had appeared flustered. Almost as if she had said something wrong.

'Shh...don't you utter such things aloud! It is bad enough as it is, must you draw attention to the fact?' Vera had admonished.

'Draw attention to what? What is bad enough?' Zinnia had asked puzzled.

'Come on, we're late. Take care little girl,' her father had wound up hastily.

And then they were gone. That was their last visit. Zinnia hadn't seen them ever since. And she missed them sorely. There was so much she wanted to ask them. A new question surfaced every other minute in her mind and she longed for answers. Questions already filled her mind like a mug brimming with water. And still they kept coming.

As she thrust her clothes into the bag, she wondered about her parents. Would they find out where she was being taken? Would they come visit her there? She already felt so lonely and discarded.

'We are all so scared. We don't understand why we stay in this Cabana, where no one ever visits us. I want my mommy…' No. 204 said, her face puckered in tearful ball.

'There's nothing to be frightened about, Lily. No one has ever hurt us here, have they? We have such delicious meals and plenty to keep us busy. So what if we are under constant surveillance and have limits on our movements? There *must* be a reason for it. Perhaps they are taking me some place where they'll explain to me what's really happening,' Zinnia said, trying to act more mature than her ten years of age. She tried to coat the obvious feeling of wretchedness with forced cheer but deep inside, despite her confident assurance, she just *wasn't* sure.

'But you four take care of yourselves, ok? Don't dilly-dally in the mornings. Eat well and go to bed early.'

'Please don't go,' Juju's voice was a whisper.

Zinnia moved forward and hugged each one of them, suddenly feeling miserable. She was the eldest among them and had slipped into the role of an elder sister with ease. She helped them dress up in the mornings, ensured that they had their meals and even sang to them softly every night till they fell asleep. Now all of sudden she would be separated from the little ones. How would they all cope without her? How would *she* cope without them? If she only knew *where* she was being sent, parting would've been much easier.

'I'll come back, Juju,' she said with sudden conviction. 'Don't worry, we'll meet again. Just keep together and don't fight. You've got to look out for each other, okay?

Here, keep my little toy doggie, that way I shall always be with you. And I'll meet you real soon.'

'Promise?' they chorused.

'Promise!'

She slung her bag over her shoulder and threw a quick last look at the room. Then, she hastened towards the Mess. She couldn't leave without saying goodbye to Peeta. Zinnia found her feeding vegetables to the Meal-Maker affixed to the wall. At first glance, Peeta didn't look much older than the lamebirl. But close observation revealed fine age lines and a slight hollowing of the eye sockets. But it was more her actions, slow and a little fatigued that gave away the fact that she had been around for a long time. She flashed young Zinnia an absent look, as she entered the kitchen.

'What is it?' Peeta asked briskly. 'And what's in the bag?'

'I've come to say goodbye,' Zinnia said, in a small voice.

Peeta halted mid-action and turned to her sharply.

'Goodbye?'

'I'm leaving…'

'What? You mean…' Peeta's expressions changed from realisation to alarm.

'I have no clue why, but I'm leaving.'

'Already?' her voice came in a frightened whisper. She clutched Zinnia's arm. 'How old are you?'

'Ten years and two months. Why?'

Peeta still looked shocked. But she turned away from Zinnia, avoiding her gaze.

'Nothing,' she mumbled.

Zinnia moved closer to the older woman, who like the rest of the Altklugs was just a little taller than her, but larger in breadth.

'What is it, Peeta? Where are they taking me?'

Peeta glanced at her full in the face, noticing the lamebirl's wavy long hair, beautiful brown eyes, heart-shaped face and the dimple in her cheek.

'You are a pretty-looking lamebirl, my dear, like a little flower. Pretty and spirited—you always give me the impression of someone...different...'

'Peeta you've told me that a thousand times before and *you* are the one who gave me the name Zinnia!'

'Did I?' Peeta looked vague. 'My memory must be failing me. I'm getting older by the day.'

'But you're only fourteen! How can you be old?' Zinnia looked perplexed.

'Fourteen is very old. I'll be fifteen next year and then I don't know...' Peeta's voice trailed.

'Where are they taking me, Peeta?' Zinnia persisted.

'To a bigger place, I guess, where you'll meet more of your kind.'

'But I'm happy here. Why do I have to go?'

'Because you are old enough.'

'Old enough? But *you* are still here.'

'That's different. I'm different and...and...you have to go. It's the rule.'

'What rule?'

'You ask too many questions for a lamebirl. Ask Supercustodian, she'll tell you.'

'She's never told me a thing before. You know how she is, barely talks...'

'Lamebirl No. 201. You have thirty minutes to report in the hall,' a voice announced in the air.

Peeta turned to her and hugged her warmly. Sudden tears pranced in her eyes.

'Listen, be a good lamebirl now. Don't do anything to provoke the Altklugs. If you are good, you'll be safe, at least...I mean...' she faltered, not knowing how to proceed.

'I don't understand.'

'You will. And one more thing, we may not meet again...'

'Why?' Zinnia cried.

'We may not, but I want you to know that I've always loved you like my daughter. Take care of yourself, okay?' The older woman brushed her tears and pushed the lamebirl away. 'Now go!'

Zinnia walked to the door, her heart heavy. She turned to look at Peeta one last time. She was standing by the Meal-Maker, staring at it absently, her round, pleasant face set in vague misery. On an impulse, Zinnia raced back and flung her arms around Peeta's thick waist, with tears in her eyes.

'Don't be sad Peeta. I'll return, I promise.'

Peeta wrapped her in a tight embrace, a faint smile on her lips as she nodded. 'Of course you will! Now go, dear. Goodbye and good luck!'

Zinnia clutched her bag and walked slowly to the hall, confusion and worry gnawing at her. She placed her bag by the door. There was one more thing she had to do before she left. She had to go to the Rose Lane.

It was a beautiful evening and the birds were in the blue sky, against the fluffy, caricatured clouds. The snow had melted giving way to a glowing green lawn. Zinnia had once wandered into this lane which was the prettiest she had ever seen. And since then she had spent time here regularly. It was one of the places that were in her permitted radius and she loved the lane.

At least ten different varieties of roses in multi-layered beds aligned and ascended like a wall along the road which winded into some skilfully crafted trees. The pond where it ended had bobbing petals with the most divine colours and it all emanated a feeling of headiness. The ruby colour of the roses burst into her vision as if she had plunged into a swirling, sparkling globe of red. The strong and sweet fragrance, the identical shapes of the flowers and the synchronisation of colours, was a treat to the eyes. Light music pervaded the air along the entire lane, the volume just right enough to tickle and soothe the senses and inspire a feeling of love. She had instantly known that this lane was different. It was more her kind—more natural. And different from the world of Altklugs which frightened her with its synthetic symmetry and challenged her sense of disorderliness. But here she felt at home.

Now as she walked down the pretty, curving road, a deep sadness filled her heart. She strolled through the trees, which whispered sweet murmurings, enveloping her in a cocoon of love and a sense of belonging. She had almost reached the end of the path and was about to step out into the open near the pond when a giggle halted her progress. Peering through the low branches, a startling sight caught her eyes. The two Altklugs were much shorter than her. But they were clinging to each other with their lips glued! She stared, stunned and aghast. Conflicting emotions stung her. Something was wrong, drastically wrong. She felt ashamed and embarrassed watching them touching each other—ashamed because she instinctively sensed that she *shouldn't* and *couldn't* do it, not now, not in this age. And these kids, much younger than her, were so comfortable in their actions. Then a thought smouldered into her mind, creating a crevice—*they* weren't children, *she* was.... They weren't queer, *she* was.

Zinnia whipped around and raced back to the Ret Cabana, her heart pumping with distress. She flopped down on the lawn, shutting her eyes to the image that forced itself through her closed eyelids. Slowly, the feeling of agitation receded though the certainty had lodged in her heart forever. She was queer. She was not at all like the Altklugs that she met or saw in the streets. She was more like the four lamebren she lived with, in the Ret Cabana.

And that is when it all became icily clear. The biggest crime in the Super-Dome of Altklugs was not to be a thief or a fraud. It was to be born a 'lamebirl' or a 'lamebroy'. With a sudden shudder down her spine, she realised, that *she* had committed that grave crime, and was about to be punished for it.

2

It was the first time that Zinnia had ventured into the real Altklug world. Her amazement completely immobilised the natural workings of her curious mind. All thoughts escaped and all expressions of astonishment felt inadequate. Only an immense wave of awe topped her feelings, and she simply stared.

She was alone in the backseat of the spinner, which flew, as it left the Ret Cabana lane and joined the main, disciplined traffic. It was as if Zinnia was sucked into the Altklug world of speed and chaotic order. Dazzling flyovers, aptly called as Skyways, criss-crossed overhead, intersecting at points creating an endless maze in the sky—a riot of colours, designs and competitive technology—leaving the ground free for the flourishing gardens, water bodies, playgrounds and houses.

Occasionally, large signboards which seemed to float from nowhere, flashed the weather report, rattler and flight timings, and the current news. Governor Tisya's short, sleek bob seemed to pop-up at every intersection on wide screens, as she announced her new retirement plan for Altklugs. Another advertisement declared how 'small was profound' and displayed a nail-sized Digi-eye for long-term storage of memories. Another shrill voice advertised and advocated the come-back of Robots. One line particularly caught Zinnia's eye, *Preceptor Amadeus's Theory of Age Progression. To know more, contact Preceptor Amadeus.* The bald face of a youngster smiled back at her from the multi-hoardings and Zinnia stared at him, fascinated.

She stuck her face to the window and watched the traffic glide by, a few inches above the skywalks. It was only when the fluorescent traffic signals embedded in them turned a hue of red that the magnetic strips of the spinners touched the tracks. After a few moments of observation, her fascination was replaced by a sense of giddiness and she reclined against the plush synthetic seat. It was a large world out there—huge, inspiring and inextricably entwined with technical brilliance. For little Zinnia, it was entirely another Super-Dome.

She longed to ask the driver where they were headed. But he was a Humanoid with an expressionless, robot-like face and looked so austere, that she dropped the idea. The Supercustodian had led her to the spinner, placed her bag beside her and wished her 'good luck' in a stiff, unnatural voice. Then before the spinner could take off, she had turned and vanished inside the Ret Cabana. Four faces peered anxiously from the window above and Zinnia waved to them. *Poor little lamebren,* she thought. She barely had time to wish a mental goodbye to her home, when the spinner had whisked forward, swallowing miles within seconds and pushing the Ret Cabana into her past.

Zinnia closed her eyes; trying to control her agitated state of mind, feeling increasingly frustrated and frightened. All through the years at the Ret Cabana, ever since she could remember, she had felt lonely. She and the four other lamebren were always an outcast, and the Altklugs had never bothered to communicate at a normal level and behaved as if they knew and understood nothing. There were so many things she couldn't understand—why people like Supercustodian, Peeta and their Exector Aerobut, just a few years older than her, seemed as if they were much, much older? Why was Aerobut so exceptionally clever and knowledgeable at just a little older age than her? Why did they appear cold and unaffected by anything they saw? Zinnia experienced frequent urges to laugh and cry.

She needed the time to be with things—flowers, trees, the rainfall every afternoon during the Rain Hour and the snowflakes in the late evening during the Snow Hour—feel it all with her hands and in her heart, and wonder at it and touch it...but her actions were regarded by the impatient Supercustodian as stupid and she had been warned on several occasions to 'behave'. But she had never *felt* stupid or felt the need to change her behaviour.

These and many more questions had racked Zinnia's brain for months. It worried her that she didn't know the answers and now, on top of it, she was being sent away. No one had asked her if she *wanted* to leave. For the first time, Zinnia realised, with a striking certainty, that she had no say at all. Was she a captive? But then, she was allowed to go wherever she pleased, within limits of course, and then no one really interfered in her decisions. Except for the meal, class and bed timings, she and the other lamebren had complete freedom. But, if she wasn't a prisoner, then why did she not have the freedom to choose where she wanted to live? Why did she not live with her parents?

'The Fountain of Life,' a voice very similar to that at the Ret Cabana floated in the spinner and Zinnia almost jumped. The spinner had left the skywalks and slowed down as it passed a flashing sign: *The Fountain of Life, Northern Quarter.* Colourful jets of water in the shape of the alphabet L, streamed in the midst of a Square. The central jet rose so high that Zinnia could only imagine the top. The entire image was vibrant, grand and elegant and she stared in fascination.

'Arriving at Northern Quarter Ret Cubicle. Please get ready to disembark,' the voice ordered again. The spinner entered a broad lane, lined with tall trees. The tree-tops were perfectly carved into geometrical shapes and even the branches seemed to be tamed into identical margins. Zinnia gazed in trepidation at the long stretch of road, at the end of which rose a towering white stone building. More trees surrounded the structure, receding into a shady background like a well-drawn sketch. The spinner circled another miniature fountain which sprouted out of a glass image of what looked like a pen. Zinnia recognised it from the K. Sensor-pic Aerobut had shown them once of these writing instruments which were non-existent now. The spinner slid to a halt before the wide-open glass doors of the Cubicle and the doors of the spinner clicked open automatically.

Zinnia clutched her bag and stepped outside hesitantly. She was barely out when the spinner glided away noiselessly. Uncertain, she stood waiting beside a large Lumino sign which read 'Northern Quarter Ret Cubicle'. The sign swayed in the cool, light breeze and the mild evening glow reflected on the glass door. A large gong resonated through the grounds of the Ret Cubicle and it startled her. A murmur of voices grew louder as a number of lamebren trooped through the entrance, chatting in low voices. They were all attired in black demi-legos and demi-sleevers. They passed her without even affording her a fleeting glance, almost as if she was invisible. Only the last girl in the group halted and stared at Zinnia curiously.

'Have you arrived from the Ret Cabana?' she asked in a soft voice.

Zinnia simply stared at the exceedingly pretty, tall girl with light green eyes, long lashes, the perfect heart-shaped face and beautiful waist-length brown tresses which were confined to a silver band. She was sporting a lovely green brooch on her black demi-sleever. Zinnia instantly liked the cheerful smile on her face.

'Yes.' She nodded at length.

'Then you should go straight in, turn right and you'll find the Supercustodian's bureau. And don't worry, she's not as frightening as she appears. Bye, see you later!' With a merry wave, the girl ran after the group of lamebren, who were now heading towards the Cubicle gardens.

Hesitantly, Zinnia stepped into the cool interiors of the mirror-lined hall. For a moment, she studied her reflection—wavy, permanently wind-blown, bleached-brown hair and brown eyes set in an oval face. Pitted against the lamebirl she had just met, Zinnia felt that she looked like a scrappy sidekick. Her only favourite feature, the dimple in her right cheek, which appeared and disappeared when she spoke or smiled, also faded into insignificance against this lamebirl's exquisite beauty. Zinnia grinned and made a face at her image in the mirror.

She turned right and was heading in the direction of the Supercustodian's bureau when a boy's voice hailed her, 'Not that way. Those are the Wash Receptacles.'

Zinnia stopped and turned to look at the thin lamebroy with a smirk on his smudged face. His eyes were tiny and his lips were thin and pursed.

'Take that door.' He indicated a door to the far end of the hall.

'Thanks,' she murmured.

'You're welcome!' He skipped away.

Zinnia headed to the shiny, black metal door and touched the button. The door glided open noiselessly to reveal ten steps. She crossed the threshold and gasped in shock. She had stepped out into the open and was face-to-face with a long, transparent wall which seemed to crawl indefinitely out of sight. But it wasn't the wall which startled Zinnia. It was what lay beyond. On the other side of the long wall, dense, huge trees entangled, wrestling for space, as if in a battle. The low hanging bushes and the dark, creepy feeling which seemed to splatter beyond the transparent border was frightening. It was like a huge black cave of ferocious wasteland opening before her. Or as if the wall was bravely trying to stop the wilderness from swallowing the Ret Cubicle.

'What do you think you are doing?' a harsh voice demanded.

Zinnia turned hastily and stumbled, 'I...I'm sorry...'

'Sorry? No one, absolutely *no one* is allowed to open this door!' Although the same height as Zinnia, the Altklug appeared tall and imposing in her white shirt and trousers. It was her angry glare that gave her the superior look.

'I was told...'

'Come right back in. And if I ever catch you nosing around the Ret Cubicle like a sneaky lamebirl, I'll have you thrown out!'

Zinnia blinked, shaken. No one had ever spoken to her like that before.

'I wasn't being nosy. I was told to take this door...' she replied slowly.

'Silence! Stop lying and step away from that door at once.'

Zinnia obeyed and the older woman clicked the door shut.

Without another word, she strode across the hall in the opposite direction. Towards the transparent Demarcator with the white frame, which Zinnia had planned to approach in the first place, if that lamebroy hadn't misguided her. Why had he played such a dirty trick on her? Obviously he knew that the lamebren weren't allowed to have anything to do with that exit. Then why had he behaved in such a loathsome manner? She wondered, frowning, as she followed the Supercustodian.

The bureau was spacious and displayed monitors on the walls—monitors which afforded a rotating view of the different sections of the Ret Cubicle and gardens, Zinnia guessed. The Supercustodian approached a touch screen and scrolled down the multi-D list.

'You are Lamebirl No. 201 from Ret Cabana.'

'Actually my name is Zinnia,' the little girl ventured.

Supercustodian did not bother to glance at her. 'You may call yourself what you please. Your number changes here. You will be Lamebirl G23,' she said brusquely. 'This is your identification tag which you must carry with you at all times. This is your padlet, it is your Personal Aide which you may use for your personal data, information and queries. You will share a room with lamebirls G10 and G11 on the first floor. She will explain the rest of the routine to you which includes class and meal timings and daily chores. Some Mudra will be loaded to your padlet, for you to use, to buy your personal stuff, like a stipend. No cash in hand. Do you understand what I'm saying?'

Zinnia nodded, accepting the blue-coloured, flip-open padlet with her number embossed on the cover.

'Do you have any questions?'

'How long do I have to stay here?' Zinnia asked.

Supercustodian turned to face her for the first time. Zinnia noticed that she had a mole on her right cheek. Her nose was long and pinched and it made her face appear very stern and angry.

'As long as is deemed necessary,' she responded in a clipped tone.

She beeped a number into her mobile unit and a voice responded.

'Yes Ma'am?'

'G10, please report and take charge,' Supercustodian spoke into her unit.

'Yes Ma'am.'

'G10 will show you around now and introduce you to your life here. There will be an Introduction Parade sharp at nine tomorrow morning in the hall. Remember, you are not to go near that Exit door again. You are not to interfere with the workings of any Altklug. You are free to move around in the Community charabanc but avoid the Water Veins. If you get a beep on your PA, it means that you are being summoned to my bureau. I have here a list of your likes, dislikes and allergies and the Meal-Keeper will serve the appropriate meals and classes will be organised accordingly. I see that you've put music and singing in your hobbies. You will receive training, as per your wishes.'

'Oh will I?' Zinnia couldn't contain her delight. 'Thank you. I always wake up with a song in my heart and then I don't know what to do with it. Supercustodian, back at the Ret Cabana, never allowed me to bring it out.'

The older woman stared at her with a hint of distaste in her eyes. 'Well, now you can, but only during class. I don't need to emphasise the need for discipline to you, do I G23?'

'No Ma'am,' Zinnia murmured.

'Good. As long you live here, I'd like you to feel at home. Oh, here you are G10. She's all yours.'

Zinnia turned and looked straight into the curious green eyes of the pretty lamebirl she had met earlier.

3

'G10?' That cannot be a forever name, it's a number,' Zinnia insisted.

'Numbers are names here and you have to be content with that.' G10 shrugged.

They were sitting in an oblong room with four beds aligned by four windows. The third bed in the corner had been assigned to Zinnia. It looked more like a bench with a fat cushion and a sleek under-head, storage-cum-cupboard space.

'We had numbers at the Cabana too, but I had a private name for each one of the lamebren. I'm going to come up with a name for you too, soon,' Zinnia declared.

'In that case, you'll have to find names for eleven of us here.' G10 smiled.

'Oh, then I will find eleven names!' Zinnia responded enthusiastically.

'Eleven of us share four bedrooms between us, lamebirls in two, lamebroys in the others—numbers 10 to 25. Actually, we were thirty but...' G10 broke off abruptly.

'But?'

'They're gone.'

'Gone where?'

G10 rose from her bed. Zinnia noticed that her every action was performed with a sort of inherent grace and rhythmic motion, very appealing to the eye.

'Come, let's meet the others in the next bedroom. Oh, here come the twins—G11 and B12.'

A lamebirl and a lamebroy strolled into the room. They looked identical in their black attire. With their snipped blondish curls, pink cheeks, blue eyes and crowded teeth, they were a perfect match and they smiled easily at Zinnia.

'Welcome to the Ret Cubicle, we hope you'll be happy here,' they chorused.

'Thank you,' Zinnia responded. She took an instant liking to their cute charm.

'G11 and B12 are twins, as you may have noticed.' G10 smiled. 'They are two years older than you. B12 plays the floflute and G11 writes poetry.'

'Oh, that's great!'

'Yes, it certainly is. Although playing the floflute outside the class is forbidden,' the lamebroy said.

'And my poetry might never be published in a thermiodical,' G11 quipped.

'Why not?' Zinnia asked.

'Because poetry is a waste of time in Altklug world and even if it wasn't, who would want to publish a poem by a lamebirl?'

'You never know what lies in the future.'

The twins exchanged a look—a quick questioning glance which turned to that of instant comprehension.

'G10, it's obvious that she doesn't really know much. Don't you think you had better tell her?' queried the lamebroy.

'Tell me what?' Zinnia frowned, her eyes fleeting from one lamebirl to the other.

'Tell you that *none* of us has a future,' a voice cut in rather bluntly.

Zinnia turned to face a cheerful lamebroy with a sweet little dimple in his chin, a pair of black, twinkling eyes and a shock of unruly hair which fell over his forehead and gave him a peppy look. He looked the same age as the twins.

'Hi! I'm B15.' He held out a hand which Zinnia shook automatically.

'Hi! But I don't understand. Why don't we have a future?'

'Look here, it's too soon to acquaint her with all the details,' G10 interrupted, hastily. 'She's just arrived…'

'Well then sooner the better. Isn't time of essence in the Altklug world?' B15 remarked.

'That's what Aerobut, our Exector said to me too.'

'Exactly.'

A big gong echoed throughout the house making Zinnia jump. It was like the roll of a drum except that it ended with a whistle.

'Dinner time,' the twins chorused.

'We'll talk later, ok?' G10 suggested. 'You'll get to see the rest of the lamebren in the Superkitchen.'

She led the way down the escalator and Zinnia found it fascinating. Following a passage they trooped into a long and plain, empty hall with a high ceiling. It was only when G10 pressed a button on the wall that a transparent, metal chair and table detached smoothly and noiselessly from the wall. Zinnia followed her example as did the rest of the lamebren who were divided on either side of the hall.

Zinnia couldn't help remembering, with a dash of wistfulness, the almost warm Mess at the Ret Cabana. Being just five of them, the forever pleasant Peeta had served them some delicious meals. A sudden ache clamped Zinnia's heart as she longed to be with her little friends and Peeta….

Now as she settled down, two tall, circular machines, laden with filled plates, appeared at the head of each row.

'This is the Server. Just look for your number and extract your plate,' G10 whispered.

Soundlessly, the Servers glided down the hall, halting opposite each lamebirl and lamebroy.

'But where's the Cook?' Zinnia asked.

'Cook? There's no cook in the Superkitchen. It is all automated. A person called a Meal-Keeper adds all the ingredients in another room to the Meal-Maker and the machines do the rest. I'll take you there one day.'

'No people around? How strange...'

'This is Altklug world, sweetie. Everything is economised, especially time and Altklug power. And no one would certainly waste time on lamebren like us. We are completely useless to the Altklugs. That they feed and clothe us is a huge favour they are doing us in the first place.'

'You mean because we are not as clever as them?'

'Not as clever? That's an understatement!' G10 chuckled, tossing her ample hair behind her. 'We are *nowhere* close to them—not in knowledge, not in intellect and certainly not in learning.'

'But why's that? We all look the same, don't we?'

'Little Zinnia, you really are so naïve...' G10 flashed an almost affectionate look. 'The Server is approaching. It waits only for thirty seconds, you have to move fast or you'll go hungry.'

Zinnia nodded, feeling very nervous, as she observed the Server's steady progress down the row. How could she ever read her number, select her plate and remove it—all in just thirty seconds? She observed G11 as she expertly slid her plate off. The closer the Server came, the more menacing it appeared. Zinnia rubbed her suddenly clammy hands against her dress.

'Be ready now. Look for the hook. I believe your plate is second-last from the bottom,' G10 hinted.

The lamebroys sat opposite to the lamebirls and Zinnia noticed the lamebroy who had deliberately misguided her. He smirked at her and Zinnia developed an instantaneous dislike for him. Two seats away from him, sat the cheerful lamebroy B15 who smiled at her encouragingly. On her right, G10 whispered encouragingly and on her left G11nodded at her. They were all so supportive yet quite suddenly Zinnia felt embarrassed—of course she could do it! It was a simple thing, wasn't it?

The Server appeared before her, and stood still like a sentinel. A big digital clock displayed a countdown, the seconds twinkling down to thirty. Numbers were tagged over each plate and Zinnia leaned forward to search for her number The clock ticked loudly and ominously, in the wordless hall.

'Second last row,' G10 repeated urgently.

Zinnia's eyes found the row. She bent forward and clutched the plate, her hands clammy.

'Find the groove and just pull it out.'

The clock began counting down to the last ten seconds and she couldn't take her eyes off the taunting digits.

'Hurry!' G10 exclaimed.

With all her strength, Zinnia tugged at the plate and it slid out, but a little too fast. It was laden with food in silver bowls and was heavy. Zinnia stared horrified as it began to slide off from her hand, on to the floor. Just then, as she struggled in vain to straighten the food bowls, a hand shot out and balanced the plate. Startled, Zinnia glanced up and stared at a uniformed Altklug. His face was grim as he gripped the plate skilfully and placed it on her table.

'Th...Thank you!' she whispered, mortified.

'You've got to be more careful, lamebirl,' he drawled, shooting her a quick look.

Sudden silence filled the room as the other lamebren stared curiously at Zinnia and the uniformed, imposing figure. Then the Altklug wheeled around and strode out of the Superkitchen.

'Whew! That was close,' G10 whispered, as she extracted her plate expertly from the machine.

'I was very lucky, wasn't I?' Zinnia mumbled

'You were super lucky,' G11 agreed. Her twin B12 was gazing anxiously at them from across the room.

'But don't worry. You'll learn,' G10 assured, an encouraging smile on her lips.

'Who was that man?' Zinnia couldn't help asking, after all he had saved her from going hungry on the very first day at the Ret Cubicle.

'I have no clue, must be some visiting Officer. They keep sending these Officers to keep an eye on us. You better eat up fast. We aren't allowed to chat while we eat.'

Zinnia nodded and tucked into her meal. She was famished and the food was delicious. What a blunder she had committed! She really had to be more careful in the future.

Thirty minutes later, the empty plates were stacked back into the Server as it made a second round and this time Zinnia was quick and alert. Then the lamebren trooped out of the Superkitchen and into the hall where a big screen was playing a docunote. Some of them settled down in the seats while others stood and now Zinnia could observe them all closely.

A tall, hefty lamebirl with a single, long braid and a shirt which seemed one size too small, was whispering secretively to a much shorter lamebirl with two plaits. They appeared like thick friends. Next to them sat a tiny lamebirl perched on the edge of the metal seat. A blunt haircut framed her pale, thin, oval-shaped face which carried a rather resigned expression. She appeared so delicate that Zinnia felt she would fall with one poof of the wind! Beside her another lamebirl had fished out a small piece of cloth and had begun stitching something, barely glancing up at the screen. Her hair was confined to a band high on her head swinging jauntily and she had very light eyebrows along with a rather snubbed nose.

On the other end, a tall lamebroy with hollowed cheeks, close-cropped hair and round glasses was impatiently pacing the floor while a stout, plumpish lamebroy with an anxious expression on his cute face, alternately glanced from the tall lamebroy to the docunote. In a corner, sat the lamebroy who had misdirected Zinnia earlier that afternoon, a bored expression on his face and his small eyes glued to the screen evoking the same dislike in Zinnia he held so far. What a bunch of lamebren they were, she thought, all dressed in black demi-legos and demi-sleevers.

'We are supposed to watch this docunote on the Altklugs every night,' B15 whispered to her. He and the twins had joined Zinnia. They stood against the wall staring at the screen.

'Why?'

'Why? Because the Altklugs have come a long way since they overtook the Singularity, that's why!'

'The Singularity?' Zinnia frowned, confused.

'It was an era when machines had taken total control of the world and ruled humans for years. The humans had rebelled and revolted and that is how the Altklugs were born.'

'But...'

'This docunote is to remind the lamebren of the greatness of the Altklugs. And mainly because they don't want us to forget that we live in *their* world.'

'Their world? It's *our* world too!' Zinnia exclaimed.

G10 and the twins glanced at each other. B15 shook his head sympathetically, a lock of hair bouncing on his forehead.

'If it were your world, you wouldn't be at the Ret Cubicle. You would be planning your retirement by now.'

'What?'

B15 patiently turned towards her. 'Okay, do answer some of these rather simple questions, will you?' He seemed to be rather enjoying Zinnia's confusion. 'Could you speak the seven major languages of the Super-Dome when you were born? And did the languages grow in number as you grew older? Did you begin your education, to equip yourself for life that is, when you were a year old?'

Soon G11 picked up the trail, 'In your third year, did you graduate and know all the sciences, and could you write K. Sensor programmes? At four, did you take up a job, make any notable discoveries? Like say Emotion-mapping or Pain-tolerance—whatever that means? Also, did you move out of your parents' house to set up your own house?' G11 stared at Zinnia keenly, her hair an array of curls.

'And at five, did you join the government or some private office and work in earnest? Around the same time, did you marry an Altklug matched for you by the K. Sensor and at six did you have your own kids…' B12 piped in, looking exactly like his twin, with his blonde curls and blue eyes.

'Married at the age of six? Do stop!' Zinnia cut in, confused.

'Well, you see, even listening to all this can blow your mind,' B15 said smugly, the dimple in his chin showing. A devilish glint in his black eyes almost gave him a rakish look.

'You mean the Altklugs...'

'The Altklugs do all this and more,' G10 supplied quietly.

'But how?'

'They are different. They are born with super knowledge. They are so clever that it is frightening. You see, their every year is biologically equivalent to our 6.25 years! It is only around thirteen years of age, that their old age really catches on. Very few live beyond the age of fifteen and only a rare handful live to be sixteen,' G11 added.

Zinnia gaped, stunned and trying to recalibrate her thoughts with the new knowledge. *So, Peeta really was old...* 'But they don't look old,' she frowned. 'I mean their faces are so brilliant, so shiny...almost alike.'

'At first sight, it does seem so. But if you look closely, you'll notice that some of them appear really tired and haggard. I guess, the outer body changes aren't drastic. Their emotions too are structured and measured. The way we talk, laugh and cry, they don't. For them tears and laughter do exist but in short measures. There simply isn't time to waste, because, according to them, there really is no need for more time,' B15 said, thrusting a hand through his untidy shock of hair.

'Have you ever seen any of the Altklugs falling ill, the way we do? No, because they never do. Everything in the Altklug world is hassle-free, systematic and disease-free. That is because everything—the trees, the rain, the snow, the landscapes, the weather—is created or engineered as per their technical data. Everything is deliberate, adult and controlled. And since they are so advanced, it is but natural that they consider us lamebrains. That is why we are lamebren girls, "lamebirls" and my twin and B15 here are lamebren boys, "lamebroys",' G11 completed.

'Wow!' was all Zinnia could say. 'You know a lot about them.'

The others looked at each other.

'We've been doing some…research,' G10 admitted.

'And that is how we learned that this world is *theirs* not ours,' B15 concluded.

They fell silent momentarily. All the questions fastened tightly in Zinnia's head seemed to be suddenly released, springing in different directions with fresh fervour. The confusion began dissolving, as awe and understanding crept in.

'So that is why we are here,' she whispered. 'That is why everyone is impatient with us and treats us like… like…we don't matter.'

G10 nodded. Her head was bent, as she traced an invisible line on the floor with her foot. The green brooch on her demi-sleever shone incongruously and daringly against the black.

'Oh, but we *do* matter. For *us*!' Zinnia exclaimed.

The others looked at her curiously.

'As if that's going to make any difference to them.' B15 scoffed.

'It doesn't matter whether it makes any difference to them. What matters is that for us *we* are important. We belong here too!'

'You don't know the whole story yet,' G10 said.

'What do you mean?' Zinnia persisted.

'Why don't you tell her about the Secret…' B15 began.

'Shh…not here,' G10 interrupted sharply.

The docunote ended just then and the Presenter, a smart-looking Altklug, signed off, promising to meet in Part 2 of the show. A hush fell, as feet shuffled. The lamebren rose and began trooping upstairs, apparently subdued by the overwhelming contents of the programme and their own thoughts.

'Bedtime,' the twins whispered.

Zinnia followed the lamebren and the Escalators carried them upstairs. What did G10 mean? They were such a combination of contradictions—helpless and frustrated one moment and so secretive the next.

The exact minute they were in their room, a voice echoed through the Cubicle.

'Ten minutes till bedtime. Lights out at nine!'

Zinnia opened her mouth to speak, but G10 placed a finger on her lips, signalling her to be quiet. Zinnia quickly changed into a night dress, feeling too wide awake to sleep. She was sharing the room with G10 and G11. The fourth bed was empty.

Back at the Ret Cabana, they were allowed to watch TV till late and since they were only five of them they could chat too. She already missed her companions from the Cabana. Not that these lamebren weren't interesting. They were quite smart and knowledgeable, and Zinnia was glad to have made some friends. Most importantly, they had answers for her hungry mind. The haze that had always surrounded her clouded thoughts, was gradually clearing up.

Sharp at nine, the central lights were extinguished. G10 switched on a small side lamp embedded in the metal frame of the bed. She was dressed in a short, flowery gown which came up to her bare knees.

'Gather around my bed. Pull those chairs lamebirls. We can talk now, provided you keep your voices low,' she whispered.

There was a knock on the door and B15 slipped in with B12. Zinnia watched bewildered as two more lamebroys accompanied them—the tall, thin lamebroy with glasses and the other shorter, plumper one with those puffed-out cheeks.

'What's happening?' Zinnia asked the twins who looked identical in their geometrically designed pajamas.

'We're having a meeting,' B12 replied.

'Of "The Secret Society",' her twin completed.

Zinnia gasped. *The Secret Society!* Even the thought was exciting. She watched as they all settled round the bed, with G10 in the centre.

'Where are the others?' G10 asked.

B15 shook his head. With his untidy crop of hair, he looked as if he had just stepped out of a sports field.

'Not interested. You know how G16 and G17 are. They don't do anything without each other. If one decides not to go, the other follows. And the rest are already in bed.'

'Never mind.' G10 shrugged. Then she turned her direct gaze on Zinnia. 'G23 or Zinnia as you call yourself, we feel that you have the courage and intelligence to join our group. We feel privileged to welcome you to join the Secret Society.'

Zinnia stared at the eager smiling faces, looking weird in the low lamp light and experienced a thrill unknown to her.

'Thank you. And I feel privileged to be a part of your Secret Society,' she responded and the others nodded. 'But what does the Secret Society do?'

The atmosphere in the room was subdued as the others glanced at G10. She inhaled deeply and began.

'Each one of us is an unwanted entity in the Altklug world. The Altklug Administrator has our complete records—our entire history, the names of our parents, our birth dates as well as our Termination Dates.'

Zinnia gulped, her throat suddenly dry. 'What do you mean?'

'It means that we are all marked. One by one, each one of us, is going to be killed or terminated. Some together, some alone, but without fail, the Dissolution Crypt is our final destination.'

Shock slammed into Zinnia and reverberated in her body, like a spinner bracing against the walls of a narrow tunnel. She stared at G10, struggling with the myriad emotions which clashed inside her. The shifting shadows in the corners of the room were gloomy and almost spectral. Beside her, she sensed the twins trembling imperceptibly. Their faces were downcast, but they were holding hands. B15 crumpled the bed sheet in a tight fist, an angry frown on his forehead. And the two lamebroys with him stared at G10 with tormented eyes. Only G10 returned Zinnia's stunned look with a steady, fearless gaze.

'And...being the eldest, I shall be the first one to go,' she divulged.

Her voice was a whisper but it seemed to explode in the silent room.

4

'As you may have already noticed, we have amongst us a new entrant. Lamebirl No. G23 will you step forward please,' Supercustodian ordered.

Zinnia stepped out of the double line standing in the mirror-lined hall for the Introductory Parade. With her pinched nose, the Supercustodian made her nervous, but she hastened to the head of the line.

'Just so that everyone knows, G23 has come to us from the Ret Cabana, which is a really small place. She would need your help in finding her way around the Cubicle as well with her duties. G23 likes to sing and will be sent to Mirella's classes accordingly. Is there anything else you would like to say about yourself?'

Zinnia was a little taken aback. She hadn't expected the liberty of a self-introduction.

'I…I…' she began.

Someone sniggered and Zinnia threw a quick look in the direction of the sound. It was the lamebroy who had misled her the previous evening. *Lorde*, she thought.

'Go on. Tell us about yourself, G23 in precisely two sentences,' Supercustodian encouraged with a nod.

Two sentences! How could she describe herself in just two sentences? Zinnia wondered, feeling constricted and trapped. Especially now, when she was just beginning to get a glimmer into who she really was, rather, trying to grapple with the oceans of knowledge that seemed to have engulfed her. She stared momentarily at all the patient faces and wondered if they were listening because they were really interested or because they didn't have any choice?

'My name is Zinnia and I miss Ret Cabana,' she said, finally.

A hushed silence packed the hall as all the lamebren wore an expression of shock. Their eyes were not trained on her but on the Supercustodian. Had she said something wrong? She glanced at the Supercustodian and her nose seemed so pinched, that her nostrils appeared stitched together. Her lips were pursed in a grim, no-nonsense manner.

'G23. That's what you are and will always be in this Ace-world. As for missing Ret Cabana, that is a wasted emotion and has no place here.' Her voice was icy and hard. 'G10, it is your duty to ensure that G23 does not fritter away time on futile jobs and her time here is used to the best of her ability.'

'Yes Ma'am.' G10 briefly glanced at Zinnia and then back at Supercustodian.

'Also, keep her by your side as your assistant, until you…' Supercustodian paused for an infinitesimal moment, 'until I say so.'

'Yes Ma'am,' G10 nodded, but Zinnia saw that her face had paled.

G10 cast her eyes down in obedience. Her long hair was confined to a silver band and she wore a lovely red brooch today. But it was the way she held herself motionless as if frozen, that made Zinnia realise that the older lamebirl was trying hard to control her emotions. *Iris*, she thought, out of the blue. The twins, who were standing right behind her in parallel lines, glanced at each other. Their blonde curls were combed well and their cheeks were pinker than ever. *Cheska and Camilla*. The usually cheerful B15 stared at Supercustodian, so hard through his shock of unruly hair, that his gaze seemed to burn through her skull. *Crispin…*

Crispin? Why not? Unwittingly, Zinnia smiled to herself, experiencing a happy gush at this wave of creativity. She had found the perfect names for them!

'Ok, back to your duties. The vehicle is waiting outside to drop Group B to their jobs, Group A into the garden, and Group C in the library. We rotate duties again next week. Also I would like to remind you that Commander Hertz may inspect the Cubicle anytime this week, so I would suggest that you all keep your padlets charged, rooms clean and attire spotless. Bosco will also be on the prowl, so I needn't say more…' The Supercustodian's tone indicated dismissal and the two lines broke up.

Zinnia stood confused. What was she supposed to do? Which group did she belong to? But her questions were answered instantly as G10 moved towards her, followed by her other new friends.

'I am in your group?' she asked, delighted as the twins joined them.

'For the time being at least,' G11 said.

'Until Supercustodian suddenly feels it necessary to break the Groups, which could happen either tomorrow, next week or never!' B12 concluded.

'Why worry about it then? We're together now, aren't we?' B15 said cheerfully and G10 nodded.

'Iris, Cheska, Camilla and Crispin,' Zinnia announced.

'What?' the others chorused, confused.

Zinnia flashed them a smile. 'I've been thinking and I have finally found perfect names for you. G10, I shall call you Iris. G11—you are Camilla and B12, Cheska. As for you B15, I can only think of Crispin.'

The others stared at her, their eyes wide in fascination.

'Iris,' G10 repeated slowly. 'I like it…it sort of does feel right on me, doesn't it?

'Perfect!' the twins agreed.

'Thank you, Zinnia,' the older girl said simply. 'I'll feel better now...when I have to say goodbye...'

'Oh shush,' B15 cut in. 'Let's enjoy our names. I've never had one before, or at least I don't remember it, since I came here when I was three years old. Besides I like the ring of mischief in Crispin.'

'Yes, I like Cheska too,' B12 agreed.

'And me Camilla! I feel as if I've had the name all along,' G11 exclaimed.

Zinnia appeared thrilled. 'See, I told you I'd find the perfect names for you. I have names for each one of the other lamebren too. See that's Reed and Berk!'

She indicated the tall, thin boy and the lamebroy with the puffed cheeks who had been present for the meeting the previous night. 'Berk has this perpetual anxious expression on his face, as if he is going to be summoned by Supercustodian any moment, doesn't he? And that's Maisie and Ivy—I haven't seen them one without the other as yet. Maisie is the one with the braids and Ivy is the tall one. And that's Azalea—dainty and fragile and she's with Cylia—the lamebirl who always seems to be stitching something.'

'Wow! You're brilliant,' Camilla chuckled.

An announcement boomed through the Cubicle. 'Group A report in the porch, Group B in the garden, and Group C in the library. Instructions await you at each point. Do not forget to keep your padlets with you. Moving around without the padlet is liable to attract Criminal Offence 226 and subject to rigorous isolation.'

'Come on, let's go,' Iris said.

'What's Lorde doing here?' Zinnia asked suddenly.

'Who?' The others turned to look in the direction she indicated.

'Lorde, that's my name for him,' Zinnia explained.

'Oh, B22! He's with us,' Crispin replied.

'What!' Zinnia looked horrified.

Lorde stood aside, ignoring them and fiddling with his padlet.

'What a name for him!' Camilla laughed.

'If I tell you what he did to me yesterday, you'll agree that it's an ideal name for him,' Zinnia said.

'Come on, everyone, to our duties,' Iris said. 'B22, please stop whatever it is you are doing and join us.'

Lorde looked up and the sullen expression on his face darkened.

'Don't order me around. You're not the boss here,' he snapped.

'I *am* in charge of the group,' Iris reminded gently.

'Yeah, only for a while. We all know what's going to happen in a few months.'

Zinnia stared at him shocked. The cheek of that boy—his arrogance and disrespect, not to mention his utter lack of sensitivity.

'How dare you talk to her like that!' Crispin cried, angrily.

'Stop it, you two!' Iris cut in hastily.

'But he's rude and ugly!' Cheska blurted.

'Let him say what he wants to. It doesn't change anything.'

'She's right. We'll all only end up being isolated, which we all know is the worst kind of punishment,' Camilla agreed.

'Come on, we have to report in flat two minutes at the garden,' Iris remarked, leading the way out of the hall.

Zinnia followed, ignoring the slow shuffle of reluctant feet behind her. She didn't like Lorde—it was an instinctive feeling, she realised. Perhaps it had something to do with the way he had behaved with her on her arrival. But also because of the way he spoke to Iris. Iris was a kind-hearted, brave girl and Zinnia had liked her instantly. If Lorde could behave roguishly with Iris, he had no sense of judgment or decency. She had to keep her distance from him.

The garden, as Zinnia had seen the previous day, was a large spread of green land as far as the eye could see. Machines of all kinds stood in a row in glass cabins with labels on then.

'Like the name suggests, Lawnrover is for the lawns,' Crispin explained. 'Trimart trims the bushes with automatic, adjustable blades for different shapes. The Plucker cuts flowers, with or without stalks, simultaneously blunting the thorns. And Cleanster is for gathering the fallen leaves and disposing them in a box.'

'You pick your choice. Which one would you like to start with? We have to shape the east side of the garden today, before Rain Hour,' Iris suggested.

Zinnia looked lost and Lorde sniggered.

'I am taking the Lawnrover,' he announced and headed towards the cabin.

'It's easy. Look, let me show you,' Camilla volunteered. She slid open the door to the cabin and quickly demonstrated the workings of the Cleanster, while the others set about their tasks.

For the next thirty minutes, Zinnia practiced the 'red button, green button' technique that Camilla taught her and was quite pleased with her pile of burnt, torn leaves. The sound of whirring filled the morning and although an urgency sat on the edge of their minds, the lamebren appeared to be relaxed.

A while later they took a break under a huge tree with red and green patterned leaves, shaped like a roof.

Iris handed out small, transparent balls of water which burst open in the mouth and quenched their thirst instantly.

'What did Lorde do to you?' Cheska was curious. 'I mean you barely know him and you've just arrived.'

Zinnia recounted the incident.

'The door to the Snarl? That is a serious offence indeed,' Camilla remarked.

'The Snarl? What is that? And why is that an offence?'

'Because *no one* is allowed to go into the deep forest—that's the Snarl! Especially the Altklugs. It's a dangerous place filled with monsters and savage brutes. We won't survive for a minute in that wild and dark jungle.'

'There's also a story behind it—we don't even know if it's true, it happened so long ago,' Iris added. 'Once, ages ago, before all of us were even born, a lamebroy escaped into the Snarl. His number was B7 but he liked to call himself Leo Leroy and I think the name kind of stuck. He simply vanished one day and was never heard of again. They searched for him but didn't dare go into the Snarl and at that time there were no Scanners in the sky. Altklugs believe that something horrible happened to him in the Snarl. They apparently discovered parts—I mean a limb and a hand, and his clothes—so says legend.'

Zinnia was listening raptly with eyes widened in horror.

'That is why no one ever dares to explore the Snarl. It is unsafe and evil,' Cheska completed. 'It was a long time ago but still no one has ever forgotten Leo Leroy, neither the lamebren nor the Altklugs.'

'And that is why it was wrong on Lorde's part to trick you into opening the door.' Crispin frowned.

Zinnia digested this bit of news. *Leo Leroy*...even the name had an allure to it and she decided to read up on him.

'And who is Commander Hertz?' she asked.

'He is Governor Tisya's right hand, a very influential man and extremely strict. He appears at the Cubicle any time he pleases,' Iris explained.

'To inspect if all is in order,' Camilla added. 'Our routine is pretty tight. Duties and classes on alternate mornings, and alternate afternoons free for extra-curricular activities. No chance for any disorder.'

'And he very well knows that we are not a danger to the Altklug world. He should stop worrying about harmless lamebren and concentrate on people like Preceptor Amadeus.'

'Preceptor Amadeus! The name sounds so familiar.' Zinnia's forehead creased in concentration.

'Oh, he's a great Thinker and has the oddest of theories, although we don't understand half of them. We almost attended one of his lectures a while ago. He lives on the other side of the Water Veins, in the Eastern Quarter—you know the tunnel that runs under the huge lake—it is fantastic, has a glass top and you have to take the glass rattler. We are forbidden to take that route unless we are with Altklugs, so we changed plans at the last minute,' Crispin said.

Zinnia suddenly remembered where she had read about Preceptor Amadeus. The evening before, while she was being driven to the Cubicle, she had spotted the large hoarding of the Thinker.

'Does he ever visit the Cubicle?' she asked.

'Nobody ever visits the Cubicle—I mean the general Altklugs never do. Not even Governor Tisya. Only Commander Hertz does.'

'Then I wonder who the Officer was who helped me with the Server.'

'Perhaps someone on appointment to assist the Supercustodian?'

'He seemed kind of nice.'

'Uh oh, don't ever mistake any Altklug to be nice,' Crispin warned. 'That word doesn't exist for them. They don't have time for such silly emotions. They're too busy doing their own thing to even notice us, leave alone acting nice.'

'Oh, but Peeta back at the Ret Cabana was nice,' Zinnia quipped. 'I mean *really* nice.'

'Then you were lucky,' Cheska dismissed the idea.

'Mirella's nice,' his twin cut in. 'She's our floflute teacher. Very strict but in a nice kind of way.'

'Yes, I guess Mirella could qualify as one,' Crispin conceded.

Iris smiled. 'Mirella's definitely good to us B15—uh I mean Crispin.'

'Oh, here's Bosco now, no chatting,' Cheska warned.

Zinnia heard the clomp of metal before she saw him. A huge man attired in a type of thin iron armour but with heavy boots, seemed to appear out of nowhere. His face was smooth and creaseless and he had the oddest eyes she had seen. Were they metal? She wondered, puzzled.

'Lamebirls and lamebroys, no time for talk, just time for work,' Bosco's speech was surprisingly soft and staccato.

'Zinnia, this is Bosco,' Iris introduced. 'He's our Security-cum-handyman.'

'Hello Bosco.' Zinnia held out a hand.

'No physical contact. No talk, only work.' Bosco nodded with the briefest of smiles and moved away.

Zinnia stared after him puzzled. 'He's...strange.'

'He's one of the last of the Singularity—the almost human-like machines that overtook the world way back. They are called Humanoids. Some were retained at the

Headquarters, Job Galleries and the Piazzars—all put to good use. They are surprisingly gentle and hard-working. Don't go by Bosco's outer appearance, he's programmed like that. Left on his own, he's the kindest person at the Cubicle,' Iris assured.

'The Singularity…I must do some reading.'

'Right now, we need to work. Like Bosco said—no talk, just work,' Crispin grinned. 'And we have the entire eastern side of the lawn to shape up before Rain Hour.'

5

'This Super-world of Altklugs is divided into five Super-Domes. The Dome is an energy field which isn't visible to the eye but which filters and protects the residents from harmful rays and elements present in nature,' Bamian explained.

The Exector looked so much like Aerobut that Zinnia wondered if they were siblings. The class was filled with twelve lamebirls and lamebroys as Bamian went on to explain the complicated world of the Altklugs.

'Some of the Altklugs travelled in time and stayed in different eras. They discovered that Earth had seasons—summer, rains and winter. The Altklugs were so clever that they mastered these weather conditions and in turn nature with geo-engineering thus harnessing the weather into a daily schedule. That is why today we have the weather hours—Warm Hours in the morning, Rain Hours in the afternoon and Snow Hours in the evening.'

Bamian's steady gaze flitted from lamebirl to lamebroy assessing their intelligence.

'Long, long ago bio-tech advancements conquered aging and human beings began to have long spans of life. This was possible because with new technologies emerging through diligent research, it became possible to grow new arms, new veins—in fact almost all body parts. Our different organs, bones, muscles, all types and colours of hair, and different types of skin could be replaced as new procedures were discovered. Everything except the heart. Stem cells, bio-printing, and genetics replaced aging skin and they strengthened frail bones and muscles, creating new versions of the body,' explained the tutor.

In class, using a slim pin which displayed his lecture in multi-D, Bamian spoke well and effortlessly. Zinnia listened with keen attention. How fascinating it all was!

'All was fine until man created the super robots, the human-like Humanoids—machines who could write books, cook, drive spinners and emulate human emotions and consciousness. These machines were so smart that with their super-fast speed and knowledge, they also began creating their own kind. And that is when the problem began and the era of the Singularity took over. Machines overtook human intelligence and began ruling the world. It was a world fraught with super knowledge but also a world of intriguing precision leading to unimaginable fear. It was a do or die situation for the humans. A need arose to think faster and better than the machines and for years the struggle continued, making the Altklugs what they are today—superior and powerful in every way possible. The Rising went on for years until one day the Singularity toppled and the Altklugs built their world around the five Super-Domes. Ours is one of them and we are connected to the other four Super-Domes in very sophisticated ways. The Altklugs did learn one lesson though. They never allowed their knowledge to create competition ever again. No robots, no clones, no more rebels...But the struggle for superiority came with a price. Age was equated with super-knowledge, efficiency and utility and thus began to be controlled. And that in a nutshell is the Altklug Ace-world today.'

Iris raised her hand.

'Yes? Any questions?'

'Wasn't one of the great grandmothers of Governor Tisya majorly responsible for the rising?'

'You are correct. She was called Governor Seeya. A charming woman, very courageous and also a visionary. She got involved in the movement as a child and as she grew older, she played a key role in toppling the Singularity. Of course, there have been many other Governors over time, but Governor Seeya will always be remembered and respected for her visionary work. We have a field visit to her Museum scheduled for this afternoon along with the Northside Altklug Knowledge Port. You will get to know more about this great Altklug at the Museum. Needless to say, I expect proper behaviour and strict discipline. No interactions with the Altklugs. Bosco will meet you at the porch at 1400 hours sharp.'

'Which leaves us barely sixty minutes to have lunch,' Crispin whispered, as the morning session ended.

'Oh but this is exciting isn't it?' Zinnia exclaimed as they headed towards the Superkitchen. 'Governor Seeya... even the name sounds formidable.'

'Apparently she was very dynamic and different...not at all like Governor Tisya,' Camilla remarked.

'But Governor Tisya is a good Governor too,' her twin pointed out. 'Look at the way she manages the Super-Dome with an iron hand. It is also because of her and Commander Hertz that there have been no revolts at the Domes.'

'I am more excited about travelling through the Water Vein. The Super-Dome is divided into four Quarters: North, South, East and West,' Camilla explained. 'Through the centre runs the Water Veins in all four directions, under the lake. But in the centre of the lake, above the cross-section of the Water Veins, is a fantastic Island Square, reachable by four beautiful bridges. All major festivals and events take place there.'

'Wow!' Zinnia exclaimed.

'That's not all. All the four Quarters are known by magnificent Fountains: Fountain of Life in the North

Quarter—our quarter, Fountain of Death in the South Quarter, Fountain of Knowledge in the West Quarter and Fountain of Conscience in the East Quarter. And you have to see them to believe their magnificence.'

Zinnia lapped up the information eagerly. The more she heard about the Altklug world, the more curious she became.

'I saw the Fountain of Life when I arrived at the Cubicle. But I'd love to see the other fountains too,' she enthused.

Zinnia glanced at Iris, but the older lamebirl did not respond. She was silent and deep in thought, barely aware of their conversation. Her head was bent and her attention seemed to be focused on the ground, as they headed towards the Superkitchen. She was sporting a lovely green necklace, which was striking as well as ornamental. Her love for accessories made Zinnia smile.

This time Zinnia was prepared for the Server and managed to pull off her plate in the nick of time. The twins and Crispin smiled appreciatively and Zinnia felt proud of herself. She was learning, slowly and surely, the lamebirl ways in the Altklug world.

The charabanc was long and metallic silver with 'Fountain of Knowledge' scrawled in huge letters on all four sides. One side whipped open like a wing to allow the lamebren to step in.

'Be seated on the left side please,' Bosco instructed and all the lamebren shifted to the left side of the charabanc. 'The right side has been reserved for the Northside Altklug Knowledge Port.'

The metallic wing slipped soundlessly into place and the charabanc took off at a breathtaking speed, zipping through the network of interconnected skyways. Zinnia caught her breath, trying not to feel too dizzy. It was as if the charabanc was participating in a race. For that matter, she was constantly aware of the continuous sense of race in the life of the Altklugs. The need to maintain speed, to keep pace with time and knowledge, to keep pace with their super-fast, breathless Ace-world, to keep pace with the six years that were rushing past their age in the single span of a year…

Minutes later, the charabanc smoothed to a halt before a dazzling building. It was the Northside Altklug Knowledge Port. Zinnia craned her neck to see the tall twin spires of the silver-coated towers. She had never seen an Altklug K. Port before and going by the jazzy outer sheen, she could well imagine the high-tech stuff inside.

A number of one-year-old students trooped inside the charabanc. One look at their polished, shiny young faces and crisp, white uniforms and Zinnia had no doubt of the vast chasm of knowledge between them. Beside the kids, the lamebren appeared like crude balls of flesh! Iris glanced up and a half smile touched her lips.

'Good afternoon, Preceptor Sven,' Bosco greeted.

Preceptor Sven nodded briefly. He was of medium height, rather pleasant-looking and an Altklug who actually seemed to possess a smile. He took the seat adjacent to Iris.

'Rest of the kids, to the right,' Bosco commanded without ceremony.

Some of the kids frowned at his tone, but some others slipped into their seats.

Preceptor Sven nodded again in acknowledgement at Iris, who turned and gazed out of the window. Her actions did not at all seem to perturb the Preceptor, because his causal smile converted to a look of frank admiration as he stared at Iris. Zinnia almost giggled. Iris was exceedingly beautiful. The green necklace added a touch of glamour to the dull black demi-sleever and lego, highlighting her green eyes. It was no wonder that the Altklug could not take his eyes off her.

The 'Fountain of Knowledge' charabanc zipped forward into the maze of bridges again. Although not a whisper escaped a single child inside the vehicle, the atmosphere was like a tight string. Only Bosco's occasional booming instructions punctuated the strained silence. While the Preceptor sat next to Iris and continued to stare boldly at her.

It was when the charabanc entered the Water Vein that Zinnia gasped. It was the most amazing sight of her life. The tunnel was long with a circular, transparent roof which displayed the blue and green stripes of the lake overhead, highlighted by long lines of multi-coloured illuminations. On a parallel track ran a see-through rattler, the heads of the Altklugs flashing by like a moving pic-chip. Zinnia couldn't take her eyes off the glistening lake, the seeping rays of the sun forming elegant, fragile patterns in the water. She noticed that all the lamebren were staring in awe at the magnificent scene overhead.

Five minutes later, the charabanc emerged from the Water Vein and slowed down. 'The Fountain of Knowledge,' a voice informed in the charabanc. Zinnia and the twins craned their necks to see the glorious fountain, the symbol of the Eastern Quarter of the Super-Dome. A jazzy lumino sign flashed the name of the fountain. Colourful jets of water sprinkled and moulded in the shape of the letter 'K' with the central jet shooting high up in the air. The blend of colour, shimmering water and white stone was graceful and ethereal, and muted whispers of awe passed between the lamebren. The Altklug kids however, stared straight ahead, barely glancing at the fountain.

The charabanc picked up speed again but within minutes jerked to a halt outside a magnificent, translucent blue mansion with a huge cupola. Zinnia stared in fascination at the intricately carved blue roof, like delicate, gilded veins forming intricate designs just under the surface. The celebrated Museum of the Altklugs!

The line was long. Altklugs in spotless white uniforms patrolled around the Museum, slim guns in their hands. Zinnia wondered at the security. Was it because the Museum housed some of the most precious artefacts of their long-gone leader Governor Seeya?

The Altklug kids took the queue first, followed by the lamebren. Iris stood at the head of the lamebren queue and in front of her stood Preceptor Sven, at the tail end of his queue. Zinnia was amused at the way his gaze travelled all round the dome, to ultimately rest on Iris's face. He seemed quite smitten by the beautiful Iris, who on the other hand, completely ignored the Altklug.

'Follow me!' Bosco commanded again and the line trooped past the huge blue Demarcators and entered the grand hall. 'From this point, you are permitted to move around on your own. Do not touch anything. Do not chat with the Altklugs. Take a look around, but be back in precisely twenty minutes.'

Zinnia found the Dome Museum so completely captivating that she forgot about everything else. Right in the centre of the hall stood a tall and statuesque sculpture of Governor Seeya. A turquoise blue gown was draped around the smooth body and a halo of blue and silver light beamed onto her. She was so unbelievably life-like that Zinnia felt that any moment the Leader would turn around and speak to her.

'Isn't she beautiful?' Camilla exclaimed, her voice filled with awe.

'Stunning,' Zinnia agreed.

Her steps automatically moved closer to the statue and for a few startling moments, Zinnia stared. An uncanny frisson ran down her spine, almost like a current, looping around her body, through her head and probed her brain as she grappled to cling to the shreds of reality. Governor Seeya was gazing straight into her eyes, combing deep through her thoughts, and filling her with a burning desire...

A sudden commotion broke out at the end of the hall and the bond of attraction snapped. Zinnia blinked, experiencing an insane reluctance to let go of the trance.

'Come on, let's see what's happened,' Cheska took Zinnia's hand.

Zinnia followed the twins, as they pushed their way through the groups and stopped short. A strange sight met Zinnia's eyes. Iris was standing beside a huge concave in the centre of the hall. It displayed Governor Seeya's kitchenware and was cordoned off from all sides by a slim, metallic blue wire. But it wasn't the pots and pans that caught Zinnia's attention. It was the way Bosco was holding off Preceptor Sven and an Altklug. The twins and Zinnia ran to Iris.

'What happened!' Zinnia asked.

Iris shook her head, looking pale and upset. Ivy, Maisie, Cylia and Azalea stood confused. Reed, Crispin and Berk were picking up green beads from the floor. *Iris's necklace!* Zinnia realised with a start.

'Now Preceptor Sven, you know the rule, no interacting with the lamebren. Not even teachers. As for you Josh, you should never have pushed the lamebroy!' Bosco's voice was calm and controlled.

Preceptor Sven's intelligent, shiny face was set in a frown. He stared at Iris, who avoided looking at him.

'I'll tell you what happened,' Crispin spoke up. His demi-sleever had come loose from his lego and his hair looked untidier than ever. 'We were studying those artefacts when that kid Josh shoved me. I lost my balance and fell against Iris. My hand got stuck in her necklace and it broke. We were collecting the green stones scattered on the floor when Preceptor Sven strode towards me and began abusing me, asking me to respect ladies and to keep my hands off Iris. As if I was doing anything!'

'You what...?' the twins looked aghast.

Ivy and Maisie passed each other quick, fearful glances while Azalea looked as worried as Berk did. Zinnia turned to Iris, who blushed blood deep.

'Forget it and let's go,' Iris mumbled her head and eyes downcast.

'Now calm down all of you. Preceptor Sven, please lead your kids to the other end of the hall. We shall meet at the charabanc in thirty minutes, right? Lamebren we have a docunote to watch. Meet me at the auditorium in ten minutes.'

Preceptor Sven shot Iris a dark look and strode towards his group of kids. Bosco sighed and shrugged. Zinnia stared in confusion at her friends.

'How weird!' she exclaimed.

'Weird is right,' Crispin agreed. 'What was Preceptor Sven thinking?'

'I said forget it,' Iris repeated looking acutely embarrassed. 'We have ten minutes to see the rest of the Museum before we go see the docunote, okay? So, let's hurry!'

Crispin handed her the beads, the remnants of the beautiful necklace, which she pocketed without a word. As the lamebren moved around the picture gallery, no one noticed that Lorde had hung behind, shooting wicked glances at Preceptor Sven.

The lamebren continued their tour across the museum, but Zinnia couldn't focus. She was troubled. Something about the way Iris had reacted disturbed her—Iris and Preceptor Sven. The Altklugs and their Ace-world had nothing to do with the lamebren. In her whole life, this was the first time that Zinnia had even shared charabanc space with the Altklug kids themselves. And yet, something strange had transpired today…something that Zinnia couldn't quite understand. She observed Iris covertly but the girl seemed to have regained her composure and in fact was quite excited about exploring the Museum. She was flushed and pretty and it confused Zinnia all the more…especially the smile in her eyes that she was trying so hard to conceal.

The auditorium was a huge place with spaced out, lush, dark arm-chairs and a lot of gadgetry attached to it. 'This is a five minute docunote on Governor Seeya. Please be seated and insert these chips into your padlets. Hold the other chip in your palm and close your eyes, please,'

The lamebren followed Bosco's instructions as they slipped into the seats in the darkened room. Zinnia closed her eyes and instantly loud cries and sharp commands filled the atmosphere. Lightening ripped the dark room, transforming it into a battlefield. Zinnia gasped as the blasts thundered into her brain and light arrows whizzed past her ears stinging in intensity. The scene was terrifying as gigantic Humanoid machines clashed with the Altklug army under a glass-like Dome. Shattering glass merged with streams of melting hot metal, filling the Cupola like red hot lava. The stench of burnt skin, the intense heat and the cries of terror, pain and agony filled her heart with horror. The entire scene seemed to erode Zinnia's heart and tears sprung down her cheeks. Then, just as suddenly, soothing music filtered into her mind and her body felt cool and began to relax.

Images rose before her eyes—Governor Seeya in a turquoise blue gown and a sparkling diamond-studded crown, looking absolutely powerful and stunning. Her black eyes were glittering as she spoke in a soft firm voice. 'Today we have achieved what we Altklugs have dreamt of for years. Peace, freedom and finally, absolute knowledge. Knowledge, which has liberated us from the uncertainty of death, of disease. Today we are in control of our destiny. Let's make a promise to ourselves not to exploit this freedom, not to abuse this knowledge and to use it to better the lives of the Altklugs and those who come under our shelter.'

Governor Seeya smiled a knowing enigmatic smile. Zinnia felt the brush of lips on her wet cheek. The Governor's piercing gaze rested on the lamebirl. Her smile vanished and the gaze grew in such intensity, that Zinnia was sucked into its depths. Governor Seeya's exquisite face loomed larger and larger, filling up her vision and finally merging into Zinnia's head. A strange sensation wrapped around Zinnia, a sort of thrill, but more like a calm and protective sheen of emotion...

Zinnia opened her eyes with a gasp. Her breath was short and she glanced, disoriented, at the others. Had the other lamebren too experienced this bizarre connection? The almost palpable and real interaction with Governor Seeya. Dim lights illuminated parts of the room. Crispin looked sober as he extracted his chip from the padlet and the twins appeared shaken. Farther on, the other lamebren shuffled uncomfortably in their seats, appearing a little dazed. Only Iris looked calm as she replaced the chips. Bosco opened a door and led them all out. He looked as unfazed as ever.

'Wow! That was some docudrama!' Crispin exclaimed, as they gathered in the hall again.

'Not something I am going to forget for a long time,' Zinnia agreed. Her mind was still reeling with the impact of Governor Seeya's speech and her look. No, it was not something that she would forget soon...

6

'I love to stitch,' Cylia explained. 'If you have any extra cloth with you, do pass it on to me. I'll cut it and make something out of it for you. I have bought the most amazing auto-needle!'

'I will. I'd love this patchwork pouch I saw in a picchip. In the olden days, people would carry stuff in them,' Zinnia suggested.

'Yes, I know what you mean.' Cylia's eyes gleamed under her almost non-existence eyebrows. 'I would love to make it for you. Oh, I'm so excited...'

'Iris is taking me to the Dome Piazzar today. Perhaps I'll buy some beautiful material for the pouch.'

'That would be super!' Cylia exclaimed. Her pony tail, held high on the top of her head, swung to and fro as she drifted away, happy in the thought of her pouch-making.

Zinnia was a little surprised at the ease with which she had settled into her new life. She had adapted to the routine within days and even the Supercustodian had toned down the waspish, sarcastic pitch that she used on Zinnia. The new faces had become familiar especially because of the names she had concocted for every lamebirl and lamebroy. She had also begun finding her way around the Dome and even discovered a Paramour Path right next to the Cubicle. Zinnia was delighted to find a lane similar to the Rose Lane at the Ret Cabana.

'Zinnia, are you coming with me to the Dome Piazzar or have you changed your mind?' Iris popped her head into the room.

'I'm coming!' Zinnia replied.

'The twins have evening duty at Commander Burdock's house, so they aren't coming and Crispin would rather sit and read instead of traipsing around the market,' Iris said as they made their way to the charabanc stop.

'I've never been to the Piazzar before, and I so want to see it!'

'It's fascinating to say the least. A world in itself. It's in the Western Quarter so you'll also be able to visit the Fountain of Conscience—it's remarkable like all the other Fountains. Amazing work of art,' Iris explained.

She was wearing a pretty crimson scarf over her black shirt. As they climbed onto the charabanc with 'Fountain of Conscience' splashed all around it in multi-colours and it sped into the skyways, Zinnia noticed that the older lamebirl looked exceedingly pretty. The little touches of colour and accessories that she added to the black common uniform, made her stand out distinctly in a crowd.

'Like my scarf?' Iris laughed, guessing at what was in Zinnia's mind.

'It's pretty,' Zinnia agreed.

'Like all my other pretty stuff. You know, I think I am the only one of the lamebren, who regularly visits the Dome Piazzar. I *have* to go there once a week. It makes me feel alive—the colours, the noise, the sheer variety—it's as if I am not in this black and white, boring Altklug Ace-world at all, but somewhere else, where all these beautiful things matter, where these gorgeous articles are a part of my life and mean something to me. That is why, every single time, I pick up a brooch, or a necklace or a scarf, whatever pleases me—I spend all my monthly quota of Mudra on it and it makes me so happy!'

Zinnia listened keenly, observing the glow of anticipation on the older lamebirl's lovely face. She really did seem to relish these visits to the Piazzar.

The two lamebren got off at the 'Fountain of Conscience' and for the first time, Zinnia saw the symbol of the Altklug Ace-world at close quarters. Five Altklug Statues supported a huge Alphabet 'C' in the centre and jets of water sprouted in a circular fashion from their hands. The Fountain rose from all ends of the C, flying so high, that as usual, Zinnia could only imagine the top. The sheer artistry of the fountain and the riot of colours was amazing. Considering that the Altklugs wasted no time on emotions, it was remarkable how they could have created this masterpiece. It was as if the monuments and fountains were trying to make up for the otherwise dry nature and monotone shades and minds of the Altklugs. Zinnia stared in awe at the huge fountain, enjoying the sprinkling of the spray on her cheeks.

'Come, let me take some shots of you at the Fountain,' Iris said suddenly.

'Shots?' Zinnia was puzzled. 'But you don't have a Digi-eye.'

'You see these boxes on the street? Well, these are digi-eyes placed for everyone to use. Just attach the cable to your padlet and shoot. Stand against the Fountain... lovely! Especially your wind-blown hair and that sweet dimple in the cheek!'

'Ok, now my turn,' Zinnia laughed.

She took some shots of Iris as she posed against the jets, holding her red scarf and smiling prettily. *Iris was such a misfit in the Altklug world,* Zinnia thought with sudden insight. A lamebirl like Iris should've been born somewhere else—far away, where life was not drab and disciplined and orderly. Where freedom meant wearing what you please, and doing what you want, but was there such a place? Anywhere at all?

The Dome Piazzar was like walking into a maze of tech-advanced shopping system. The shops themselves were spread over several towers, the tips of which seemed to vanish into the sky. Zinnia was so taken aback with the sheer magnitude of it all, that she had to take a breather.

'These towers have stores, sorted according to commodities in alphabetical order. We'll have to take the internal charabanc which will pick and drop us at our desired store,' Iris explained.

They stood in the centre of a Square with long queues of high-rise towers all around them.

'It's all automated of course and it took me a while to figure it out. It *can* get a little daunting if you don't have help.' She grinned. 'Come on, there's the charabanc, hop in. Just speak the number of the store that's all. I want to pick up another scarf and my favourite store is on the 85th floor, store No. 55.' The older lamebirl demonstrated, as she spoke into a screen, which instantly displayed her instruction.

The charabanc set off at a steady pace, passing rows and rows of shops. The variety of the merchandise took Zinnia's breath away. Machines to design and turn your cloth into dresses, automatic hairstyles, limb replacement units, stores and stores of nutritional 'food' packets, colour and size-changing umbrellas and clothes for the weather hours, a variety of padlets, digi-eyes and screens, ranging from the tiniest to the largest, portable, foldable and adjustable furniture which you could carry anywhere, even in your handbag—Zinnia could only gasp in amazement. Iris seemed to enjoy the younger lamebirl's astonishment.

'It's fun, isn't it?'

'It's dazzling,' Zinnia agreed. 'I've never seen so many shops before...and do the Altklugs really use all this beautiful and...and mind-boggling stuff?'

'Yes they do, in their after-hours, at home. The rest they export to the other four Domes across the planet. Oh, here's my store. Come on!'

No. 55 was a place Zinnia would never forget. In one sweeping moment, she grasped why Iris was the way she was—*she had no choice*. The store tempted every lamebirl instinct in her, arousing the finest feelings. There were scarves, jewellery, shoes, clothes, handbags—each vying for attention in colour, shine and attraction. Iris immediately moved to the scarf section and touched a turquoise blue scarf of the softest variety.

'Beautiful, isn't it?'Admiration dripped through her tone.

'It is,' Zinnia admitted. 'And it will look lovely on you.'

'I'll look pretty, won't I?' She draped it against herself with a candid smile.

'You already are very pretty, Iris,' Zinnia assured, amused. 'But the scarf will make you look exquisite.'

'Aw, you are sweet Zinnia.' Iris gave the young lamebirl a quick, affectionate hug.

She punched her padlet number into the machine and the Mudra from her account was transferred to the store. The machine then released the Scarf, which Iris folded and pocketed.

'Hello!' a voice hailed.

Startled, Zinnia and Iris turned around.

'Preceptor Sven!' Iris exclaimed.

'Ah...you are...G10, right?'

Zinnia could simply stare. Preceptor Sven smiled pleasantly at them.

'Yes, I am and she's Zinnia. For that matter, my name is Iris.'

'Iris—what a beautiful name! It suits you.'

Iris blushed. Zinnia stood awkwardly, uncertain of what to do. Were they allowed to talk to Altklugs? Why was Preceptor Sven behaving in such an easy, familiar manner?

'So good to find you here,' he continued amiably.

'Yes what a coincidence, isn't it?' Iris said.

'Iris, I think we better leave,' Zinnia admonished, nudging the older lamebirl.

'Been shopping you two, haven't you? You must be tired. The Dome Piazzar can be a little exhausting after the initial excitement of shopping is over,' the Altklug continued.

He glanced from one lamebirl to the other, his gaze resting longer than necessary on Iris, apparently awaiting her response.

'It's a fantastic place and shopping is a pleasurable activity.'

The older lamebirl smiled shyly at the Preceptor. Zinnia's heart began to thump erratically. She had to stop this exchange of pleasantries, she had to *do* something. Instinct told her that it was not appropriate.

'Excuse us, Sir, but we really have to leave,' Zinnia cut in. 'We are already late.'

'But…' Iris turned to Zinnia, a frown topping her beautiful face.

She opened her mouth to protest but the look on Zinnia's face made her falter.

'Come on, I still have to buy some material for Cylia,' Zinnia insisted.

She literally dragged the older lamebirl by the hand, wanting to increase the distance between the Preceptor and them for some strange, mysterious reason. Zinnia sensed a resistance in her friend's body language and hoped earnestly that Iris would not hold back and continue to chat with the Preceptor. After all, he *was* showering her with special attention and keen interest which no lamebirl had ever experienced before and most certainly not from an Altklug. Wasn't that an offense in the Altklug World? Zinnia suddenly experienced a frisson of fear...

But mercifully, Iris followed her friend mutely.

'Goodbye!' she exclaimed rather belatedly over her shoulder.

Preceptor Sven bent his head in acknowledgement, his manner grave and controlled.

For the rest of the evening, Iris was meek and had lost her exuberance for shopping. Zinnia sensed the change in her mood but maintained a stoic silence. She bought some material for Cylia, following Iris's brief instructions. Her mood swings puzzled Zinnia a bit. There was so much to learn from Iris—her desire to help everyone, her sensitive nature and yet sometimes Zinnia sensed a restraint on her part. As if she was holding back something, something she wanted to keep strictly to herself...some secret... some desire...

But then, didn't they all? Wasn't each lamebirl and lamebroy unconsciously doing the same? Weren't their dreams and desires suppressed and crushed under the great pressure of the superiority of Altklug existence? Wasn't the Secret Society a result of this need to burst out from under the pressure? Hadn't she herself experienced a restless energy inside of her?

Being the oldest, Iris was simply more expressive than any of the other lamebren, Zinnia concluded. She had seen more of the Altklug Ace-world than any of them, so she was prone to being more reactive and reflective than any of the lamebren. Satisfied with her analysis, Zinnia allowed the puzzle to slide from her mind. It was dark when the two of them returned to the Cubicle, just in time for dinner.

'I feel so weak, I have no clue what is wrong with me,' Azalea whispered so softly that she could barely be heard.

As Iris fussed over the lamebirl, Zinnia hovered in the background. Azalea was a delicate and fragile lamebirl and the weakest of the lamebren. Iris made her comfortable on the bed, gently arranging the covers around her. Zinnia hung back, watching the exchange.

'Thank you, Iris. You do know we aren't allowed to lie down during class hours.'

'I know, but it's the class with Mirella and she'll understand. Do rest, you know it's the Heat Hour which does this to you. With Rain Hour, you'll feel better.'

'Don't you think nowadays they are missing the Snow Hour? I do so love it, although it gives a terrible burn in the head. Do you think the Snow Hour is getting delayed?'

Iris shook her head briefly. 'Everything is right on time, dear. Nothing is missing and nothing gets delayed here. You must've miscalculated.'

'Yes, I probably did.'

Azalea turned grateful eyes on Iris, who smiled in understanding. Berk appeared just then, looking plump and earnest with an almost perpetually anxious face, followed by the other lamebren.

'She's right. The Snow Hour has shifted. I noticed it too. Is that what is making you sick?' he asked, looking fretful.

'Yes, is it?' Reed confirmed, adjusting his spectacles.

Maisie and Ivy also regarded Azalea with concern. Reed and Ivy were the tallest of the lamebren and made even Bamian uncomfortable with their height, Zinnia suspected.

'No, it's not,' Iris cut in firmly. 'It's a temporary feeling and it will pass. Come on, let's all leave her alone to rest. Don't we have Mirella's class?'

Iris literally hustled everyone from the room. Berk threw a frown in Azalea's direction.

'Take care,' he flung at her.

Zinnia liked Mirella on sight. She had the kindest face she had seen so far on an Altklug, even kinder than Peeta's at the Ret Cabana. And she had a lilting voice, smooth and musical, which uttered only the most encouraging words. Her white, floating dress was starkly in contrast with the norm of the Altklug world uniform and she looked angelic.

'My notes say that you like music and you like to sing, is that right G23?' She looked directly at Zinnia.

The lamebirl nodded, a little shyly.

'And the notes also say that you wake up every morning with a song in your heart and you don't know what to do with it?' Mirella's curious gaze was steady on the little girl.

'Oh, they put that down too in the notes?' Zinnia was surprised.

'They put down everything in the notes. Even your thoughts.'

'Even my thoughts?' Zinnia was startled. Iris and the others hadn't warned her about this.

Someone sniggered at the back of the classroom. It had to be Lorde!

'Well not all the time, of course and only if you are in the vicinity of the Thought-Reader which not all the Altklugs have access to, anyway. So, don't worry. You must have heard about the Memory Porters? Well, you can put your memory in chips for future reference or for the reference of generations if you so wish. But again access is only to Altklugs. Anyway, I'm digressing. I hope that this class will help you understand what you can do with the song in your heart.' Mirella smiled briefly and turned away. 'Now G11 are you ready with your poetry tutorial and B12 with the floflute?'

The twins immediately rose and ran to the head of the class. Mirella took a transparent seat by a large screen. A hush fell on the class as Cheska raised the floflute to his lips. A sound so sweet rose from the instrument that the taste spilled into Zinnia's mouth and filled her senses. Her eyes closed spontaneously as she savoured the magical notes which swirled through and around her. Cheska played the instrument with ease and a meditative ardour which revealed his love and dedication. Finally, when the music stopped, the silence that followed was loaded with appreciation. Mirella clapped loudly.

'Wonderful, B12! I am amazed at your improvement,' she declared.

'Thank you.' Cheska looked abashed, but a shy smile revealed his crooked teeth.

'G11, you may begin your poem now.'

Camilla ran a tongue over her dry lips. Her glance swept across the classroom and came to rest on Iris.

'This poem is dedicated to my friend G10 or Iris, as our new friend Zinnia calls her,' she began.

'Iris—that's a nice name.' Mirella flashed a look in Iris's direction and nodded appreciatively.

Camilla cleared her throat and smiled across at the older lamebirl. Then in a voice filled with emotion, she began her poem.

'I watch helplessly as they come and go,
Touching my life with a special glow
With a hungry mind and a hungry heart;
They enrich my life, as they depart.

I watch them disappear into a haze
Touching my heart in, oh, so many ways
Teaching me love and the art of giving,
And making me, a better being.

I'm not an Altklug, just a lamebirl in the Dome
This isn't my world, nor my home
Soon, I will have to say goodbye,
Without asking how, when and why…'

'Stop this nonsense, this instant!' a harsh voice cut in rudely.

Startled, Zinnia turned to see a bald man standing by the door. He wore a pristine white uniform with badges loaded on his right shoulder. Beside him stood the Supercustodian, wrath printed all over her pinched face. Mirella rose at once, as a frightened Camilla faltered in her recitation. Cheska edged towards his twin.

'Excuse me?' Mirella frowned.

'I absolutely forbid you to continue this class, Mirella,' Supercustodian remarked. 'I am lucky to have chanced in on this hour to witness this atrocity and I am sure Commander Hertz will agree with me.'

'Totally. No more poetry, no more whatever it is that you teach!' the Commander rasped.

Mirella stared at them, her head held high.

'And may I know why?'

'You may not, Mirella,' Supercustodian continued, a gleam of hatred in her eyes.

Mirella glanced from her to the Commander. 'May I remind you that as an Altklug teacher, I have full powers to take this class.'

'You do, but I too have the full power to inspect the result of your teaching and I find it unsuitable for the lamebren.'

'Unsuitable!' Mirella exclaimed. 'And what was so unsuitable about a floflute performance and poetry, may I ask?'

'The nature of the contents of the poem Exector!' the Commander was sarcastic.

'This class was formed with one goal in mind—self-expression. Unleashing of bottled-up emotions which would dissipate any feeling of antagonism and hatred, and I think we are very nicely achieving that goal.'

'Are you?'

'Would you rather one of the lamebren directly ask you the questions in her mind?' Mirella asked, her hands folded.

'She or he would be quashed without preamble.' The Commander's voice was low and menacing.

'Precisely. A situation which could arise and gather momentum if we don't have classes such as the ones that I conduct. Commander, with due respect to your opinion, I request you to leave me to handle the lamebren. I think I know them better than anyone here.'

Commander Hertz stared at Mirella for a long moment. The Exector returned the look, unwavering in her stance. It was as if unspoken words were being rayed into each other's brains. Finally, the Commander wheeled around and marched out of the class. The Supercustodian gawked after him in surprise.

'Now, if you will kindly allow me to continue my class?' Mirella raised an eyebrow cynically.

The Supercustodian flushed deep red but stood her ground. The button on her padlet blinked a bright red. She glanced at it and raised a triumphant look at Mirella.

'A lamebirl is missing. Where is G18?' She turned a sharp piercing gaze on the class.

A look of surprise crossed Mirella's face as an ominous silence filled the room.

'G18?' Supercustodian repeated.

'She ditched class!' Lorde stood up and spoke. 'And G10 asked her to.' He pointed an accusing finger at Iris.

All eyes turned on Iris who sat motionless, with her head bent. Supercustodian fixed her with an angry gaze. A quick look of worry flashed across Mirella's face.

'G10? Is that right?' Supercustodian demanded.

Iris rose slowly, her beautiful face flushed. A red brooch adorned her black top, twinkling as it slanted.

'She...she's not feeling too well. She's in the Cubicle...'

'Not well!' Supercustodian expostulated. 'Nobody is ever unwell at the Dome. *Unwell!* How dare she break the discipline of the Ret Cubicle! And who asked you to give her permission to miss her class?'

'Exector...' Iris began and her voice was trembling.

'I did,' Mirella spoke up. 'I knew she wasn't well and allowed her to stay in her room.'

'You did?' Supercustodian's gaze narrowed in suspicion,

Mirella's frank gaze met hers across the room.

'Yes and now if your Inspection is over, I would like to continue with my class.' Mirella's voice was cold and uncompromising.

The Supercustodian stared at the teacher, her nose pinched with anger and frustration. Then with a whisk of her gown, she strode out of the room. Zinnia expelled a breath and it was only then that she realised that she had sucked it in. She glanced at Iris who was staring at Mirella, her eyes moist with unspoken gratitude. For a fraction of a second the teacher returned the young lamebirl's look, then angled towards the class.

'Who's next? B22—you were quick to stand up and point a finger at G10. Now let's see if you are smart enough on the floflute,' Mirella remarked.

Lorde squirmed out of his chair, his face set in a sulky frown and moved towards the head of the room. Cheska passed him the floflute, a faint smile on his lips as the twins took their seats. Zinnia leaned forward to see and hear better. Could Lorde play the floflute? Her curiosity was satiated within seconds. Lorde raised the floflute and touched it to his lips. A loud, tuneless croak filled the room, followed by a spontaneous burst of laughter from the entire class. Lorde blew into the floflute again, puffing out his cheeks and the others laughed louder. He paused and a dark look crossed his face.

'Laugh all you like. Make fun of me. One day I'll get back at all of you!' he scorned.

Mirella raised an eyebrow. 'B22, that is quite enough. Go back to your seat at once. Instead of issuing threats—which by the way is completely unacceptable in the Altklug Dome and prone to charges under Section 411, please practice the floflute more. At least you'll get good marks at the end of the term.'

'Good marks—as if I care!' B22 scoffed. 'Who cares how much we get! Or if we pass or fail? In the end it's the Dissolution Crypt for all of us. Even for your favourite G10 or *Iris* as that newcomer calls her.'

A deep frown surfaced on Mirella's forehead and her eyes flashed in anger.

'B22! I won't have such talk in my class.' The Exector lost her cool. 'If you aren't careful, I may have to order the Isolation Chamber for you.'

This time it was Lorde's turn to pale. He shuffled to his seat and slumped into the soft cushion. Zinnia glanced at Iris. Her lips were trembling and she was staring at the floor.

7

'How can he!' Zinnia exclaimed, feeling hot with rage.

'He can and he did,' Crispin said gloomily.

Iris did not utter a word and the twins glanced at her anxiously.

'But the *Isolation Chamber...*' Camilla began.

'It's horrible!' Cheska shuddered as he finished in a terrified whisper.

Zinnia reread the message on Iris's padlet, indignation and fury choking her.

G10 remanded to Isolation Chamber from 0900 hours to 2100 hours for abetment to indiscipline.

By Order—Commander Hertz.

'I'm sure this is *her* doing. Commander Hertz wasn't even present when Supercustodian discovered that Azalea was missing in class,' Zinnia declared.

'Whatever, *whoever!* Iris did nothing wrong and Mirella did side with her in class,' Crispin pointed out, his cleft chin jutting out in defiance. 'The matter was sorted out. What perfect underhanded behaviour of Commander Hertz, to issue such a punishment for so little a crime.'

'It wasn't a crime even. Azalea was genuinely not well. I was there, I saw it,' Zinnia said. 'Iris only did what any caring person would do. And the Isolation Chamber—I don't even know what that means.'

The other lamebren turned to her, suddenly aware of her ignorance.

'It's a metallic room with no windows,' Crispin said.

'And not larger than a bathroom,' Camilla cut in.

'And it's airless and stifling, like a torture chamber,' Cheska completed.

Silence fell between them as the image of the dark, claustrophobic room rose before their eyes. Zinnia gasped, her breath stifled with anger and frustration.

'We've got to do something. Let's go to Mirella, she'll put in a word for Iris. She can revert the order, can't she?'

'Orders once issued cannot be reverted,' Iris spoke for the first time. She appeared calm and controlled.

'Not even Mirella can do it?'

'Not *even* Commander Hertz!'

'Then what do we do?'

'Not we, *I* am going to do something.'

Crispin, Zinnia and the twins stared at her.

'What do you mean?' Crispin frowned.

'I am going to attend Preceptor Amadeus's lecture this evening,' Iris stated calmly.

'No, you cannot!' Camilla's eyes widened.

'You'll be penalised,' her twin warned.

'I'm already penalised for something I don't deserve. Then I may as well break the rule and *do* something that I've always wanted to do—listen to Preceptor Amadeus speak.'

'But we have a field visit to the Northside Altklug Knowledge Port this afternoon. We've been ordered to assist at the Graduation Ceremony,' Crispin reminded.

'I know, so I'll go after the field visit. Don't worry, I'll manage.'

'But what about the Water Vein? You'll have to cross it and you know we've been forbidden to do that.'

'I am fourteen. The sleep chamber awaits me round the corner. You think I'm now going to worry about what is forbidden and what isn't?' Iris asked, her eyes flashing.

The fierce tone in her voice surprised everyone. Iris had never spoken in this manner before.

'Besides, it was one of the tasks of the Secret Society, remember? To attend Preceptor Amadeus's lecture and take some notes. Well, I am determined to do it.'

'I'll come with you,' Zinnia offered.

The twins turned to her with a start. 'Are you out of your mind? Do you know what happens if you're caught?'

'I just saw what happens when you do something good. Apparently, it can't be worse, can it? Besides we have the full freedom to move around as long as we don't interfere with their lives. So why should I fear to venture out?' Zinnia questioned.

Iris looked delighted, 'You sure?'

Zinnia nodded. 'Positive!'

Crispin and the twins glanced at each other, troubled expressions etched on their faces. Iris was reflective for a few moments. Then her face clouded and she shook her head.

'No, Zinnia, I'll go alone. I can't allow you to break rules. Supercustodian has especially made me responsible for you. It will never do if I lead you to mischief.'

'But...'

'No buts,' the older lamebirl interrupted firmly. 'Let me go alone today. I promise I'll share every word the Preceptor speaks, with all of you.'

Crispin appeared relieved and the twins nodded in agreement. Reluctance was stamped on Zinnia's face. Iris had *wanted* her to go with her, but her sense of responsibility had made her change her mind. Or was it something else? A sudden feeling of unease stirred at the back of her mind. Iris was doing the right thing, wasn't she?

The Northside Altklug Knowledge Port was now familiar to Zinnia. These were the same students who had visited the Museum with the lamebren. As soon as they reached the K. Port, Bosco divided them into groups. Iris, Crispin, Maisie and Ivy were dispatched to the kitchens to assist with the party food preparations. Berk, Reed, Azalea, Lorde and Cylia were sent to the entrance with decorations. Zinnia was bracketed with the twins and led into a huge hall.

'You have thirty minutes to clean up and decorate the stage. The Graduation Ceremony will begin in sixty minutes from now. Governor Tisya will be here sharp at 1600 hours, so you lamebren better hurry.' Bosco handed them palm-size vacuum cleaners.

Zinnia and the twins set to work. The stage was already arranged with deep-cushioned, lightweight arm-chairs in a semi-circle. A flashing white screen acted like a big backdrop to the stage. It displayed a multi-coloured, glittering message: A warm welcome to Governor Tisya! Zinnia paused in her cleaning and stared at the words for a long moment. Something was missing in the message, some warmth.... On an impulse, she picked up the laser-tip attached to the screen and drew a half moon under the dot of the 'i'. A child-like pleasure filled her and she smiled. The 'i' now looked like a stick sketch of a person but the picture was so small, it almost looked like a dot. Surely not a soul would notice it and yet it gave the welcome note, some much needed cheer.

'Zinnia, what are you doing? We've got ten minutes left. Hurry!' Camilla called and Zinnia rushed back to them.

She felt inordinately pleased with herself for some inexplicable reason.

When Bosco returned, the stage was spic and span and he nodded briefly in approval.

'To the back of the hall, you three. The kids will now be taking their seats.'

Zinnia and the twins obeyed, joining Iris and Crispin and the other lamebren at the far end of the hall. As the Altklug kids filled the huge hall, Zinnia stared at these two-and-a-half-year olds all set for their Graduation Ceremony. They were attired in white uniforms with polished hair, unblemished faces, and intelligent eyes. They all looked like exact replicas of each other. Zinnia could barely separate the boys from the girls. Two years! She couldn't even remember what she felt like when she was two. Her reminiscences were way too hazy. All she could recall were juxtaposed moments of joy and security in her mother's arms, spurts of emotional discoveries and then awe and fear of the world. And here were these kids—the exact opposite of her memories. Confident and accomplished, they had completed their education and were all set to conquer the professional world. For a moment, she experienced an acute sense of helplessness and vulnerability. The chasm between the kids and lamebren was too great for her to imagine. How could they ever compete with this degree of knowledge and progress? No wonder the Altklugs thought the lamebren were retarded and useless. They were different, in every conceivable way possible. And the difference began in the mind and heart…

Sudden buzzing filled the hall and all heads angled towards the entrance.

'That's Governor Tisya,' Crispin whispered in her ear.

Zinnia instantly turned in the direction of the bustle. A lady as tall as Iris swept past them. Her hair was cut so short around her head that for a moment Zinnia thought she was bald. Her white dress was so tightly moulded around her body that it was difficult to make out if she was wearing trousers or a gown. It fitted her like a metallic armour. Her movements were swift yet unhurried and she carried an air of total control and command. Behind her, Commander Hertz marched in a solemn manner. Zinnia watched fascinated as she swept between the aisles and climbed on to the stage. The Altklugs clapped as an audiocrone immediately slid in the air and positioned itself before her.

'Sit down kids,' the Governor began and her voice clear and sharp, vibrated from all the corners of the K. Port. 'Today is an important day in your lives. You will now step into the real world with your invaluable chips of knowledge and aspirations. But remember, you will be received with respect and awe as long as you dedicate your lives to the betterment of the Altklug Ace-world. You too will reap the fruits of your hard work and involvement. Progress and development will take on a new meaning for you. The future is yours to build or yours to destroy. The real world does not tolerate laziness, indiscipline or stupidity. It is tough and brutal but only if you allow it to be, so step into the real world with a clear vision—the vision of a powerful Altklug Ace-world in sync with science, knowledge and technology, a world of limitless possibilities and perfection, a world which we have all sworn to enhance. So, step into it with an aim. Step into it with a plan. Step into it with zero tolerance for wastage of time. Use every day, hour, second to give the world your best. To give *our* world *your* best...Good luck!'

A deep, stunned silence followed the thundering speech and then the audience broke into a rapturous applause. They rose spontaneously and Governor Tisya nodded. In that instant Zinnia understood why Governor Tisya had such a hold on the Altklug Ace-world, why she had been elected time and again to lead this perfect Dome of super knowledge. It was because she was the epitome of the inherent qualities of the Dome. She was a Leader, a Communicator and a Dictator! She was incomparable...

Governor Tisya rose to leave and suddenly she halted. She turned her back on the audience and stared at the backdrop screen.

'Who did this?' Her voice was as cold as the Snow Hour.

Commander Hertz instantly moved forward and she exchanged a few words with him. He nodded, glanced at the screen and then took the audiocrone. His entire demeanour was unrelenting.

'Who wrote the message on this screen?'

A figure hastened forward. 'I did, Sir.'

'Preceptor Sven, what is the meaning of this, rather insolent act?'

'What act, Sir?' Preceptor Sven appeared a little non-plussed. 'I have no idea what you are talking about.'

'Kindly enlarge the word—Governor Tisya!' Commander Hertz ordered.

In that instance, Zinnia's heart began thudding a wild tattoo. The Governor had noticed the half-moon she had drawn on her name!

Preceptor Sven magnified the word with the remote in his hand. Immediately the entire hall could see the tiny half-moon under the dot of 'i'. Enlarged, it looked more like a stick drawing than she had imagined.

'Now do you understand what I mean?' the Commander enquired with sarcasm.

'I didn't do that Sir and I wrote that message myself,' Preceptor Sven replied calmly. 'But I *can* look up the monitoring record to see who did it.'

'Then do it this instant,' Governor Tisya commanded.

Zinnia broke away from the group. The other lamebren glanced at her surprised, as she hastened down the aisle. Crispin and Iris frowned while Bosco stared, uncomprehending.

Zinnia's feet acted of their own volition. She ran down the aisle, her heart pumping with trepidation. All Zinnia knew was that she had to own up. A voice at the back of her mind screamed that this was dangerous, that she would be dismissed to the Isolation Chamber, but her legs had taken on the role of her conscience. And now they refused to listen to reason, fear or anxiety. Several heads turned in astonishment as she approached Preceptor Sven.

'You don't need to check your records, Sir. I did it!' she confessed, breathlessly.

Preceptor Sven wheeled around to see the lamebirl, alarm reflecting on his face. Governor Tisya and Commander Hertz looked taken aback. At the back of the hall, Iris, Crispin and the twins gasped. Zinnia was crazy—what was she saying?

'*You* did it?' Preceptor Sven confirmed.

'Yes, I did. I'm sorry, I didn't mean to hurt or insult anybody. I just thought the message needed a bit of warmth, so I...I added a half moon under the dot. That's what I do all the time on my K. Sensor. Draw half-moons to show love.'

A deadly silence followed this confession. The kids in the hall caught their breath. The lamebren at the back of the hall squirmed sensing the doom that would befall Zinnia. Before Preceptor Sven could respond, a sarcastic laughter rung out from the stage. It was Governor Tisya.

'Love, warmth, half-moons—wasted emotions! Spoken like a true lamebirl,' Governor Tisya hissed. 'You played mischief with my name. You deserve a punishment that will act as a deterrent to anyone who dares to take such a liberty ever again.'

Her piercing gaze clashed into Zinnia's innocent face, befuddling the lamebirl's brain. The instantaneous protest on the tip of Zinnia's tongue was quashed and she simply stared back at the Governor.

'Governor...' Preceptor Sven began on a hesitant, quick note but the top lady of the Dome raised a hand and silenced him.

She turned to Commander Hertz and they consulted in low tones for a few moments. There was a tight band in Zinnia's chest. She wanted to break the band and speak out, but her legs were trembling and her tongue felt powerless.

At length, Commander Hertz stepped forward. 'As a penalty for acting rashly, you are herewith commanded to clean all the Wash Receptacles in this K. Port before you leave today. The mechanical cleaning devices will be turned off, no one will help the lamebirl and no one will speak to her till the task is done.'

'Oh...!' A ripple of diverse exclamations ran through the kids. Some sniggered, some whispered, while others just stared at the lamebirl with candid contempt.

Zinnia stood rooted to the spot, shocked beyond words. Clean all the Wash Receptacles? How demeaning, and... and...humiliating. All because she had tried to put some warmth into a message? Perhaps it had been wrong... perhaps it didn't fit the Altklug code of ethics...but *cleaning Wash Receptacles?* How completely unjust! Tears of frustration sprang into her eyes and her heart protested in anguish. But her tongue was in knots and her mind in an abyss.

Without further ado, Governor Tisya and the Commander stepped off the stage and walked past Zinnia, completely ignoring her presence and the kids followed in their steps. Preceptor Sven stared at Zinnia fleetingly and shook his head. Zinnia couldn't understand if it was in sympathy or plain reproof. Someone thrust her out of the hall and down a corridor. Zinnia turned, hoping to see her friends but they were far behind in the hall. She saw a wave of a hand. Was that Crispin? But she was hustled forward, down a narrow white corridor to a sling of white doors. A motorised cleaner was thrust into her hands and she was alone in a long string of Wash Receptacles. Zinnia inhaled deeply, brushed away the tears, shut her mind against thoughts and set to work.

8

The street directional arrow claimed the time as seven, when Zinnia climbed off the Community charabanc. The Rain Hour was over and the roads were wet and shining. The Wash Receptacles had taken a long time to clean and it was only when the automatic machine had passed the 'spotless' verdict and a green light had shone above the door that she was allowed to pass through the locked doors. She had walked down the empty corridors, under the dim, florescent blue-green lights which bounced off the glass walls, and a sense of eerie loneliness descended on her.

The K. Port Humanoid had hailed the Community charabanc and Zinnia had climbed in, without a backward glance at the Knowledge Port. The charabanc was empty and within minutes had dropped her off at the Ret Cubicle. But Zinnia hesitated to go in, stalling, to glare at the small fountain in the shape of the pen, at the glass doors and the lumino sign of the Cubicle. In the pale evening light, the Cubicle appeared like some kind of a lone monument. Dinner time was still ninety minutes away—she wouldn't be missed. Zinnia had no desire to enter the sterile premises of the Ret Cubicle. She experienced a sudden urge for fresh air, gallons of it, to breathe and wallow in until she could flush the stench of the Wash Receptacles. She wanted to dig her hands into the soft earth and bury her head between the flowers. She wanted to erase every memory of the task she had just performed.

She ran towards the Paramour Path, the love lane she had spotted earlier. She remembered the one at her last home and wondered if this one would be similar. Weren't all Paramour Paths supposed to serve the sole purpose of creating the feelings of harmony and love? Zinnia felt so lonely that only the ambience of the Paramour Path would allow her some semblance of peace and warmth.

The leaves on the trees were fresh green with the tender gloss of a newborn leaf. The street lamps which lit the road from below, illuminated the path with subtle yellows and oranges setting the mood for the Paramour Path. Scores of flowers provided a riot of colours and their sweet scent attacked her nose with vehemence. The moment Zinnia stepped into the lane, her hair lifted with the moderated breeze and her spirits instantly rose. She closed her eyes momentarily and soaked in the mood. This, for her, was the real world. A world filled with flowers and trees and the beautiful lake surrounded by light woods, a world where even the Altklugs were left unattended, to relax and love, and emerge invigorated to pursue their structured lives. A world where hidden digi-eyes did not follow them, trying to pinch and unearth their deepest secrets, the only place without prying, political eyes. Zinnia loved the Paramour Path.

She strolled down the path, touching the soft petals of the flowers to her face and listening to the sounds of chirping, regulated through the audio stream. Up ahead, she could see the water of the lake glistening in blue and green stripes. She ambled towards it, chose a flat, stone seat and sat gazing out at the lake's serene water, its gentle ripples calming her. What a beautiful place this was! If only she could sit here forever. She never wanted to return to the Cubicle, where she felt stifled and angry all the time. She missed Peeta from the Ret Cabana, her young friends, and her Mom and Dad and she longed to cry. But after the initial rush of tears at the K. Port, suddenly her tears seemed to have dried up.

Thoughts reeled into a loop in her head. The harsh, humiliating punishment for a crime which wasn't one…the unfairness of it all.... The fact that she was a mere lamebirl to be shoved around in the Altklug world, became stark and real now. *No, this wasn't just an Altklug Ace-world. She* was born here too! This was *her* world too. *The Altklugs needed to realise this!*

But how? How could she ever make them understand that she belonged here too? She could imagine the twins and Crispin smirking—trying to make an Altklug understand? She *must* be crazy! And yet there had to be a way

Suddenly a light giggle broke into her trance. A couple emerged from the woods, hand in hand and so engrossed with each other that they did not even notice Zinnia. At the lake they paused and Zinnia broke into a sweat. They began kissing, passionately and with a crazy abandon... Zinnia closed her eyes swiftly, memories of the first kiss she had witnessed in the Ret Cabana Rose Lane resurfaced in her mind. She felt hot and flushed. She felt like an intruder—like she wasn't supposed to witness this display of physical bonding, like she had to leave this couple to their private world of love and passion.

She rose hastily and stumbled, dislodging a wet rock by the bank. Immediately the couple drew apart. Zinnia froze. *O God...it wasn't...it couldn't be...*Her mind whirled in a tizzy, as she tried to grapple with the shock. Then she whipped around and broke into a run, her heart pumping with shame and guilt.

'Zinnia wait!' A voice called out.

Zinnia chose not to listen. She *couldn't* listen. Her mind was reeling with questions and disbelief. There was no space for more.... But the girl caught up with her and put out a hand.

'Wait Zinnia, please!'

Zinnia halted in her tracks, panting with an urgency she couldn't understand. She couldn't bear to hear the words that would come as a form of explanation. Words which she knew would cause her more unease than relief.

'I can't Iris, I can't...'

'No Zinnia, please listen to me!' Iris begged.

Zinnia caught sight of another figure, appearing behind the older lamebirl like a shadow. And she gasped. What in the world was Iris up to?

'Sven—this is Zinnia—you know her, you met her at Dome Piazzar and this afternoon at the K. Port...' Iris turned to the Altklug.

A look of surprise crossed Sven's intelligent face and he nodded.

'Could you excuse us? I need to talk to Zinnia alone. Do you mind?'

Preceptor Sven glanced from Zinnia to Iris, then nodded. He appeared abashed.

'We'll talk later. Goodbye!'

For a moment, Iris watched him depart down the Paramour Path, then she turned to Zinnia. In the fading evening light, her face looked almost ethereal.

'Come with me,' she said and caught hold of Zinnia's hand.

'You don't have to, Iris,' Zinnia cut in hastily.

Iris didn't respond but led her back to the spot by the lake where Zinnia had sat peacefully moments before. She took the seat and patted the space beside her. Zinnia obeyed. For some strange reason, she felt more like a child in front of the older lamebirl, incapable of coping with any conversation. Iris no more seemed like just another lamebirl now. Suddenly she had taken on the image of an adult. In fact, Zinnia realised with a start, Iris was more like a woman now. She stared at the bright red brooch on Iris's shirt, a blush creeping up her face as she noticed that it had turned crooked. She felt inadequate and incompetent to exchange any thoughts on what she had just witnessed. Iris noticed Zinnia's gaze on the brooch and a small smile lit her face. She straightened the brooch gently.

'Preceptor Sven and I are in love with each other,' she said simply.

Zinnia sucked in a sharp breath. *In love? Could this get any worse?*

'We've been seeing each other for a year now. We met at the Northside Altklug Knowledge Port and we meet here secretly.'

'But...but you are only fourteen!' Zinnia blurted out.

'Yes, I am fourteen who is going to be killed at fifteen!' Iris retorted bitterly. 'I've lived almost all my life in that Ret Cubicle. You think I am not aware of my age? I think of it every single day, every single hour. I can't sleep at night thinking that when I wake up I would've lost another precious day of my life and that I'm one more terrifying day closer to my death!'

Zinnia was at a loss for words. The dread, the ache of anticipation of one's death—each one of the lamebren was to experience it. But Iris was the first in their group. How could Zinnia debate such an impending feeling of closure?

'Iris, you are still young, like all of us lamebren. You can't really be in love?' But even as she uttered the words, Zinnia knew that it wasn't true. Iris was *not* like the rest of them.

'I've had my periods for the last whole year! I'm an adult in human terms.'

'Periods?' Zinnia appeared confused.

'I forgot—you wouldn't know. Ask Camilla. She's just started. But that's not the point. The point is that Sven and I love each other.'

'But he's an Altklug! You can't...I mean it's not allowed...'

'We are both aware of it. The impossibility of the situation. A lamebirl and an Altklug! It is betrayal on his part and sacrilege on mine,' Iris concluded in an emotionless tone, staring far out at the lake. She turned to face Zinnia. 'But how can we control our feelings? We love each other! Love isn't something that warns us before happening. It simply creeps in on us unawares and strikes on the sly.'

'But what if someone discovers...'

'We've been very careful. In public, we ignore each other; we barely talk to each other.'

Zinnia remembered Preceptor's Sven's continuous stare on the charabanc trip to the Museum and the scene he created inside the Museum. Far from subtle...

'It's all too risky Iris.'

'I know. It really *is* difficult what with the constant digi-eyes picking up every action of the lamebren and the chips that monitor the Altklugs. The memory chips that they have to replenish all the time.... It *is* risky, all of it, but I can't help it! *We* can't help it. There's just no other way. We have to meet, we have to talk...I'll go mad if I don't see him, he means too much to me!'

Zinnia kept quiet, a splinter of anxiety beginning to prick in her mind. Iris was too far gone to see reason, but Zinnia wasn't. She could see and understand—all too clearly that the older lamebirl was not only playing with danger but putting herself all out in the path of peril. She was too wrapped up in love to realise that she was teetering between a life-and-death situation. If Iris and Sven were caught.... A small act of disobedience had led to the Isolation Chamber, what could a blossoming love between a lamebirl and Altklug lead to? A love which was a brazen contempt of all Altklug rules? Zinnia shuddered as a snowy hand clamped her heart.

'Iris...' began Zinnia cautiously.

'Look, do you see this on my wrist?' Iris indicated the silver elastic metallic band she always wore on her wrist. 'This belonged to my mother. I still remember that day. She had come to visit me one last time, before she was sent to the Dissolution Crypt. Being an Altklug, she had to take special permission to see me. This band was hers and she gave it to me that day, on an impulse. She asked me to keep my beautiful hair tied, so that it wouldn't attract unnecessary Altklug attention. This is all I have left of her—this band, which I wear on my wrist all day, and then sleep with it under my pillow. I did keep my hair tied like she earnestly advised, but it didn't work. Like it or not, the Altklugs *did* notice *me* and I noticed *them*.'

Iris was silent for a moment as she studied the silver band which glinted in the moonlight. 'I want to *live* my life, Zinnia,' she added, vehemently. 'Live my life to the fullest. In a short while, my expiration date will draw near. I want to do all the things that I've wanted to do before that. If I have to die, let me die with the satisfaction that I've lived my life the way I've wanted to. Not the life the *Altklugs* want me to live—drab, servile and like a slave! Look at the way they treated you this afternoon. Wash Receptacle cleaning for adding a variation to a name? That's why I want to die with a satisfied conscience. Don't you see, Zinnia? If I don't meet Sven and experience and share the love in our hearts, I'll die anyway!'

The anguish in her voice cut into Zinnia's heart. Suddenly the older lamebirl burst into tears and clung to Zinnia. She sobbed hard, her entire body shaking with misery.

'I don't want to die...I want to marry and have children and I want Sven to be the father...' she sobbed.

Zinnia was silent. Her young mind was a tight-strung ball of emotions, powerless to cope with the outburst. She wanted to console Iris but the right words seemed to be cluttered at the back of her mind. She wanted to stroke her hair and help her ease her pain and fear, but her hands merely held onto Iris's hands in a tight, clammy clasp while anger whistled in her head. Strong, beautiful, cheerful, kind Iris who needed love and wanted a life, was instead miserable and being pushed slowly towards a forced death under the Altklug rules. She was right about their existence—they were all slaves. Slaves of the Altklug system, slaves of a destiny framed by the Altklugs and slaves of a life with no future...

At length, the sobs receded and Iris sniffed. In the moonlight, her long hair was illuminated into a silver halo and her cheeks shone with the wetness of the tears. Her beautiful eyes were aggrieved and pensive. 'Promise me something, Zinnia?'

'What is it?'

'I've tried to be brave all my life. All the lamebren think I'm wonderful. Promise me you won't tell a soul of our conversation, my breaking down...about us meeting here, or about Sven and me? At least until...my date... after that, I don't care...I guess...'

'I'll never tell a soul of what passed here today!' Zinnia said fiercely. 'Not now, not ever...'

Iris broke into a weak, watery smile. 'You're a good girl, Zinnia. Good, strong and focused. If you had the right backing, you could've been our hope...'

'Hope? Hope for what?' Zinnia appeared confused.

'Nothing,' Iris dismissed. 'Zinnia, thank you! For listening. Who listens to a frustrated lamebirl anymore?'

Zinnia smiled. 'I do and I will. But you're welcome.'

'Let's go, shall we? It's almost Dinner hour. I have to give all of you an update on Preceptor Amadeus's lecture—yes, I did attend it. And then I have the Isolation Chamber tomorrow to look forward to…'

Zinnia glanced at her quickly, but she was still smiling and Zinnia wondered if a single meeting with Sven could make Iris regard the threat of the Isolation Chamber with cheer, what would a life with him do to her? Well, love did have a way with life…

9

'Today we may feel that we are living in a perfect world. But are we really?' Preceptor Amadeus passed a cruising gaze over the gathered Altklugs. 'More than some billion years ago, life on this planet passed through phases of evolution. On a large scale, human life was totally different from what it is now. All those who need detailed information can avail our vast library of chips at the Main KlugBiblio which has a stock of history collected via satellites over millennia. It is chronicled under "Earth History".'

Preceptor Amadeus looked imposing and distinguished despite his rather short stature and his bald head shone under the hall lights. Zinnia felt as if she was right there in the bright hall—the murmur of the crowd, the heat of anticipation in the air and Preceptor Amadeus's voice speaking right into her head.

'But for now, let me present before you a brief picture of life as it was in some phases of evolution. At one point, human life was riddled with inequality, various dividing systems, poverty and untimely painful death. Everything depended on money and what it could buy. Corruption was rife which led to more damage and strife. Life was at its worst with misery, pain and fear—the highlights of human existence.

'Simultaneously, scientists were making new discoveries and major developments in Biotechnology and then Nanotechnology. But millennia passed before these two could change human life forever.

'Gene Therapies and Bio-printing started enhancing the ability and appearance of the humans. This led to one of the biggest discoveries ever—Reversal of Ageing. It was at this point that the first indications of the possibility of age being reversed were seen and soon organs, bones, muscles, hair and skin could be reconstructed, veins and arteries could be re-grown. It was magnificent and humans began conquering age.

'Biotech and Nanotech were so superiorly developed that death rates decreased rapidly from decade to decade. Then the prosthetic or non-biological body parts became affordable—which meant that the human bodies became as strong as machines. But it was when humans learnt to transfer consciousness from broken human bodies into new ones that the first step towards eliminating death began. But it was several years later that sudden and unexpected death was conquered. Also simultaneously birth-rate reduced. With an indefinite span of life, the desire to give birth to children to further the family name became redundant.

'On the job front, automated, superior systems eradicated the need for humans in jobs and a spectacular molecular nanotechnology industry came into being. The success of humanity was also in its prosperity, but at the same time, commerce began to get redundant too.

'This was also the time when people seriously began taking effort at eliminating poverty. They began by experimenting with monthly allowances for the poor leading to larger amounts and finally over many, many years, basic necessities like food, medicine, clothing, vehicles, housing, public facilities became freely and easily available. Earth became a commerce-free world, which meant that stress and worry over earning for a living became obsolete. By the way, if you need to know anything that happened on this earth since it came into being, its past, its varied cultures, people, history, books—it's all stored in the DNA section of the Sensorlib.

'Anyway, human existence became a life filled with happiness, affluence, intelligence, and humans began to enjoy a lifespan which can almost be called immortal.'

Preceptor Amadeus paused. There was a hush in the hall. It was a silence laden with respect and Zinnia sensed the controlled breathing in the room.

'Today we have to understand that this is the life I would call perfect. Stress-free, happy and filled with the knowledge of a free existence. So let me ask you all a question—today, are we all happy? Are we stress-free? And by we, I mean we all—the Altklugs and the lamebren. Are they happy? Are they free? No, they are not. They are under the constant burden of aping the Altklugs, of matching their intelligence, of trying to be *like* the Altklugs. Whereas my question is—why *should* they? Why can't they just be them? They are special and why can't they remain special? Why must we regard them as lamebren and treat them like dirt? And thus I come to the main issue—why can we not consider Age Progression for them?'

A murmur rose from the audience—a murmur of unrest, of concern, of unvoiced confusion. Preceptor Amadeus glanced at them all, his gaze piercing and scrutinising. The image flickered and dimmed and the voices receded from Zinnia's head. Iris switched off the holo-view and stared at the lamebren. The members of the Secret Society were present in the Cubicle Tory. It was well past their bed time but none of them were sleepy.

'What do you think?' she asked softly.

In the low light of the Cubicle, the lamebren looked tiny and vulnerable. Camilla and Cheska in their similar pajamas and their curls, looked zapped. Crispin was frowning, a restive hand fiddling with his untidy shock of hair. Reed's eyes behind his glasses were downcast and

Berk appeared more anxious then ever—both had their mouths open in awe. Zinnia struggled to emerge from the trance of Preceptor Amadeus's magnetic lecture.

'He is fantastic!' she expressed, warmly.

'And brave,' Crispin stated, flatly. 'I am surprised they haven't put him in confinement as yet.'

'He was amazing! The Altklugs were taken aback by his direct, no nonsense attitude. He is charismatic, I tell you,' Iris praised.

'And he is garnering a lot of support,' Cheska added. 'Perhaps one day he may even achieve his objective.'

'If he isn't stopped for good before that,' Berk remarked, a little glumly.

'He's got supporters, solid backing too,' Camilla pointed out.

'Whatever, whenever!' Berk shrugged.

'But still, it's great to hear him speak,' Iris cut in. 'He is so inspiring!'

'But how can we make use of it all?' Zinnia asked. 'We can't join him, can we?'

'Of course, not!' Crispin remarked. 'That would be the end of us all. If the Altklugs ever get wind of the fact that we are interested in Preceptor Amadeus and his theories, we would be regarded as Betrayers—and Betrayers face a fate worse than the Dissolution Crypt.'

'Don't scare her, Crispin,' Iris cut in hastily. 'We cannot be labelled as Betrayers ever. We are too insignificant in their eyes, so let's not imagine the worst.'

'We can keep ourselves updated with his philosophy. You never know when it might prove useful,' Cheska suggested.

'I don't get it,' Zinnia frowned. 'We lamebren have always been warned to stay out of the lives of Altklugs.

But we have never been stopped from being creative or productive, have we? So why would they stop us from trying to learn something new?'

'They want to give us a chance of developing into *an Altklug*. You know like a late bloomer…so we get good education, opportunities for development, till the age when they realise, for a fact, that we are a hopeless case,' Reed spoke up.

'And this—Preceptor Amadeus's theories are not just something new—they are revolutionary and dangerous. They may even shake the foundation of the Altklug world,' Iris said quietly.

'But then why is he still allowed to go on?'

'Because he is too popular to be insignificant and Governor Tisya is very careful with her policies. She will not do anything to jeopardise the peace in the Altklug Dome.'

'However, I bet she's thinking of ways to put an end to it. We just don't know about it yet,' Crispin prophesied.

'She'll have to be really very smart about it then. Because from what I saw today, Preceptor Amadeus and his theories are here to stay,' Iris declared.

Zinnia observed the lamebren who were all deep in thought. Not one of them had referred to the Wash Receptacle punishment of that afternoon, preferring to relegate it to the background and Zinnia was grateful for their thoughtfulness. Iris seemed calm and there were no signs of their encounter earlier that evening, neither of her outburst nor of the anxiety of the Isolation Chamber the next day. She seemed composed and in a way even happy. How unpredictable she was sometimes and yet she was such an inspiration to Zinnia. She possessed a strength which Zinnia doubted if any one of the lamebren possessed. And yet she had been foolish enough to fall in love with an Altklug. How in heavens was she ever going to hide her true feelings from the world and more importantly, how would the Altklug world react, if they ever found out?

Outside the window, snow fell gently, noiselessly but a shiver ran down Zinnia's spine.

That night, Zinnia tossed and turned in bed. Her thoughts swung from Iris to Preceptor Amadeus's speech, making her fidgety. The other two lamebren were fast asleep. For all her tumultuous emotions, Iris seemed to be in a deep slumber, one hand tucked comfortably under her pillow. Finally, Zinnia rose and stood by the window, sweeping away the curtains and clearing the white frosty sheen that had gathered on the glass. The window overlooked the entrance to the Cubicle and the long drive way. In the illuminated lamps, the entrance looked stark except for a van. It was a black van with no windows and nothing written on it. *Like a big black box*, she thought with a frown. She had never seen this vehicle at the Cubicle before. Who could be visiting at this hour of the night? She stood for moments staring out at the van, when a sudden wave of fatigue found its way through a big yawn. *Time for some sleep*, she decided and returned to her bed.

The mournful siren awoke her with a start, the slow high-pitched sound creeping into her consciousness and shuddering her awake. Startled, her eyes shot open and for moments she remained almost paralysed in her bed, staring at the plain white ceiling. The Siren of Departure... the heart-wrenching wail seemed to etch a lingering bitterness into her mind. *The Siren of Departure?* But that was played only to announce the departure of...Zinnia jerked up in bed, her head spinning with the thought. But who? She frowned clapping her hands over her ears to block out the hateful screech and simultaneously looking for Iris. She would know, she realised and turned to see if the older lamebirl was awake. But Iris's bed was empty. Camilla sat up in her bed too, appearing bewildered and lost. She rubbed a hand over her sleepy eyes and thrust another through her untidy curls. Outside the window, a crimson dawn stained across the sky.

'What's happening?' Camilla murmured groggily.

But before Zinnia could respond, a cool voice announced through the Ret Cubicle, 'Lamebren, gather in the Hall at once.'

Zinnia and Camilla glanced at each other surprised, suddenly wide awake. They joined the other lamebren trooping down to the hall. Everyone appeared sleepy except Cheska and Crispin who were alert.

'What could this mean?' Crispin frowned.

'It's never happened before, has it?' Cheska asked.

His twin shook her head. 'Not that I remember.'

'But where's Iris?' Zinnia wanted to know, as they formed queues before the dais in the mirrored hall. She sent a searching look across the room, but Iris was nowhere to be seen. Had Supercustodian sent her on an errand early morning?

The tick-tack of shoes announced the Supercustodian's arrival. She stood in a pool of soft orange rays of the dawn and appeared grave and unsmiling. She stared at the lamebren solemnly for a moment.

'We would like to inform you that from today there will be a change in the management amongst the lamebren. Until now, G10 had been in charge of your group. From now on, another lamebirl will take charge, since G10 won't be here anymore.'

Zinnia flashed a quick, confused glance at the twins and Crispin. Iris won't be here anymore? And no more in charge? Had she been sent to another Cubicle? But wasn't she remanded to the Isolation Chamber for the day? Then why the sudden change of plan? Questions crowded in her brain, pining to be answered.

Supercustodian continued to gaze at them gravely, her pinched nose scrunching closer. The mole on her cheek seemed to twitch ominously. 'G10 has been sent to the Dissolution Crypt.'

Exclamations reverberated in the hall. Shock slammed into Zinnia so hard that the blood froze in her body. For a moment, the world tilted around her. Iris sent to the Dissolution Crypt? No, she must've heard wrong. Iris still had another year to go. Today she had to report to the Isolation Chamber, not the Sleep...*The siren! It was for Iris...* Sudden understanding streaked into Zinnia and a tight band squeezed against her chest as the horror of the truth sunk in. Her throat constricted as the words repeated in her head—*Iris sent to the Dissolution Crypt!*

'But, why?' The words were out of her mouth before Zinnia knew it.

All the lamebren gasped.

Supercustodian turned to drive her down with a cold, cruel look. 'Why? You dare question an Altklug for a reason?'

'Ma'am, G10 still had a year before the Expiration date,' Crispin spoke up. His eyes were moist and a hint of anger glinted in them. His dimpled chin stuck out with determination. 'We just want to know why her date was advanced, that's all.'

Supercustodian turned her hawk-like gaze on the lamebroy. 'Governor's orders, *that's why* and that's all you need to know. Now back to work. G11, you will replace G10 in her duties until further orders.' She nodded at

Camilla who was staring at Supercustodian wildly while tears poured down her flaming red cheeks fast.

The tick-tack of the Supercustodian's boots receded into the office. The hall echoed with a stunned silence after her departure. The silence was so profound that Zinnia could hear the clamour of her heartbeats, drumming in her ears. She continued to stare at the slanting orange rays of the sun. They seemed brighter and had shifted position through the hall window.

Camilla burst into sobs. 'No, no...' she repeated, holding her palms over her face in distress.

Cheska rushed to his twin and flung an arm around her. Crispin stared at Zinnia. The others shuffled their feet, uncertain and fearful.

'This can't be,' Zinnia murmured, almost to herself.

'But why so sudden?'Crispin blurted out in anguish.

Zinnia knew why, this was the punishment...no warning, no announcement, a rapid clean-up of a messy situation. And Preceptor Sven? Was he too punished in a similar manner? She wondered bitterly.

'We didn't say goodbye to her,' Azalea sobbed and Cylia sniffed. 'She was such a wonderful lamebirl, so caring and loving!'

Zinnia stared at them and a sudden sense of choking filled her. Almost as if someone was throttling her with their bare hands and cutting off her breath. She whipped around and rushed out of the hall and into the cool, crimson haze of dawn. The lawn felt wet under her bare feet. Zinnia inhaled deeply, gasping for breath. Her cheeks were wet but she didn't remember crying. She brushed the tears away but they refused to stop, filling her heart with a roar she could not control. *Iris...in the Dissolution Crypt?* Gone *forever*? But...but...the disbelief refused to go away.

The suffocation was blinding her. She flopped down on her knees and hid her face in her hands. Iris's voice echoed in her head, like a torture machine, *'I don't want to die…I want to marry and have children and I want Sven to be their father…'*

Poor, poor Iris—so much in love, such a dear friend… she had taught Zinnia to find vibrancy and colours in the black-and-white world of the Altklugs, she had given wings to hesitant dreams and courage to timid minds. She had broken tradition to enrich the vision of the lamebren and had brought excitement into reality, and most importantly, she had evoked smiles on sad, lost faces and introduced a spring of harmony in their desynchronised existence in the Dome. Dear Iris, so full of a desire to live and punished so cruelly for that desire, her beautiful life cut short by a whole year just because Governor Tisya had passed an order.

The words repeated in her head till she wanted to pry them out with a piercing ray and force them into oblivion. Force this whole episode into oblivion. She didn't want to think, feel, or live…suddenly, a flame of anger and pure hatred burst inside Zinnia. She longed to go right up to Governor Tisya and tell her on her face that what she did was wrong. That she had no right to play around with the lives of the lamebren. That the lamebren too were human beings and deserved to live the life they wanted. That Iris deserved to live a life she desired…with Sven! But Zinnia *couldn't*, and she wouldn't because then she too would be punished and then perhaps sent to the Dissolution Crypt and not a soul in this Ace-world of Altklugs would try to stop her from dying. Just as no one had stopped Iris from dying…

Zinnia suddenly rose. Iris had pointed out the digi-eyes that were placed in boxes on the street for public use.

She opened one of the boxes by the garden, extracted the digi-eye which fit in the palm of her hand and attached the thin, thread-like cable to her padlet. Then she faced the digi-eye and took a deep breath.

'Last night Iris was sent to the Dissolution Crypt. We were all asleep. I didn't hear her leave, I was so fast asleep. Iris was my dearest friend, my *best* friend. She left so silently as if she was an illusion. But she wasn't. She was a lovely person, in love and with a great desire to live. Her life was cut short for some reason, whatever the reason… I don't know…but would any reason ever be worth enough to cut a life short? Why do the Altklugs have the right to play around with a person's life? Why is it so easy for them to do that? Why is it so easy to control us lamebren? To pick at us, throw us, make us live or make us die—all of it so simple and unquestioned as if what we feel, say or do just doesn't matter. Isn't it unfair? I know that these are questions which will most likely remain unanswered, simply because no one is being held accountable. And in the meanwhile Iris is gone. No more seeing that beautiful, kind face…'

Her voice choked on a wave of anguish…Her lips trembled as she switched off the digi-eye and replaced it. Her eyes were still streaming with the pain of loss, but speaking it out loud had provided an iota of release. Dawn had passed and the day was fully awake. And Zinnia knew that from now on, she would never really be able to sleep.

Mirella had still not arrived when Zinnia slipped into class. The lamebren were huddled around tables in silence but their moist eyes spoke volumes.

'I knew it was coming!' Lorde announced, suddenly.

His voice was clear with the aim of garnering pointed attention which he did because all the lamebren turned to him, astonished.

'Knew *what* was coming?' Crispin asked, the hint of a warning in his voice which Zinnia noticed at once.

'She had it coming, what with her and that Altklug,' Lorde sneered.

'What!' Crispin's eyes flashed.

The twins exchanged aghast looks. Ivy and Maisie bent their heads and Azalea closed her eyes, appearing faint. Reed and Berk shifted uneasily in their chairs. Cylia began fiddling with her padlet. Only Crispin stared at Lorde, eye to eye, daring him to utter another word.

'Don't look at me like that. *I* didn't do anything wrong! *She* did and that's why she's gone. They couldn't wait for her to be the right age. They had to send her in early and without warning. It was her fault!' Lorde remarked, his nose in the air.

This time everyone in the room paused in their respective actions and stared at Lorde. Zinnia's heart was filled with loathing.

'And serves her right too,' he finished with a triumphant gleam in his small mean eyes.

He really hated Iris, Zinnia could see that now. Any person who could revel in another person's death could only be described as inhuman. Lorde had proved that today...

Crispin approached him with venom in his eyes.

'Get out of here this instant,' he hissed. 'You dare say a word against her and I'll skin you and I don't care if I have to go to the Isolation Chamber for that. She did so much for each one of us and you ungrateful brat... you don't deserve to be in the same room as us. Go on, get out!'

Lorde stood his ground for a minute, then with an arrogant half-smirk turned but stopped short. Mirella was standing by the door. Her face was like a tight mask. A shocked silence followed. Zinnia knew that curiosity had been peaked about Iris and Sven, but not a soul from the lamebren would mention the indiscretion out of respect to Iris. But Mirella?

'You,' Mirella pointed a finger at Lorde. 'I want you to meet me this instant in the Klugsage Room. The rest of you can have an off.'

With that she wheeled around and marched off, her head held high in anger. Lorde looked taken aback and the triumphant gleam was replaced with fear. He threw a pleading look at the class and realising that it was futile to hope for support from them, he slowly trudged out of the room.

10

It was shadowy and murky and the trees seemed to block all vision. The path was narrow and wet and Zinnia could barely see her next step and yet she plunged through the dark. Her heart pounded as branches brushed across her face, clawing and leaving a mark. But she didn't care. She couldn't stop. A ring of anticipation seemed to grip her as her footsteps quickened. She broke into a run, rushing through the dark undergrowth, her heart beating a tattoo, not of fear but of a strange expectation. Something was waiting for her at the end of this forest, something inimitable, something unique. She was breathless and panting. Suddenly the edge of the forest appeared with a hint of light filtering through the closed-in trees. Zinnia stepped out of the forest and into a beautiful clearing with grass so fresh and dewy that it bounced off the light; flowers bordered the clearing like a round garland, the multi-coloured flamboyance a splash in the eye. But Zinnia wasn't looking at any of it. She was staring at the sky. The most magical colours streaked across the sky. It was a long rainbow which arched like a graceful bow and vanished into a bright blue sky. The colours glowed with an in-built fluorescent light and she gasped. The sight filled her heart with a deep pleasure and an immense peace. And in that moment, her eyes flew open. For long disoriented moments, she stared at the ceiling. As awareness crept in, swallowing up the dream and the rainbow, bits and pieces of that feeling wedged in her mind. The memory of her dream was like a warm fuzzy ball inside her heart and Zinnia held on to the feeling of joy and happiness.

She glanced at the empty bed beside her. *Iris*...she sat up with a jerk. A pain throbbed inside her and she closed her eyes tightly. How could she ever live, day in and out, without her favourite lamebirl? Iris, who had befriended her and shown her the Dome and guided her with her knowledge and understanding—how could she ever wake up every morning and face that empty bed and the day without her beloved friend Iris? With all their brainy discoveries in their Ace-world, had the Altklugs devised a cure for heart pain? Discovered a medicine which would decrease the pain of loss and lighten the emotional trauma of irreversibility? She had forgotten to ask Iris that.

Zinnia stared at the untouched bed. Then impulsively she kneeled down and opened the cupboard under her bed. Iris's stuff had been cleared out and her padlet had been confiscated. The empty cupboard was a terrible reminder of a life gone by. Zinnia shut the cupboard and slowly lifted the pillow. Nothing. For a moment, she floundered. Then, impulsively, she lifted her own pillow and stared in surprise. There it was—the metallic band which was Iris's mother's last gift and which she either wore on her wrist or kept under the pillow at night. Except that before parting she had slipped it under her pillow, like a last message from the lamebirl. She had said goodbye. But more importantly, she had wanted Zinnia to remember her...

A sense of deep loss pervaded Zinnia's entire being. Like a giant hand had clutched her and squeezed out the flow of life-blood in her. Zinnia knew in that instant that if she didn't do something she would die. She felt an immense pressure inside of her which threatened to burst if she didn't do something concrete, something conclusive. Iris had to be the last lamebirl to be sent to the Dissolution Crypt. She had to stop it, somehow, anyhow. She sucked in a quick breath as, out of the blue, everything fell into focus with a snap. She was not going to sit back, awaiting the day which would announce her termination moment. She did not wish to count every day and every hour the way Iris had done and perhaps each one of the lamebren was already doing, consciously or sub-consciously. She did not want to live with that dread, she wanted to live, just the way Iris had wanted to...but how? It was something she would have to figure out and fast. Time in the Altklug world was limited. She slipped the band onto her wrist staring at it reflectively. Now Iris would be with her forever. Her dreams, her aspirations, her desire to live would now be Zinnia's goal in life. Iris would not only be remembered by her, but by every being in this Altklug Ace-world....

'Why are we sent to the Dissolution Crypt in the first place?'

'I don't know clearly but it has something to do with development,' Crispin said.

'That isn't very helpful. Didn't the Secret Society find out?' Zinnia asked.

'The Secret Society, as you can see, is of no use!' Cheska said bitterly.

'We could do nothing to save Iris—doesn't that tell us a lot about the futility of our society?' Camilla added.

They all fell silent. Any mention of Iris and none of them could speak for moments.

'I think the best thing to do is to research it in the Sensorlib,' Crispin suggested. 'We have free access to it, provided Mirella permits.'

'That's a good idea. I'm going there right away. Anybody wants to join in?' Zinnia rose.

'No, we have to leave for duty at an Altklug house soon,' Cheska glanced at his twin. 'We were informed that this is a special job and Commander Burdock has particularly asked for us to be assigned at his house. The charabanc will pick us up in fifteen minutes.'

'I think I'll just sit here a while.' Crispin shrugged. 'Reed and Berk said they would join me here. They want to discuss something.'

'Okay then, see you at dinner.'

Zinnia sat at the padlet feeling excited. Mirella had allowed her to use the Klugsage room padlet which housed encyclopaedias of information. She knew exactly what she had to find in that data which spanned information since the inception of the world. She had to hunt out the reason—why year after year, the lamebren were sent to the Dissolution Crypts.

Five minutes later, she had her answer. The padlet provided her with umpteen options and versions and she sorted it by 'most reliable'. The paragraphs that came up were so interesting that Zinnia enlarged them into a big screen.

> *The lamebren are humans who represent an age which has long gone past in the lives of the Altklugs. They are a reminder that an equation has gone wrong, at some point in the time of conception. The combination of the conception rays and the three-month pregnancy period are a crucial period in the life of the mother. All care has to be taken to ensure a safe delivery. But despite all precautions, sometimes, a baby is born which just doesn't respond to all the Altklug cues. It is slow in development and filled with useless emotions. Maturity is slow and speech is delayed. To talk in numbers—a lamebirl or lamebroy has to be 6.25 years to match the intelligence of a year-old Altklug. This difference in the mental and physical age, make it difficult for the two to co-exist.*
>
> *In fact, by the time the Altklugs reach the end of their productive years, edging towards retirement age, the*

lamebren just begin to gain maturity—an awkward equation where it's difficult to balance the odds and evens. While the Altklugs quit the world by the age of fifteen and sixteen, the lamebren enter adulthood whereby they are sent to the Dissolution Crypts, in order to match their life-span with that of the Altklugs. Allowing the lamebren to live beyond their termination dates and the ensuing repercussions are a matter of intense speculation and debate.

Altklugs have formed their own perfect world which hinges on knowledge, technological and nano-biological developments. If the lamebren are permitted to live out their complete ages, it would upset the perfect equilibrium attained in the Altklug Dome and worse, it would initiate a reversal in the process of development, taking the Dome back to the rudimentary existence of by-gone millennia—a life unimaginably tough and riddled with disease and death.

Zinnia paused, her heart beating in excitement as she digested the information. She had gained two very important points through the article. First, the reason why lamebren were terminated and second, most important fact that lamebren could live longer in years than the Altklugs due to their slow biological development. *Could live longer if they were permitted to*…Which meant that if the lamebren were not sent to the Dissolution Crypts then they could enjoy life, just the way Iris had imagined and pined for…

Once the Cubicle lights were out, the lamebren gathered in Zinnia's room—the twins, Crispin, Reed and Berk. As they pulled chairs around Iris's bed, the door opened again and in trooped Maisie, Ivy, Azalea and Cylia.

'When Reed told us, we couldn't resist. We want to be a part of the society,' Ivy explained in a whispered tone.

Crispin nodded and indicated for them to pull more chairs.

'I've called this meeting for a reason,' Crispin began. 'First of all, let's maintain silence for our dear departed G10, also known as Iris.'

The lamebren looked solemn as they bowed their heads in subdued respect. The bed-side lamp glowed with eerie concentration. Snowflakes fell outside, piling one on top of the other to form a neat layer. A couple of minutes later, one by one, they opened their eyes.

'Zinnia here has something to say. In fact she is the one who has called this meeting,' Crispin explained and all heads turned expectantly towards the lamebirl.

Zinnia cleared her throat. 'I am a new entrant to the Secret Society which has done wonderful work with their research so far. Unfortunately, we've all seen the way Iris was snatched away from us. It has been a great loss to me—and to all of us. But since then, I've been thinking. Why can't we *do* something about it?'

'What can *we* do?' Azalea asked.

'How could we have prevented Iris from being sent to the Dissolution Crypt?' Reed added.

'Especially since it was done with such cunning in the middle of the night,' Ivy agreed.

'And more importantly, who can stop the Altklugs from doing what they do? We are just "nobodies" for them,' Cylia reminded.

'I understand these feelings. I felt the same for a long time—I was confused and helpless when I had to leave the Ret Cabana and was brought to this Cubicle. When I came here, I got to understand the Ace-world of the Altklugs. But all along, I felt that despite all these rules and classifications, I *had* a say. I had been in a way fearless—until Iris was taken away. Not only was it a shock, it changed something in me. I realised that I was becoming afraid. Afraid of the same thing happening to me, to others, afraid of losing all of you...you who have become my family...and then it struck me. This was exactly what the Altklugs wanted us to experience—fear—fear of them, fear of being caught doing the wrong thing. Fear of what would happen if we interfered in their lives, if we ever rebelled!'

'Rebelled,' Berk appeared shocked. 'I wouldn't dream of it.'

'Me neither,' Azalea added. 'Even the thought sucks the strength out of me.'

'Please, let's hear her out first,' Cheska interrupted, frowning. 'Zinnia, you want to elaborate?'

Zinnia looked at him gratefully. 'Yes I do.'

She turned to face all of them. The twins looked eager, Crispin encouraging, and the others extremely sceptical. 'We all are aware that we have termination dates. But, we now also know that just as Iris was sent to the Dissolution Crypt, anyone of us can be just picked and sent too, right? Unless we fight for our survival and put up a resistance, you and I could be the next on the list. There is no one to stop them, except us.'

'How can we stop them?' Maisie asked, confused. With her two pigtails at odd angles, she looked very young and innocent.

'Maisie is right. The Altklugs are far superior to us in every possible way,' Ivy, her best friend added.

'Not in every possible way,' Zinnia corrected, quickly. 'We *do* have something that they don't have.'

Crispin looked at Zinnia with interest. Even the ever doubtful Berk leaned forward.

'*Time,*' Zinnia pronounced.

'We do?' Crispin asked with hope in his voice.

'Yes, we have the capacity to outlive the Altklugs. We can live on for years *if* we are not terminated as per their convenience.'

A stunned silence ensued as they all stared at Zinnia in wonder.

'Is that true?' Camilla confirmed.

'Yes, I've just read up on this topic.' Zinnia told them about what she had read in the Sensorlib. 'The Altklugs actually should fear *us* and not the other way round.'

'Wow!' Crispin whistled.

'That is...something...' Cheska remarked.

'Still, what can we *do*?' Berk insisted.

'He's right. Even if we do have the power to outlive them, we *can't* and they won't allow us to,' Cylia agreed.

'That is exactly what we need to figure out. How can we use this knowledge to our advantage? Ideas, anybody?' Zinnia glanced at the lamebren one by one.

The blank faces spoke volumes. None of them responded.

'What if one of us tried to escape?' Zinnia suggested softly.

A collective gasp ensued. Zinnia too, was surprised at herself. Escape? How in heavens had this idea cropped up in her mind?

'Escape! You must be crazy to even think about it,' Ivy spoke harshly. 'You have no idea what you are talking about!'

'Escape is out of the question,' Reed said. 'Because, first, there's nowhere to go and second, even if anyone tried, they would be caught within seconds.'

'He's right,' Crispin agreed. 'The streets, all public spaces are under surveillance and every single action of the Altklugs is recorded and stored. So is ours. The Dome is a fool-proof world.'

'What about the Snarl—the forest outside the Dome?' Zinnia asked.

The twins stared at Zinnia in wonder, their lips slightly parted, revealing their crooked teeth.

'You aren't serious right?' Cheska asked.

'Look, all I'm doing is studying the options.' Zinnia shrugged.

'The Snarl? Have you forgotten Leo Leroy? Well, we haven't. You really have to be mad to step out of the Dome and into the forest. Survival chances are nil. There are wild animals and all kinds of monsters in the Snarl. Even the Altklug Ace-world, despite all the restrictions and the continuous fear of death, is a better place than the Snarl,' Maisie scoffed.

'Which is precisely why the Altklugs don't worry about us escaping and also why the Diaphanous Seal fencing isn't monitored at every exit,' Ivy added.

'In short, there is no means of escape,' Cheska reinforced.

'Which is alright because no one's trying to flee,' Crispin concluded on a note of relief.

Zinnia was silent. While the others continued their exchange through whispers, her mind replayed Ivy's statement and a train of thoughts was unleashed...Had Iris ever thought of escaping with Sven? Would she have eventually done something as foolish as try to elope? But elope where? There wasn't a safe corner in the Altklug Dome, the Sky Radars covered every inch of the Dome, and nothing was undetected. What chance did Iris have? What chance would any of them have, if they ever planned to escape?

The meeting adjourned and the other lamebren returned to their rooms. Zinnia slipped into bed, willing herself to sleep but Iris' empty bed made her restless.

'Zinnia, you aren't asleep, are you?' Camilla asked softly.

'No, why?'

'There's something...I mean...I want to ask you something.'

'What is it?'

Camilla sat up in bed, and pressed a restless hand through her ample curls.

'Have you ever been assigned work at Commander Burdock's house?' she asked.

'No, so far I haven't been assigned to any house—except the K. Ports. Why?'

'Well, actually, it's just that he's a little odd...'

Zinnia heaved herself on her elbow and looked over at Camilla. 'What do you mean? Odd in what way?'

'No, I guess it's just my imagination,' Camilla brushed it off.

'Imagination? Please explain,' Zinnia insisted.

'I don't know. It's just that Commander Burdock makes me a little uneasy. Whenever Cheska and I go over to his house, he works in his study and asks me to sit in one particular chair while he works. Cheska is sent to assist in the garden, never inside the house. And all I do is sit and do nothing!' Her voice sounded awkward and uncertain.

'That's strange,' Zinnia replied reflectively, studying her friend. In her own rather cute way, Camilla was good-looking. The blonde curls and the crooked teeth added to her personality instead of marring it. She appeared older since Zinnia's arrival, her body looked curvy and the permanent pink glow on her cheeks added a charm to her personality.

'Perhaps, he's probably just wondering what to assign to me when much of the workload is taken care of by their Humanoids. This has happened twice and somehow I don't really like it. I feel so drowsy there, sometimes so relaxed that I never realise when time has passed by. But finally when I leave, I feel sort of strange, tired and with a body ache. Perhaps it's all the inactivity,' Camilla concluded.

'Possibly,' Zinnia agreed.

'Good night then, sweet dreams.' Camilla smiled and lay down in bed.

'Good night.'

But Zinnia didn't sleep for a long time. For some bizarre reason, the conversation with Camilla had nudged an instinctive distrust for Commander Burdock and for the first time, she experienced a twinge of worry. She would talk to Crispin about it, she decided. Finally, as thoughts dulled into an ache, she dosed off into a restless slumber.

11

'There is going to be a change in the order of things,' Supercustodian announced.

The lamebren were gathered in the mirrored Hall, alert and attentive in their straight lines.

'As I call out the numbers, please step away from your line.'

As Supercustodian read aloud the numbers from a padlet, Cheska stepped aside with Reed and Maisie. The other lamebren stared at them. Camilla turned white and Zinnia's heart began to pound. What was happening? Surely, not again...

'You have thirty minutes to pack. You three will now be staying in the new Ret Cabana in the Northern Quarter,' Supercustodian said. 'Please ensure that you carry your padlets with you and take all your belongings.'

A stunned silence followed. Zinnia whipped around to see Camilla clutch Cheska's hand.

'No please, let him stay with me. I...I can't live without my brother,' she beseeched, the tears beginning to flow swiftly.

Supercustodian turned cold eyes on her, her pinched nose pointed and ugly. 'How many times do I have to tell you that tears are a waste of emotion, G11? And bonds reduce the efficiency of a person. It would do you good to remember that our Ace-world is all about optimum efficiency.'

'Ma'am please!'

'Thirty minutes!' she announced again. 'And the rest of you, to your classroom.' With that she tick-tacked out of the hall.

Immediately the lamebren gathered around Cheska, Maisie and Reed who appeared bewildered. Camilla clung to her twin, the tears pouring freely.

'It's alright,' he comforted, but his usual pink face was white and tense.

'No, it's not. They are taking you away from us—just like Iris!' Camilla cried.

Ivy held Maisie's hand and Berk hovered around Reed. Only Lorde stood back from the group, watching the protests and exchanges with a look of contempt in his eyes.

'Is that true?' Berk asked, gazing anxiously.

'No, it's not,' Crispin spoke up. His voice was firm and controlled. 'I think I know what they are doing. They are trying to break up the groups. Cheska and Camilla, Maisie and Ivy and Reed and Berk—it's like trying to break up a pack,' he explained on a bitter note.

'And we can do nothing to stop them,' Cheska concluded, with a sigh.

'Not now perhaps,' Zinnia said.

'Not ever!' Azalea shook her head. 'We were born losers and we will remain losers.'

'No!' Zinnia snapped. 'We are *not* losers and never will be, you'll see. But for now, it is important for all of us to be strong. Cheska, Maisie and Reed—you will remain strong, won't you?'

Reed looked thinner than ever as he towered over the rest of them. 'We don't have a choice, do we?'

'Look, I think we had all better disperse. We have to be in class in five minutes and these three have to pack,' Crispin said sensibly.

'I am not leaving Cheska!' Camilla's voice was fierce with determination.

'Listen twin, I'm going to be fine. We are all going to be fine. The new Ret Cabana is just ten minutes away from here. We'll be meeting all the time and besides, I'm sure this isn't a permanent arrangement.'

Zinnia observed as he consoled his sister, his hand on her shoulder. With their curly heads propped together in shared whispers, she could understand their physical as well as their emotional bonding. A wave of sympathy and anger drove through her. What if it was not a temporary but a permanent arrangement? Why should they be separated? They were twins after all, they needed each other. For that matter why separate best friends Ivy and Maisie, and Berk and Reed either? What kind of a game were the Altklugs playing? Whatever it was, it was mean and cruel, with complete disregard for the feelings of the lamebren.

'Ok lamebren, get going,' Bosco appeared and began hustling them away. 'Back to class all of you!'

'I'm going up with Cheska to pack,' Camilla declared, her tone defiant.

The others thought it wise not to argue. The lamebren hugged Cheska, Reed and Maisie, whispering goodbyes, under Bosco's watchful eye. An unspoken understanding seemed to bind them. As the group separated and the rest of the lamebren moved to their classroom, Zinnia experienced an acute sense of anxiety. They would see Cheska, Maisie and Reed again, wouldn't they? She wished Iris was with them that moment. Iris, who always softened the impact of reality, protected them and gave them strength. She touched the wrist band as an ache of longing descended on her. *Iris*...

Zinnia was absent-minded in class and barely heard a word of what Bamian was explaining, about how dreams could be harnessed to solve problems and make discoveries. She sat up when Camilla appeared by the classroom door, her eyes red-rimmed and swollen and her cheeks a bright red. Bamian glanced up at her and without a word consulted his padlet.

'G11—you are late.'

'I'm sorry—my brother and the others…'

'Yes, yes I know—they have been transferred to the new Ret Cabana,' he cut her short impatiently. 'Sit down, I was about to demonstrate something to the class.'

Camilla slipped into her chair and bent her head over her padlet.

Bamian placed his padlet on the shiny metallic table and searched the faces of the lamebren.

'You, come forward,' he ordered.

Berk rose and with small steps, hastened to the front of the room.

'As you already know, Altklugs have taken giant leaps in terms of knowledge and technology. What you don't know is the *extent* of that leap. Today I am going to demonstrate a small experiment. It is about dreams. Dreams, as you lamebren know them, are thoughts that form an in-cohesive whole in the brain while we are sleeping. Today we have harnessed these thoughts and channelised them into constructive means. Sometimes, we have been lucky to turn the dream into a discovery by expanding on it. Are you following me?'

He glanced at the lamebren over his glasses and at that moment looked so much like Aerobut that Zinnia was convinced that they had to be related.

'So, let's begin. Shut out all light!' Shutters dropped down over the windows, plunging the room into darkness.

'B18, close your eyes. Now you are fast asleep.'

As Berk closed his eyes, within seconds he seemed to sway gently. Zinnia watched fascinated.

'Now let's see what this lamebroy is dreaming about...'

Bamian pushed a button on his padlet and immediately a light flickered in the room, like a projector and images danced in the light. Zinnia's eyes widened in amazement. A quick series of images flashed by—Reed smiling, a van without anything written on it, Reed sleeping in the dorm, pulling plates out of a server, Reed at Governor Seeya's Museum...

'Okay enough! Shutters open, B18 please wake up...' Bamian was smiling, looking very pleased.

Berk opened his eyes, looking a little dazed and confused.

'You can return to your seat now.'

The lamebroy stumbled back, uncertain on his feet with disorientation.

'What we just saw was totally fascinating. When B18 was asleep, his dreams consisted of visions of his friend, his activities, his insecurities. Dreams in this form are psycho babble as we call it and would serve self-analysis, but are totally useless in terms of psycho-techno advances. On the other hand, if you were to test an Altklug dream, you would find something completely different. His thoughts do not manifest into a dream—which is a lamebren prerogative—but would manifest into what we call a thought-harness process. The thoughts would consist of work, of theories, of discoveries, sometimes subconscious which can be harnessed and 'logicalised' into reality. This thought-harness process has been very important in the psycho-techno advancement of the Altklug world. Am I making sense?'

He threw a shrewd look across the classroom, assessing and gauging the absorption of knowledge.

'Any comments? B15?'

Crispin rose. 'Sir, you mean to say that psychobabble is not present in Altklugs?'

'That's right. It is a tight competitive world out there. Altklugs have to perform with optimum efficiency to justify and support their existence in our world. Which means, their life would have no space for idle thought like you lamebren have. No idle thought, no over-reactive emotions, no bonds—the perfect equation to erase psychobabble. The perfect definition for cent percent success.'

Zinnia raised her hand.

'Yes, G23.'

'But Sir, what if you were to find psychobabble in one of the Altklugs? What happens then?'

'Then, he would probably be sent to the Lab for analysis, which I may tell you, is not a pleasant affair,' Bamian shrugged.

'What about Humanoids?'

Bamian looked surprised. 'Humanoids are as close to Altklugs as they can possibly be which was why Altklugs had it so difficult to overthrow the Singularity years ago. But at the same time, they do reflect psychobabble and when they do, the situation can be a little dangerous.'

'How is that?'

'Humanoids are machines which copy human behaviour and emulate their emotions. But being machines they are programmed to be used with minimum emotions. If at some point their programming is overturned, like it did in the era of the Singularity, they can overtake the humans. But that isn't possible now. The Altklugs are far too smart to ever allow Humanoids to rule the Dome again. Besides, a lot has changed since then. Today we live in a futuristic world where simulations are an inherent part of our life and which, day by day, have become difficult to separate from reality.'

Bamian looked at the blank faces of the lamebren.

'Okay, let me explain. You all saw what B18 was dreaming about. With simulation—an art which Altklugs are perfecting—B18 can experience the same trauma and fear of losing his friend as if it had actually occurred. But that is a temporary phase unless you want to continue to live in that simulation. And Humanoids, I believe, are incapable of experiencing simulations.'

Zinnia flashed a quick look at Berk, who had his eyes cast to the floor. The poor lamebroy's innermost fears were being publicly discussed as if they were as simulated as the emotions of the Altklugs. Bamian's tone was casual and indifferent and it hurt her deeply.

Camilla raised her hand.

'Yes G11.'

'Sir, is psychobabble wrong? Because now that my twin has been sent to the other Ret Cabana, like Berk here, all I can think of is him and his safety.'

'Same here. I shall keep wondering if my friend is alright too,' Ivy spoke up.

Bamian glanced from Camilla to Ivy, a frown on his face. 'Safety? Why should you bother about their safety? That Ret Cabana is well-equipped, it has good Exectors and the jobs assigned would be dignified, I presume.'

'But I won't be able to meet him!' Camilla exclaimed, frustrated.

'Which would add to your efficiency quotient, I am sure,' Bamian concluded, coolly.

Camilla stared at him, an expression of helplessness on her face. She exchanged a quick look with Ivy, who appeared equally lost. Zinnia felt annoyed. How does one expect an Altklug to understand that life exists beyond 'being efficient'?

'The Governor must've made the shuffle for a good reason. We must learn to trust her judgment. Well then, class is over for today. Tomorrow I shall do another exercise with you.' With that Bamian picked up his padlet and marched out of the room.

Lorde rose and followed the teacher while the rest of the lamebren remained in class. Zinnia approached Berk and placed a gentle hand on his shoulder. He glanced up, a thick glaze of unshed tears in his eyes.

'We'll find a way to bring them back,' she promised.

Commander Burdock's house was like a huge square box. The rooms were demarcated by transparent walls, laden with curtains. Furniture slid in and out to create space and adjust around corners and walls, in monotones of grey. In contrast, the garden was flourishing with exotic varieties of flowers in all shades of orange which Zinnia could only smell and not identify. As she worked with the Lawnrover and the Trimark, Plucker and Cleanster, she wondered what task Camilla had been delegated.

Camilla had been assigned to Commander Burdock's house and since Cheska had moved to the new Ret Cabana, Zinnia was ordered to accompany Camilla. The look of relief on Camilla's face when Zinnia's name had been announced for duty with her to Commander Burdock's, had brought back the conversation she had had with the lamebirl the previous night.

Now, Zinnia turned off the Lawnrover and listened for sounds from inside the house. Commander Burdock lived alone, so it wasn't surprising that she could hear nothing. A little curious, she edged towards a window which was tiny and low. Through the soundproof sliding panel of the window, she caught sight of Commander Burdock at his table, his head bent and writing on his padlet. Right opposite him sat Camilla, her hands crossed in her lap demurely but her eyes glazed and unfocused. Zinnia watched the scene, perplexed. Why did the Commander insist that Camilla sit before him doing nothing? Altklugs very rarely paid any attention to any of the lamebren, then why this special treatment to Camilla? Even as she puzzled, suddenly the shutters of the window dropped down, blanking out all view. It startled Zinnia. For moments, she stood staring at the shutters, a sense of unease gripping her.

On an impulse, she headed to the main door and crept towards the Commander's room. Pausing at a glass window, she inhaled deeply and slowly peeped inside the room. What she saw singed her like a burning beam. The room was dark but vision was still possible. Commander Burdock was seated in the same position, except he was leaning forward, an odd, excited look on his fleshy face. So was Camilla, but her eyes were now closed and her face tilted at an angle. However, Zinnia was not looking at her. Her attention was riveted to the images that were being projected over the lamebirl's head. For a moment, her young mind couldn't grasp what was happening and then like a jolt, instinctively she knew.

Simulated images…simulated feelings…like the kind Bamian had explained in class except that this was different…this was *wrong* and far more horrifying! Camilla was making soft moaning sounds and swaying sensuously. Her instinct screamed voicelessly in revolt and her skin crawled. The images shook her to the core. Sweat broke out on her forehead and for a moment she shut her eyes, she had to think...*think*...should she barge in and stop this wicked scene? But then she would be banished, perhaps even to the Dissolution Crypt and then that would be the end of it all. Or should she just rush back to the Cubicle and complain? But who would listen to her or believe her? And what about the amount of shame it would bring Camilla? Trapped in her own confusion, Zinnia lost precious moments. She couldn't just stand here doing nothing. She had to stop this...now...forever! She had to *do* something! Anger and frustration clamped her in a grip. And then, out of the blue, she knew what she had to do.

She rushed out and snapped the public digi-eye from its box. Fumbling with the cable, she adjusted it quickly to her padlet. Then switching the digi-eye on, she hastened to her previous vantage point. The window afforded a plain view of what was transpiring inside and Zinnia trained the digi-eye on the Commander. She covered as much as she could keeping Camilla's simulated visions out of shot. She took a close shot of the Commander's greedy, lusty eyes and groping hands, then panned to shoot Camilla's face and trance. Revulsion and bile rose inside her, choking her, but she curbed it...she had to do this...she had to be strong if she had to protect Camilla, she told herself repeatedly.

Finally, satisfied that she had enough proof, she hastened out again, unplugged the digi-eye and returned to the Lawnrover. But her palms were sweaty and her heart was pounding painfully. Her mouth tasted dirty and she wanted to spit and rinse. She closed her eyes to the stark images but the scene repeated itself with renewed clarity. So now she understood why the Commander specifically asked for Camilla to be assigned to his house, why she was always asked to sit and do nothing and why Cheska was always doing duty outside in the garden. All this while, the Commander had been *using* Camilla...that monster of an Altklug!

When Bamian had said that the lamebren did not understand fully the extent of the giant leaps of knowledge the Altklugs had taken, could he have ever meant this? Could all those leaps of knowledge justify this—the maligning of a lamebirl's honour? Or the smear of disgracing an innocent?

Poor, poor Camilla, she would feel terrible when she knew. For no fault of hers, shame and dishonour would dog her all her short life. Every moment would be an accusation and every day would be a trauma. When she knew...*if* she knew...*that's right,* Zinnia thought with sudden, clear realisation, *if* Camilla knew...but then she *needn't* know...she needn't be put through hell...and Cheska? What about him? Always so protective about his twin...If only Iris was here, she would have known what to do, whom to speak with, she would've taken control and relieved Zinnia of the heartbreaking burden that had suddenly befallen her.

Ten minutes later, Camilla appeared at the entrance of the house, her face drawn and drained. 'Hi! The Commander said we may leave early if we wish,' she announced. 'Are you done with the lawn? Seriously I feel so guilty—there I am, doing absolutely nothing and here you are, working your butt off. And yet I feel kind of tired, you know.'

Zinnia couldn't speak. The lump in her throat felt the size of a moon. She felt as if she would burst with the force of her bottled-up emotions, but she didn't. She had to face this issue with the strength of a lamebirl. She had to go back to the Cubicle and think. One thing was for certain, Camilla should never know about what had transpired. Most importantly, she could never ever return to Commander Burdock's house. And it was up to Zinnia to ensure that.

12

Zinnia watched the snowflakes fall through her bedroom window, soft and beautiful, like the glowing petals of snow. Landing on the ground soundlessly and merging with others to thickly coat the snowy road. A tear slowly rolled down followed by another and soon streams of them were gushing down her cheeks. And all the while, she stared at the snowflakes and admired them like a parallel disconnected activity in her mind. She cried hard, emptying the apprehensions, the agony and frustrations from her mind and heart. She cried noiselessly. She didn't want to wake up Camilla who was sleeping like a child. Camilla had worried and fretted about Cheska and had finally dozed off. Zinnia wanted to protect the lamebirl from further hurt, just the way Iris would've done. When the tears dried up and her sobs had converted into sniffs, Zinnia made up her mind. She had to share her secret and the sooner she did it, the better it would be for her dear friend Camilla.

Zinnia had to sit through Bamian's class, with a patience she had not thought herself capable of. She had to struggle to keep her attention on his lecture as he demonstrated how technology had ensured new body parts with minimal invasive techniques. Finally out of sheer annoyance, she raised her hand.

'Yes G23,' Bamian turned his attention to her.

'Sir, do you believe that this Ace-world—this Dome is a perfect world?' she asked.

A look of astonishment crossed the Exector's face. 'Yes, it is as perfect as perfect can be, without a shadow of doubt.'

'But then that would depend on the definition of perfection, wouldn't it?'

'Take any definition you like: the highest degree of a quality; an exemplification of supreme excellence; an unsurpassable degree of accuracy or excellence—the Altklug Ace-world fits each definition,' Bamian replied with a superior smirk.

'What about "freedom from fault or defect"?' Zinnia asked.

The rest of the class turned to face her, confused and yet alert. Crispin tried to catch Zinnia's eye, warning her to be careful. He was quick to notice the rebellious gleam in her eyes.

'That too, my dear lamebirl. The Altklug Ace-world is superior and protected from any kind of technological vice and free from faults. But for a matter of an interesting discourse, are you suggesting that there are faults in the system?' Bamian's tone was mild, but he looked at Zinnia keenly.

'What I am saying is that mere strides in technology does not make an Ace-world. It is the Altklugs who do and Altklugs are humans, aren't they? Wouldn't they make mistakes?'

'Humans who make mistakes are not Altklugs.'

'But what if they do?' Zinnia insisted.

Bamian hesitated, for fraction of a second. 'If they do, which is the rarest of occurrences, then swift and immediate action would be taken to replace that element from the system. There are no cracks in the Altklug world. It has been perfected over years and years of research and human existence is at its best in this Dome.' Bamian's tone brooked no argument but Zinnia was satisfied.

She sat down and passed the anxious Crispin a quick reassuring smile.

The expression of sheer disbelief on Crispin's face said it all. He shook his head, as he grappled with the realisation. A shock of unruly hair fell on his forehead as he paced the floor.

'The nerve of that Altklug!' he finally exploded. 'The creep…the…the…!'

His face was flaming with fury and at his inadequacy to find the exact words to express his horror.

Zinnia put out a hand and stilled him. 'I know. I went through the exact emotions. And I've been awake all night, wondering what to do about it. Whom can we trust? Who can we go to? The Supercustodian?' she suggested, her voice thickly laced with doubt.

'Supercustodian!' Crispin sneered. 'You would be deported to the Dissolution Crypt or worse still to the Lab, before you can take your next breath.'

'I thought so too.' Zinnia sighed. 'Then who?'

'Bamian too would be useless. He's too practical and would probably think Commander Burdock is a genius.'

'Back at the Ret Cabana, I would've spoken to our Peeta. She was a warm and understanding Altklug—not that it would've been much use though.'

'Mirella!' Crispin snapped his fingers at the idea.

Zinnia's eyes gleamed. 'You're right. Mirella would listen. She would make an effort to understand. Let's go right away. You will come with me, won't you?'

'Of course I will! This is for Camilla…'

Zinnia smiled at Crispin and nodded. She felt a load off her shoulders, now that she had confided in Crispin.

The Klugsage room was devoid of any fussy flourishes. The only embellishment was the big Altklug emblem on the wall—a combination of the four Fountains. Three uncluttered metallic tables aligned a wall and at the farthest end sat Mirella. She looked small and approachable as Zinnia and Crispin stood waiting at the glass Demarcator. Crispin pushed a button and Mirella glanced up at them. Without a word, she slid open the Demarcator and Zinnia and Crispin entered the Klugsage room.

Zinnia's hands were clammy and she felt nervous. This was a big step, disclosing Camilla's predicament to an Altklug. It was almost like breaching Camilla's confidence, although ironically, she was totally unaware of the situation. But if at all anyone could help her, it would be Mirella. However, she was still an Altklug and a strict one. How would she take an accusation against a Commander? What would her reaction be? Would Mirella believe her?

'Yes, G23 and B15, anything the matter?' Mirella asked shrewdly.

Crispin glanced at Zinnia who gulped apprehensively.

'Yes, Exector.'

'Is it urgent? Because I have a class in ten minutes...'

'Yes, Exector.'

'Okay. Make it quick.'

'I would like to show you something, Exector.'

Zinnia opened the screen of her padlet and angled it towards the Exector. Mirella frowned, impatience stamped on her face. But as soon as her eyes rested on the images, she sucked in a quick breath and the look of impatience was replaced by one of incredulity. Zinnia observed the Exector, as her eyes widened and narrowed. Mirella watched the recorded visuals carefully and for once the controlled mask of non-committal indifference slipped. At length, when she glanced up at Zinnia, compassion reflected in her eyes.

'I won't ask you how you recorded this. Without a doubt, this episode is in very poor taste. We need to take immediate action before acts such as these contaminate the Altklug Dome and repute. I need to think this out.'

Zinnia was silent. Mirella had reacted in exactly the manner she had hoped. Sensitively and without much fuss.

'I will have to consider this very seriously. Commander Burdock is a much-respected Altklug and the Altklugs uphold his high standing in society. You will have to give me some time to handle this.'

'But Exector, Cami...G11 will be sent back to Commander Burdock on assignment soon and we...'

'No, she won't. I shall speak to Supercustodian,' Mirella cut in smoothly. 'In the meanwhile, speak to no one of this. We will have to maintain strict secrecy, you understand? This would mean a high-profile investigation and in our world that means a lot. Now go back to class. Tell them I'll be there in ten minutes.'

But ten minutes later, Mirella had still not arrived. Instead, Bosco appeared to inform the lamebren that Mirella had been called away and they would not have class that day. Crispin and Zinnia walked out into the garden, so as to be out of earshot.

'What do you think?' Zinnia wondered.

'Like she said—it's high profile. They would all probably have a meeting since Commander Burdock is a top-level guy. It would be difficult to accuse him of something so debasing.'

'But I have the holo-view.'

'Which is the only reason why Mirella had to forward this issue, I guess. But my only concern is for Camilla. Remember what happened with Iris? The fault lay with Preceptor Sven as well, but it was Iris who was sent to the Dissolution Crypt.'

'You mean...' Zinnia appeared shocked. The thought that Camilla may face the same fate as Iris hadn't even occurred to her. 'No, that was different. They loved each other—wait, you knew?'

A half smile touched Crispin's lips. 'I am neither blind nor deaf. I tried to warn her, but she pretended as if she didn't know what I was talking about.'

'Poor Iris...' Zinnia's voice trailed. She missed the beautiful lamebirl badly. If only Iris was alive.

'Iris was reckless. She probably just got tired of the Altklug Ace-world, living and obeying their set of rules and conditions. I think, she simply wanted a world of her own,' Crispin guessed.

He had no clue how close he was to the truth, Zinnia thought. *Slaves,* she had called the lamebren. And now more than ever, Zinnia could see how right she had been.

'Anyway, it won't be the same with Camilla. After all, this is exploitation, not an act of mutual consent,' she remarked.

'And that is precisely what the Altklugs are going to ask us—how do you know that it wasn't an act of mutual consent?'

'Because then Camilla would *know,* wouldn't she?'

'She could be lying as far as their argument goes.'

'No!'

'We are dealing with Altklugs here. They would go to any extent to protect their image of a perfect world. Commander Burdock is a chink in that world. They would either root him out or cover the chink so expertly that it would never show,' Crispin concluded.

Zinnia was silent. She suddenly felt very uneasy. What if Crispin was right and Camilla had to take the blame for something she wasn't even aware of? Oh dear! Had they been wrong in going to Mirella for a solution?

'I think we'll know in sixty minutes what the Altklugs are planning to do—play it fair and do justice or play it biased and cover up their chink,' Zinnia said gloomily.

'All I know is, if things don't work out in our favour, I promise you I won't allow Camilla to go the Iris way. I'll take her and escape into the Snarl!' he said in such a fierce voice that Zinnia was a little taken aback. And yet she was reassured. Crispin was a real friend.

But sixty minutes later there was still no news from Mirella. With every passing hour, Zinnia's worry quadrupled. Why hadn't Mirella got back yet? What was going on in the top circles of the Altklug Bureaus ? She wished she knew. If only there was some way of finding out.

By dinner time, Zinnia was so tightly strung with anxiety that food tasted like snow. She and Crispin kept Camilla by their side, under some pretence or the other. Since Cheska wasn't around the lamebirl was grateful for their company. They had just finished dinner and the Server had marched away with their plates, when Bosco appeared in the Superkitchen.

'G23 and B15, you have been summoned at once,' he announced.

Zinnia's heart skipped a beat.

Camilla frowned and looked at them and so did the rest of the lamebren.

'Now what...are they taking you two somewhere?' her voice was almost a wail.

'Sh...no, I'm sure it's not that,' Crispin said swiftly. 'Don't worry. We'll be back. Supercustodian must have some query that's all.'

Zinnia couldn't help noticing how protective Crispin had become of Camilla ever since Cheska's absence. And it was a good thing, because right now, Camilla needed all the support she could get. They hastened after Bosco as he led the way to the hall. Supercustodian was standing by the entrance doors of the Cubicle.

'Come on hurry, get into the spinner!' she ordered.

Zinnia flashed Crispin a look. Where were they being taken? Suspicion clouded her anxiety, but then she brushed it away. No negative thoughts. She was more curious now, than afraid.

They were rushed into a long black spinner and it swept down the silent roads which appeared like lit ribbons. Zinnia raised an enquiring eyebrow at Crispin but he shook his head. She grasped that they ought not to talk.

Within minutes, the spinner slid into parking and the door flung open. A Humanoid shepherded the lamebren into a glass elevator and up they went at a speed so fast, that Zinnia's head swam. It was only when they stood outside a diamond-shaped glass room, which jutted out of the building like a tilted crown, that Zinnia realised where they were. Governor Tisya's office!

Her hand slid forward and held Crispin's for a few seconds, gaining some much needed courage from the touch. Then the glass Demarcator glided open. Zinnia and Crispin were ushered into one of the most beautiful rooms the lamebirl had ever seen. The entire Altklug Dome twinkled below them against a velvety, black backdrop. Commander Hertz was pacing the floor and Governor

Tisya was seated in an ink-blue metal armchair which adjusted automatically every time she moved. Zinnia noticed her green eyes for the first time but she looked just as tall and graceful with close-cropped hair and an armour-like white dress.

'B15 and G23,' the Humanoid announced.

'Thank you, Bozo,' the Commander acknowledged and Bozo left.

As the door glided shut behind them, Zinnia experienced the briefest of anxiety. Why had they been summoned to Governor Tisya's office?

Commander Hertz turned to face them.

'So, who is the one who has witnessed this scene?' he asked, without preamble.

'I have, Sir.' Zinnia spoke up.

'Can you tell us what you saw?'

Zinnia took a deep breath. 'Yes Sir. I was working in the garden and I wondered what Cam...G11 was doing so I looked in through the window.'

'You mean you were spying?' Governor Tisya cut in sharply.

'No Governor, I wasn't. G11 had told me earlier that Commander Burdock makes her sit in a chair doing nothing and she found it very odd. That is why I thought I would just check on her.'

'Go on, what did you see?' Commander Hertz prodded.

Zinnia explained what she had witnessed to the best of her ability. She could feel Crispin flinch beside her as she narrated the incident but not a muscle moved on the Altklugs' faces.

'You are sure you haven't made this up?'

'I haven't made it up, Sir.'

'And how do we know you haven't? After all, you are the same lamebirl who had messed with the Governor's name at the Graduation Ceremony.'

So they remembered her!

'I was only trying to add more dignity to the welcome note. I had no intentions of insulting the Governor,' Zinnia's tone was apologetic but firm. 'And I haven't made it up, because I have proof—a holo-view recording.'

'And who has the recording?'

'I do.'

'We need to see it,' Governor Tisya said.

Zinnia nodded. She synched the padlet with the big screen in the office and played the clip. Moments of silence ensued as the two Altklugs watched the recording. Not a single emotion flickered on their faces. Not a sound escaped their lips. Their faces were frozen in an impassive mould. Only their eyes followed the activity on screen. When the recording ended, Commander Hertz passed the Governor an almost imperceptible glance.

'This byte reveals nothing,' Governor Tisya snapped. 'Where are the simulations you mentioned?'

For the first time that evening, Zinnia experienced a twinge of uneasiness. She flashed Crispin a quick look. He looked a little worried too.

'I deliberately avoided taking those images. It...it wouldn't have been proper...I mean for G11.' A faint blush crossed her face. She felt awkward even discussing it.

'Commander Burdock is a top-level Executive in the Dome. We need solid proof before we take any action against him,' Commander Hertz said.

'All this byte shows is two people having some fun!' the Governor shrugged.

'It shows only *one* person having his fun. The other is a victim of his fun,' Zinnia corrected, in a quiet tone.

'Unbelievable! For your information, we spoke to Commander Burdock and he denied using the lamebirl. He said she was the one who initiated it. What do you have to say to that?' Governor Tisya leaned forward and fixed a sharp green gaze on the lamebren.

'He's lying, Governor,' Crispin spoke up for the first time. 'I've known G11 for many years now and she would never do such a thing.'

'How do we know that you two aren't lying?'

'We aren't lying because we have nothing to gain from it. But Commander Burdock—he has a lot to gain by lying,' Zinnia remarked.

Commander Hertz looked at the Governor directly for the first time that evening. She nodded.

'If we decide to take action against Burdock, you will have to promise us not to utter a word of this episode to another soul in the Dome. And, you will have to erase the byte right now, before us,' he said.

Zinnia glanced at Crispin. She knew that his mind was on the same track as hers.

'We promise that no one would know about Commander Burdock.'

'I hope you understand that the consequences of breaking that promise can be really harsh,' Governor Tisya reminded.

The lamebren nodded.

'And will you erase the holo-view?'

Zinnia hesitated. It was foolish to erase the only proof they had before any action was taken against Burdock.

'I'll erase it the moment I hear that justice has been met.'

For the first time, the Governor flew into a twinkling laughter. Even Commander Hertz smiled, amused.

'You dare state conditions, lamebirl! Do you know that this instant I can confiscate your padlet and put you into the Isolation Chamber? Or pack you off to the Dissolution Crypt and no one will ever hear of you again?'

'I know you can, but you *won't*. Because the Altklug Ace-world is a perfect world and these actions would mean that you want to curb justice. And curbing justice is the first sign of a weak and imperfect world.' Zinnia was surprised at the calm tone in which she spoke. Inside she was trembling and her senses seemed to be scattered. Where was this logically profound knowledge coming from?

'You are smart for a lamebirl but be careful. I may not always be in an accommodating mood. Okay, go back to the Cubicle now. We'll see what can be done. And Mirella will make sure that you have erased the holo-view.' Governor Tisya turned her back on the lamebren in dismissal and stared out at the carpet of lights below.

'Thank you, Governor and Commander!' Zinnia managed before Bozo materialised almost magically and hastened them out of the office.

Zinnia flashed Crispin a smile. She couldn't believe it. Had they actually emerged victorious? She couldn't fully appreciate their win just yet. Not until she could talk it out with Crispin.

13

'You know what, no more duty with Commander Burdock,' Camilla announced. 'Supercustodian just told me that my duties would now be reshuffled. Can you believe my luck?'

She grinned from ear to ear in relief. Lunch was just over and Zinnia and Crispin were seated on the lawn, talking. Crispin glanced at Zinnia and smiled in tacit understanding.

'That is good news,' he agreed.

'Isn't it? No going to that stuffy man with goggling eyes! He gave me the creeps I tell you. And specially with Cheska not around, I didn't want to be in that house. Doing nothing at all—what wastage of time! Well, see you in Mirella's class.'

She sailed away happily and Zinnia felt an inner flow of joy. This was definitely Mirella's doing, she thought. Mirella understood and unlike other Altklugs, she cared for the lamebren. But Zinnia still had to hear from the Exector about the action taken against Burdock.

It was already afternoon and Bamian's class had progressed as usual—full of knowledge about the Altklug world. Zinnia had been distracted, the memory of the previous night and the interaction with the Governor herself, still fresh in her mind. Where had the courage to face the top boss of the Altklug Dome sprung from? It hadn't been easy...but she and Crispin had still done it! She remembered how he had stood up for Camilla—unfortunately Camilla would never know it. He really was the best friend anyone could hope for.

'You did the right thing,' Crispin remarked.

'*We* did the right thing,' Zinnia corrected.

'No, that's not what I meant. I meant recording Burdock and Camilla and not the images. And also not letting her know what had happened in that room. *That* was the right thing to do.'

Zinnia shrugged. 'I couldn't. I kept thinking of what the truth would do to her—I didn't want her to live her life in shame and horror. I want Camilla and all our friends here to be content and happy and live their lives the way they want to.'

'I know what you mean.' Crispin nodded.

'Now, if only Cheska, Maisie and Reed could return to the Dome, I'd feel so much better,' she added. 'Have you heard anything from them?'

'No. The connectivity between the padlets has been disabled. But we will. I'm sure that there won't be a problem keeping connected with them,' he assured.

'I guess you're right. But what about Mirella? Why hasn't she got in touch with us regarding Burdock as yet? I'm dying with curiosity. What do you think they will do? They will have to take immediate action, won't they? They do work very fast anyway, don't they?' Her questions had a twinge of anxiety. And yet, somehow, Zinnia had faith in Mirella. She would see it through. She would ensure that justice would be done.

Before Crispin could respond, a gong resounded through the Cubicle and the two of them rose at once. Zinnia was optimistic. The gravity of the issue and last night's visit to Governor Tisya's office were too significant to be side-tracked. Mirella would definitely revert with more information. Hopefully, it would be good news that some concrete action had been taken against Commander Burdock.

Mirella was punctual and carried on with the class, without the slightest indication of the previous day's events. Zinnia waited impatiently for the class to get over. She wanted to thank the Exector for her timely intervention. If she hadn't spoken on their behalf, Camilla would still be allotted duty at the Commander's house and would have continued to be his victim, without her knowledge.

'G23 and G11, please come to the Klugsage room,' Mirella requested, as class ended.

Zinnia's heart jumped in anticipation as the two of them hastened after her. Zinnia felt hope bubbling inside her.

Once in the room, Mirella shut the Demarcator and turned towards them. Her usually cheerful face was grave.

'I have some bad news for you.'

Zinnia's heart sank. Something was not right!

'I'd like you to know that suitable action had been taken against the Commander, but unforeseen circumstances have thwarted progress. Commander Burdock has outright refused to step down from his post and in fact has declared that if he is forced to resign, he will sue G11 and you two for maligning his reputation.'

Zinnia and Crispin gawked at the Exector in disbelief.

'How can he!' Crispin expostulated.

'He *can*. He has the right to defend himself.'

'But...but Governor Tisya said...' Zinnia began, indignantly.

'You have to understand that it's a very delicate situation. Commander Burdock insists that he has been tempted by G11. Unfortunately, your byte is not good enough proof to register otherwise.' Exector Mirella pursed her lips and shook her head.

Zinnia stared at her as if she had spoken in a foreign tongue.

'The holo-view byte is not proof enough? What more did they want?' she asked, anger beginning to hammer at her temples.

'I'm sorry I can't do much more than this. It is now up to you two to decide. Do you want to pursue this matter and file a formal charge against Commander Burdock or would you like to withdraw the accusation?'

'We cannot withdraw the accusation,' Crispin spoke up. 'And it is really unfair that the byte proof cannot be used against the Commander.'

Mirella glanced from Zinnia to Crispin, a sympathetic look on her face.

'This means that Commander Burdock is so powerful that even the Governor cannot touch him,' Zinnia remarked slowly.

'That is, of course, untrue. No one can be or is more powerful than the Governor. But that is beside the point. The fact is he *can* be touched if *you* decide to file a case. You can fight this legal battle if you believe in your cause. But I have to warn you that the legal battle will be long and tedious, and poor G11 will be dragged through the whole trial until the day you actually gain victory—*if* you gain victory.' Mirella paused and her dark eyes flitted from Crispin to Zinnia. 'On the other hand, if you don't file charges, then I can assure you that Commander Burdock will never set eyes on G11 again. For that matter, it is an Altklug promise that none of the lamebren will ever go near him.'

Zinnia met Mirella's steady gaze unflinchingly. She read so much more in the Exector's eyes than she was revealing.

'An Altklug promise?' Zinnia couldn't help repeating. 'Like the one Governor Tisya made last night?'

Mirella folded her arms. In her white robe, she appeared as angelic as ever. 'From what I heard, Governor Tisya wishes to see justice done. She does not issue false promises and does not raise unnecessary hope. Give it a thought. You have until tomorrow morning to take a decision.'

'This is outrageous!' Zinnia exploded, the moment they were out in the garden. 'I can't believe that last night was just a farce! They made us believe that they are playing it fair. But in reality, they are threatening us that if we pursue this, we will be entangled in a legal battle. And we all know who will win the court battle in the end, don't we?'

'Why am I not surprised?' Crispin remarked almost to himself. 'It was too good to be true, anyway.'

'This is blackmail. If we sue Burdock, the Altklugs will ensure that he wins the case. So much for being fair and perfect!'

'The Altklugs were never fair. Why did we think that they would be in the first place?' Crispin wondered. He thrust a hand through his dishevelled hair. 'In all my years at the Cubicle, I haven't seen anything fair about the way they operate. If they were fair, we would be free in the true sense of the word. If they were just, we wouldn't be regarded as lamebren and inferior and they wouldn't have decided our termination dates! There is nothing fair about the Altklugs.' The anger and bitterness lay thick in his voice.

'What do we do now?' Zinnia asked. She suddenly experienced a wave of helplessness.

'Do we have a choice?'

'I guess not,' she agreed, slowly. 'If we file charges, there is no guarantee that the legal battle would be fair. Because it is obvious that Governor Tisya has made her choice. She prefers to side with Burdock, despite his crime.'

'That's because she has more to gain from supporting him than supporting us. Who are we after all? Just lamebren with expiry dates.'

'You are right. Besides, we also have to think of Camilla. She should not be dragged into all of this.'

'Then our decision is made. We will not pursue the subject anymore,' Crispin concluded, his voice devoid of emotion.

Zinnia glanced at him. She sensed his anger, frustration and pain—a reflection of her own emotions.

The Paramour Path was beautiful as ever and the perfect balm for Zinnia's disturbed mind. But today, she barely noticed the play of colours, the lilting sounds of birds and water as she sat staring out at the lake. This was the same spot where she had discovered Iris with Sven and look what had transpired immediately that night. They had smuggled Iris out of the Super-Dome and straight into the Dissolution Crypt. No chance to say goodbye, no time to object. Not that anyone would've dared to oppose it, not then at least...but what about today? Would it have been any better? Could she have found the courage to take a stand against the Altklug decision of punishing Iris? No one would've paid heed to her objections but she would have at least tried?

All said and done, all lamebren including Zinnia, were in awe of the Altklugs. They were far superior to them in knowledge and technology And what did the lamebren have? Nothing—yet she felt that she would've been there for Iris, perhaps thoughtlessly, perhaps driven by sheer love for the lamebirl. But she would've stood up for her, just like she was trying to stand up for Camilla now. But just like this time, that time too would've been hopeless.

The Altklugs had absolute power and control, and used it indiscriminately on the lamebren who had no one on their side. There was just no controlling and stopping them. Or unless there was...Zinnia paused in her thoughts—Preceptor Amadeus! What if she approached him and informed him of Commander Burdock's behaviour? Would he be able to help?

Something soft brushed against Zinnia's leg and she jerked, startled out of her thoughts. Then she almost screamed. A pair of honey-brown eyes was staring at her from a tiny frame of golden fur. Zinnia gasped. If she wasn't mistaken she had seen different versions of this animal at the Zoelter. It was a puppy! Exactly like the little furry toy her parents had given her. She was still staring at it with shock when the puppy advanced with a wagging tail, tongue hanging out and lifting a tiny paw. Something in his stance was so inviting, that Zinnia spontaneously took the uplifted paw. Instantly he licked her hand. With a small cry, Zinnia dropped the paw and jerked her hand away, rubbing it against her dress

It gave a low, insistent bark and continued staring with his beautiful eyes.

'Hello!' Zinnia said softly. 'How did you get here doggie?'

Once again he raised his paw and whined in reply. He looked so endearing, that she accepted it. This time she was ready for his lick of friendship. She patted his head boldly and within minutes, the puppy had jumped into her lap. Zinnia laughed as the golden bundle cuddled up in her lap.

'I can't believe this! A doggie in my lap. Oh my goodness! You are the cutest. I'm going to call you Doodle.'

The puppy seemed to accept his name as it rested his head between his paws, his eyes glued to her face.

'Eeeeks! What are you doing?' Two voices cried out simultaneously and Zinnia glanced up to see Camilla and Crispin staring at her in horror. She laughed.

'Meet my new friend Doodle!'

'New friend? Where did you find it? What will you do with it? You know you can't keep it at the Cubicle. Supercustodian would never allow it,' Crispin shot out all in one breath.

Zinnia laughed. 'Come and meet Doodle first, both of you. And Crispin, you can be practical and all adult-like later okay?'

The two lamebren edged closer a little cautiously, but Doodle jumped out of Zinnia's lap and began prancing around them playfully. Crispin sat down and fondled the pup but Camilla kept her distance, eyeing the animal warily.

'He's cute,' Crispin admitted.

'But what will you do with it?' Camilla asked.

'I can't possibly leave him here where there's no food and no one to care for him,' Zinnia decided. 'I'll have to take him to the Cubicle.'

'You can't do that. Supercustodian will confiscate it and send it to the Zoelter,' Camilla pointed out. 'Or worse, have it killed. It is a potential disease carrier according to them—all animals are, which is why they are kept away from the Altklugs.'

'You mean they are potential emotion-evokers! Look at the way the puppy made me smile and feel happy. I forgot everything the moment I touched him. I think the Altklugs are actually more afraid of being sucked into the positive gamut of emotions—perhaps that's why these doggies are remanded to the Zoelter,' Zinnia replied with sudden insight.

'Whatever! The point is you can't take it to the Cubicle,' Camilla insisted.

'If the pup is here, his mother must also be around,' Crispin realised. 'I think it must have strayed in from the Snarl. The Diaphanous Seal runs very close to the other end of the lake. The pup must've left his mother and strayed into the Super-Dome.'

'Then what do we do with it? We can't take him to the Cubicle and neither can I leave him here. And Snow Hour will start in a while. The pup will freeze and die!' Zinnia exclaimed, the thought making her shudder.

Both Crispin and Camilla looked at Zinnia with helpless eyes. They knew she was right but what could be done?

'We'll have to take him back to the Snarl,' Zinnia declared.

The other two looked aghast.

'The Snarl? You must be crazy!' Camilla shrieked. 'No one goes to the Snarl. It's too dangerous. Remember Leo Leroy? The lamebroy who never came back and whose body parts were found?'

'Camilla's right. The Altklugs are forbidden to go into the Snarl too,' Crispin agreed.

'The Altklugs aren't allowed, but no rule says that the lamebren can't go to the forest?'

'I'm not sure if there is. Although Supercustodian has warned us to keep away from the Exit door in the hall.'

'Look, what difference does it make to them? If we do get lost, so be it! For the Altklugs, it's just one less lamebirl or lamebroy to be concerned, if we go the Leo Leroy way,' Zinnia concluded triumphantly.

'But the point is that the Forest is considered very dangerous and there are monsters and...' Camilla repeated.

'Do you have another option?'

'No, but the forest?'

'Seriously Zinnia,' Crispin began in his most practical voice.

'Don't "seriously" me!' Zinnia cut in. 'Do you have another option?'

'No,' Crispin admitted, reluctantly.

'Then, we *will* have to look for his mother in the forest. If you can't accompany me, it's alright. Just point the way to me,' Zinnia spoke stubbornly.

She picked up the pup, who whined but settled snugly in the crook of her arm. She sensed his love and a kind of peace settled in her heart.

'Look at the trust this little one has shown in me. I cannot betray his confidence.'

'What's happening here?' another voice cut in.

Zinnia turned around in surprise.

'Cheska!' Camilla shrieked and rushed to hug her twin.

Cheska, Reed and Maisie grinned widely. Cheska looked exactly like his twin. Reed appeared taller and thinner and Maisie's braids seemed to have grown in the past few weeks.

'So thrilled to see you three!' Zinnia exclaimed as Crispin hugged them all.

'The Paramour Paths aren't under the digi-eye scan, so we thought we'd meet Camilla here,' Cheska explained.

Zinnia glanced at Camilla who turned a shade of red.

'I...I was going to tell you that was why Crispin and I were here, to meet them but you found the pup and...'

The other lamebren instantly saw the pup in Zinnia's arms and everyone started talking at once in excitement. After the initial inhibitions were voiced, ideas were brainstormed as to what was best for it.

'We would've offered to take it to our Ret Cabana, but the place is stricter than the Cubicle. Besides, the new Ret Cabana is kind of different. There are rooms in which we aren't permitted to enter, there's twenty-four-hour security outside these rooms. We are just eight of us including lamebren brought in from the other Cubicles, but there's something fishy about the place. Of course, it doesn't concern us. We have been given duties and our meals, so that's fine. Although why exactly we've been shifted to that Ret Cabana is still a mystery to me,' Cheska intoned.

'Easy—to break up friendships,' Crispin remarked. 'Oh, here come Ivy and Berk!'

Once again, first, there was a lot of happy hugging followed by squealing over Doodle. The pup seemed to enjoy all the attention as it licked and woofed and snuggled deeper in Zinnia's arms. When the excitement had died down, Crispin glanced at Zinnia and nodded.

'I think Zinnia is right. We have to find Doodle's mother. We cannot allow it to starve here in the Paramour Path. So you sit down and chat, while Zinnia and I go into the Snarl and look for the mother. She can't be far away.'

A hushed silence followed this suggestion.

'You sure?' Cheska frowned. 'Leo Leroy...'

'Don't worry. We won't go far. Besides, this part of the entrance isn't monitored, so we'll be in and out un-noticed. You don't have to wait for us. See you all later.'

Zinnia waved to the others as they sat down by the lake to exchange notes. Camilla looked so happy to meet her brother. There must be a way to bring these three back to the Cubicle, she thought idly. But she would think about it later. She had Doodle to think of first.

Crispin led the way round the edge of the lake till they arrived at the running Diaphanous Seal. The contrast in landscape was startling. On this side of the wall, the Altklug Super-Dome was polished, controlled and beautifully manicured. On the other side, the Snarl sprawled dark, dangerous and unruly. Crispin and Zinnia glanced at each other.

'You are determined to do this, aren't you?' Crispin confirmed.

Zinnia nodded, but her heart had begun to thud erratically.

There was a small slit where one part of the transparent wall ended and the other began—the gap was wide enough for a thin kid to slip through. Crispin slid through and Zinnia followed, a thrill of excitement running down her spine. They had entered the Snarl!

14

The Snarl was an attack on the senses with sharp odours and a thick foliage which seemed to close claustrophobically with every step. Zinnia clutched Crispin's hand in a tight grip, as he cautiously tread over fallen branches.

'Be alert and keep your eyes on the ground. There could be crawlies you don't want to step on and be bitten,' he admonished.

As their eyes got accustomed to the patchwork of shade and light, shadowy shapes solidified into thick, impenetrable foliage. Branches crouched low and gnarled trunks twined and entwined into a mesh of branches. The sheer variety of the green shades amazed Zinnia and she couldn't help comparing it with the myriad colours of the Altklug trees. There was something cosmetic about those, she realised, now that she had come face-to-face with the real thing. Everything about the Snarl was raw, unpolished and wild and a little frightening too, she admitted.

'Let's call out to the dog,' Crispin suggested.

'Yes, let's,' Zinnia agreed, glad to hear the sound of their own voices, in the eerie silence.

'Doggie, doggie!' Crispin called, apprehensively.

They edged their way forward, through what looked like a tiny path. Doodle struggled in her arms, so Zinnia released him on the forest floor which was a latticed carpet of tree roots and fallen leaves. He immediately began sniffing the ground and scampered ahead, his little tail wagging like a flag.

'Hey Doodle, wait!' Zinnia hastened after the pup.

'I think he's leading us to his mom,' Crispin guessed.

They followed the tiny, furry body, as he happily jumped over the roots and dodged the low-hanging branches, a contrast of golden brown against the dark, rich greens. Zinnia stopped to catch her breath, and stared in awe around her.

'I've never seen anything ever, quite like this, have you? Just look at those clusters of flowers! And there, the ivy seems to have covered the entire tree. And what an inviting bunch of fruits, are those really bananas? And that round one? Would it be okay if we taste one? This is all so different from our world. So—sort of—raw, unplanned, wild and yet, kind of real. Isn't this simply amazing?' Zinnia gushed. She couldn't help staring at this whole new world around her.

Right above, between the gaps in the thick foliage, a blue and orange sky peeked invitingly. A sense of déjà vu swamped her and she suddenly remembered her dream. Hadn't she been running through a deep forest just like this one? Would there be a magical rainbow at the end of the forest, like in her dream? Another wave of excitement spiralled through her and she glanced at Crispin.

'It is breathtakingly beautiful. And dangerous too, I'm sure,' Crispin reminded.

A flock of birds suddenly rose from the branches, the flapping of their wings so close and clear that both Zinnia and Crispin ducked instinctively.

'Wow! That was a little scary, I thought the famous forest monster had appeared.' Zinnia grinned sheepishly as the birds flew to another treetop.

'Come on, let's not lose focus. We want to find Doodle's mother as soon as we can, so that we can return to the Cubicle. It's dangerous out here. Listen, is that him barking?'

'Woof, woof!' The bark was excited and seemed to come from a distance.

'I think he's found his mother,' Zinnia figured. 'Come on!'

Zinnia and Crispin plunged through the overgrowth. The joyful barking continued and Zinnia forgot her fear. She was eager to see Doodle meeting his mother.

The shadows were punctuated with patches of streaming light and the two of them ran towards the thinning trees. Just on the edge of the clearing, they suddenly stopped short. Zinnia stifled a scream with her hand over her mouth. A most startling sight met their eyes. Standing in the clearing, was a tall and huge figure of a man, the size of four Altklugs aligned one on top of the other. His face was so wrinkled that his eyes seemed to be lost in the folds of the skin and he had the longest beard she had ever seen. It entangled with his long white hair. He was holding a large stick and leaning slightly over it. He wore a long gown of some coarse material which was a mix and match of different colours. Who was this towering species? Was it a human and why did he appear so weird and different?

Instinctively, Crispin held Zinnia's hand in a protective grip. He too was staring at the man, who would have appeared sinister but for the fact that Doodle was prancing around at his feet. An older dog was licking Doodle lovingly. Finally, they had found the mother!

The man smiled, his wrinkles increasing three-fold and the lamebren stepped back quickly.

'No wait, don't be frightened!' he spoke in a gruff voice. 'I'm a friend.'

Crispin and Zinnia glanced at each other.

'You brought the pup back to his mother, didn't you? That was kind of you. He is very naughty—goes off on his own, the little one, leaving his mother Deedee. I've been looking for this little chap for a while now.'

His piercing gaze rested on them alternately.

'I'm Leo Leroy and I live in the Snarl.'

'Leo Leroy!' Zinnia and Crispin exclaimed together, their faces frozen in shock.

'But you...you...' Crispin stammered.

'You escaped from the Altklug Super-Dome years and years ago. And you were dead and parts of your body were found...' Zinnia burst out.

Leo Leroy broke into laughter and the sound of his guffaw echoed through the forest.

'What imagination the Altklugs have,' he chuckled. 'I *did* run away, yes, but I'm fine and now I live far away, deep into the forest where the Altklugs cannot hunt me down.'

'No one lives in the forest. It's too dangerous,' Zinnia said.

'*I* do and the forest is dangerous only for the Altklugs, not for normal beings like me and you.'

'You know about us?' Crispin asked, surprised.

'I know about you and the Altklug Super-Dome yes, although they are totally unaware of my existence.' Leo smiled. 'Come sit down here by this tree and let's talk.'

He walked slowly and with a slight limp, leaned his stick against a fallen branch and seated himself. Immediately both the dogs, settled down by his feet, which seemed to be covered in some kind of wooden invention. Zinnia and Crispin hesitated for a fraction of a second, then Crispin nodded at Zinnia. They perched themselves on Leo's left, keeping a safe distance between them.

'I am delighted to meet both of you. What are your names?' He looked at them kindly.

'I am Zinnia and this is Crispin,' Zinnia replied. 'Do you really live in the Snarl?'

'Yes I do. I've lived here for sixty years now.'

'Sixty years!' both the lamebren exclaimed.

'Yes, sixty long years filled with wonderful experiences.'

'No one can live that long,' Crispin scoffed.

'I'm not lying if that's what you are implying.' Leo's eyes crinkled in amusement.

'We live up to sixteen years and none of us has ever lived beyond that age.'

'Now, you are completely wrong there. Altklugs live up to sixteen years. But you, on the other hand, you "lamebren" as they call you, can live for many, many years. Look at me, I am like you and I'm old and seventy!'

The lamebren appeared confused.

'Which means that you must have been around when the Singularity was toppled by the Altklugs,' Crispin realised.

'Smart boy. You know the Super-Dome history well. Yes, I was around. I've seen Governor Seeya and know how hard she fought to bring back the Altklug regime. Brave lady…Governor Tisya is not a patch on her, I must say. Anyway, we'll talk about that later…'

'But you aren't a lamebrain, like us, are you?' Crispin asked.

'I'm not a lamebrain and neither are you.' Leo smiled.

He really appeared very kind and gentle, Zinnia realised, now that they had got used to the wrinkles on his face.

'I don't think I understand. In the Super-Dome we are considered as lamebren and we are all born with termination dates.' We are going to be killed one by one,' Zinnia explained patiently.

'You are not a lamebrain and definitely not born with termination dates, those are *given* by the Altklugs—it's just the Altklug manner of handling issues,' Leo dismissed. 'Look let me explain. People like you and me, we belong to a normal world. You were just unfortunate to be born in the Altklug Super-Dome, where you are treated like a lamebrain.'

'What is a normal world?' Zinnia asked, frowning in concentration.

'A normal world is where people live out their natural years. Look at me, I am seventy and perhaps would live on for a few more years. But you will only really understand it once you live it. Live it, have children and create your own normal world. Only then will you be really safe. It is a life filled with love and emotional attachments—an "imperfect life" with ups and downs.'

'But how can we be normal? And can we live such a life with the Altklugs?' Zinnia wanted to know.

'Hmmm...I have my doubts. You see, in the process of materialistic and technological advancement and perfection, the Altklugs have lost the charm of being normal beings. They have turned almost into superior robots and that is why, cocooned in their "perfect techno-domains" they cannot relate with you and understand you children. When their lack of understanding overpowered their thinking, they preferred to regard you as a lamebrain. But don't think that you have no rights. You do and if you ever need them, just go to the Main KlugBiblio and look them up.'

Zinnia and Crispin listened attentively. The old man's gruff voice was low and slow. He glanced at them and smiled occasionally and one of his hands constantly fondled the big dog Deedee.

'I want to bring about a change in the Altklug Super-Dome. How can I do that?' Zinnia asked, suddenly.

Leo appeared amused. 'Change the Altklug Ace-world, eh! That's a huge task, but not necessarily impossible. You see the biggest problem with the Altklugs is that they are born as adults, because childhood and childlike innocence has been eradicated from the Altklug life. So perhaps, you can begin with something that will evoke their emotions? And I mean *childlike* emotions—not adult ones. Since they are born so adult-like, they are unaware of what childlike emotions mean. They have to *learn* to be children.'

'But how? How does one invoke the childlike emotion in an adult?'

'Well, the whole intention is to create and awaken this innocence which is now completely non-existent in their lives. Think back into your early years. What brought on the purity of emotions such as joy, anxiety, and tears? The Altklugs should do the same thing that would recreate this innocence, these emotions. They should take pleasure in the simple acts of life—play in the park, or play games, love animals. There's innocence when you fall and cry and innocence when you need your mother. Innocence when you need to cuddle with your parents, innocence when you get your math wrong. It would also be good to show them what old age means—because that would show them what it means to be fearful and insecure.'

Zinnia and Crispin listened in fascination. Leo seemed to know so much about the Altklugs!

'I'll try but I can't see the Altklugs being fearful and insecure,' Zinnia said, reflectively.

'That's sad but true and the crux of the issue. They are too deeply imbedded in their craft and knowledge to allow insecurities to run free. Plus they have their own method of dealing with fear and insecurity. Their methods are time-tested and politically motivated.'

Zinnia glanced at Crispin. Leo seemed to be the right person to ask for advice about Burdock. She raised her eyebrows at him and Crispin instantly caught her silent query. He nodded.

In the next few minutes, Zinnia had explained the entire Camilla-Burdock episode to Leo. His eyes were thin slits as he listened to the story with a great deal of attention. He sat motionless and his head was bent in concentration.

'We had hoped that Mirella and Governor Tisya would help us resolve this issue. But instead they have threatened us,' Zinnia concluded.

Leo was silent for a few moments. Then he glanced up at the lamebren.

'Camilla doesn't remember or know a thing about what happened to her?' he asked, finally. His voice was carefully emotionless.

'I don't think so,' Zinnia replied.

'The Altklugs are cunning and this is classic Altklug problem solving method. Skilful and yet biased and overpowering. They first assured you and hinted that they would take care of the problem, which meant that you would not make a hue and cry about it to all and sundry. Then they cornered you, taking you by surprise, warning you of dire consequences if you took legal action. If you still decide to go against their threat, it won't take them long to send you three to the Dissolution Crypt.'

Zinnia and Crispin exchanged looks. So, they had interpreted the situation correctly.

'Well, my advice to you is to back off. Camilla will not be sent to Burdock again, the Governor would see to it. And you two have to learn to forget what happened.

That is the only way now. Let them think that they frightened you off.'

'But...' Zinnia protested.

'I said forget, not forgive,' Leo cut in quietly. 'Leave the rest to the Universe. The Altklugs may not believe in the power of the Universe but I do. The Universe, or God as some preferred to call it, behaves in strange ways. But as far as you two are concerned, the matter is over. Tomorrow you tell Mirella that you are ready to drop the subject and all's well that ends well. Will you do that?' Leo studied Zinnia's face keenly.

The lamebirl nodded.

'I know that you are spirited, you care for your friend and want to see justice done. But justice can be met in a number of ways. The Altklugs have their style and manner of executing it, and the Universe has its own. Save your energy and spirit for bigger matters, my dear. You are going to need it—all of you.'

Leo's sharp, assessing gaze glided from one face to the other.

'We will, Sir,' Crispin assured.

'I think it is time for you to leave. Just keep together and stay strong. If you should ever need me, you can use this drum. See, this is a natural hollowed bark of a tree. Here's a stick. Try this rhythm which will be our contact code.' Leo played a sample rhythm on the bark which echoed loudly through the trees. 'Here try it.'

Crispin imitated him—dhun, dhun, dhun-dhuna-dhun—and succeeded to an extent. Zinnia tried and her effort made Doodle tilt his head and bark.

'It will get better with practice.' Leo smiled. 'If you play this code, I'll hear it. I live some distance away but the sound carries easily through the forest and I'll turn up as soon as I can.'

'Goodbye, Sir,' Zinnia said. She kneeled down and hugged the puppy. 'And you will look after Doodle for me, won't you?'

Leo gave a nice hearty laugh. 'Yes, I will. His real name is Sunny, but from today he shall be Doodle. You two take care and remember my words. Stay strong!'

15

'I think we've taken a wrong turn,' Crispin remarked. 'The trees don't look familiar at all. In fact, this part of the forest appears terribly ferocious.'

All light had faded and the Snarl was murky and dark and the trees hovered like ghostly figures all around them. A cool wind slithered between the foliage making an eerie sound. Crispin halted in the path, and Zinnia shivered.

'No we haven't, look, there's the Diaphanous Seal!' she exclaimed in relief.

The Snarl during night time was gloomy and particularly frightening. They hastened to the gap in the wall, eager to escape the interminable blackness and the chill in the air. Crispin squeezed through the wall first and Zinnia followed. It was colder in the Altklug world with the Snow Hour about to begin and Zinnia rubbed her arms to gain some warmth.

'Wait. It *was* a wrong turn,' Crispin whispered.

'What do you mean?'

'We aren't at the lake. We're at the Ret Cubicle.'

Zinnia noticed the ten steps leading to the black metallic door. This was the same door she had opened on the very first day of her arrival.

'You're right. What do we do now?'

She had barely finished talking when, to her great horror, the metallic door slid open. Supercustodian! They were going to get caught! And there was nowhere to hide…

But it wasn't Supercustodian, another Altklug stood by the door, looking directly at them. Silhouetted against the light inside the Cubicle, his face was completely shadowed. He stood with his hands on his hips and stared at them.

'I saw you on my screen,' he said.

'We...we're sorry, we kind of lost our way,' Crispin spluttered.

'Lost your way? Where? You weren't in the Snarl, were you?' He didn't wait for them to respond as he turned and led the way inside, into the warmth of the Cubicle.

Crispin and Zinnia followed, taking the steps two at a time. Once inside the hall, the metallic door slid shut again. Zinnia could see the Altklug's face now. He was the same Altklug who had helped her with the Server on her very first day. She stared at him, wondering who he was.

'We...actually...' Crispin hedged.

'We were curious so we walked along the Diaphanous Seal,' Zinnia cut in quickly. 'We didn't mean to be late for dinner.'

The Altklug faced her. A small, half-smile touched his lips and his eyes crinkled at the corners pleasantly. She wondered how old he was. He was as tall as Crispin and dressed in the usual uniform. And yet...it was in that instant that Zinnia had her first doubt. He was an Altklug, wasn't he?

'You're just in time for dinner. But I must warn you, the glass wall or the Diaphanous Seal is for your safety. Do not cross it and do not be out in the Snow Hour. The next time I will not be so lenient,' he remarked and then he marched away.

Zinnia frowned after him. The authority with which he spoke indicated that he was someone important. Was he appointed as a Preceptor? A residential one this time? Her doubts were cleared after dinner, during their meeting in the dorm room.

'Our new Supercustodian Colonel Kripton,' Camilla informed. 'Our old Supercustodian has been posted to the New Ret Cabana. Poor Cheska and the others—she's such a nasty woman! What did you think of him, by the way?'

'He seemed pretty okay to me,' Zinnia said, careful not to voice her suspicion. She was almost certain that the Colonel was not a complete Altklug. But she would sound foolish if she said so. After all he was the Supercustodian and she had nothing to substantiate her suspicion.

'I hope so. But tell us—did you find Doodle's mother?'

'Not only did we find Doodle's mother Deedee, but we found someone else too—someone mysterious and cool,' Crispin grinned.

'Who?' Berk asked.

'Hold your breath—we met Leo Leroy!'

Berk's eyes bulged. Azalea's mouth flew open and Ivy and Cylia, stared.

'Leo Leroy!' they exclaimed.

'Shh...voices down. Yes, Leo Leroy.' Crispin smiled, thoroughly enjoying himself. 'But listen to the whole story first...'

The interest of the lamebren was piqued at once and they eagerly gathered around. As Crispin narrated their adventure, Zinnia found the expressions on their faces very amusing. Ivy was attentive, Camilla in awe, Berk totally astonished and Azalea appeared dazed.

'Leo Leroy,' Cylia repeated in amazement. 'The boy who escaped! And who everyone thought was dead. Wow!'

'Isn't it amazing that he actually survived in the Snarl? And survived for so many years that he's really, really old,' Crispin said.

'But then the legend about finding his body parts…' Ivy frowned.

'I believe that was created to dissuade other lamebren from escaping into the Snarl,' Crispin guessed.

'So, "old age" for us is different from that of the Altklugs,' Ivy observed.

'It certainly is. The Altklugs look no different whether they are four or fourteen. But Leo looked *strange*. Wrinkled skin, gnarled hands—almost as if the body was withering away,' Crispin explained.

'And yet he was nice—I mean he wasn't repulsive or dirty or horrible. He was kind and gentle, and spoke with such knowledge. It was not the Altklug kind of knowledge. It was—more human, more normal—our kind of knowledge.'

'Wow!' Berk expelled a breath.

'But where does he live? What does he eat?' Ivy asked practically.

Crispin and Zinnia looked at each other.

'We completely forgot to ask him these basic questions. Zinnia you should have thought of asking him about his life,' Crispin remarked pointedly.

'Actually I should have, but in the excitement of finding him and sharing our thoughts with him, I forgot. After all it was the first time someone was actually listening to us, believing in us and guiding us, so I guess it just slipped out of my mind. But why didn't you, Crispin? You could've also done the asking! I was already talking too much,' Zinnia retorted.

'Ok, you two stop squabbling,' Camilla cut in smoothly. 'Now, what next?'

'We discussed this on the way back and Crispin and I have come to the conclusion, that we have to do something concrete about the future of the lamebren.

We cannot allow the Altklugs to terminate us at their will,' Zinnia said.

'Easier said than done,' Berk muttered.

'Yes, it's tough Berk, but we have to begin somewhere. First, we have to stop thinking that the Altklugs are superior to us. And secondly, we have to realise that if we want to be safe, we need to live longer than the Altklugs.'

'But Preceptor Amadeus has been trying to change the mindset of the Altklugs without success for some years now,' Ivy pointed out. 'Hasn't he been propagating Age Progression?'

'Preceptor Amadeus talks of Age Progression, yes, but in a scientific manner. He wants to experiment. I am talking about the humane angle to it all. Plus our right to live as long as our bodies permit.'

'The Secret Society has two main agendas now—one is to formulate a plan to ensure the safety of the lamebren, not just in this Cubicle but the other four Cubicles across the Super-Dome, which is a long-term plan,' Crispin said. 'The second one, more urgent, is to get Cheska, Maisie and Reed back here. Does anyone have any ideas?'

In the dim light of the lamp, the young faces of the lamebren appeared innocent and reflective.

'Can't we request the Supercustodian to bring back Cheska and the others?' Camilla suggested.

'Or ask Mirella? She seems nice, too,' Cylia said.

Crispin and Zinnia flashed each other another quick glance. So much for Mirella being 'nice'. Although she had appeared sympathetic when she had forwarded the message from the Governor, she had seemed to be doing her duty a little too well, Zinnia thought. No one could be trusted in the Altklug Super-Dome— *absolutely no one!*

'We could try asking Supercustodian Kripton, but why would *he* listen to *us*? And why would he override the instructions of Commander Hertz?' Ivy wondered.

'Exactly my thoughts,' Crispin agreed.

'We need to *show* them not tell them that those three are needed here,' Zinnia added.

'How can we show?' Azalea asked.

'I think she's right!' Crispin appeared excited. 'Any amount of *telling* is useless with the Altklugs. We'll have to create a "need" for them here.'

'Think, think—of what use are those three to the Northern Quarter Ret Cubicle?'

No one responded as they all racked their brains for an answer.

'The problem is that the lamebren are of no use to the Altklugs. They just keep us alive to project that they are being fair with us,' Ivy said bitterly.

'You're right, but that isn't the truth any more than the fact that the Altklugs are superior to us,' Zinnia replied, in a firm voice. 'I've just thought of something else. Didn't Cheska say that some of the rooms at their Cubicle are guarded by security personnel?'

'You're right. Why does a lamebren Cubicle need security? What is in the rooms? And more importantly, why have some lamebren been transferred to that Cubicle…' Crispin's voice trailed.

For a moment everyone was silent. A sudden sense of unease filled the Cubicle Tory. Did the transfer of some of the lamebren have anything to do with the guarded rooms? And what exactly was happening in those rooms?

Zinnia and Crispin remained standing while Mirella fiddled with her padlet. Finally she glanced up at them. In her white robes and kind face, she really appeared so different from her other stone-faced colleagues.

'Yes. Have you decided what you want to do?' she asked.

'Yes Exector. We have decided that we do not want to go the legal route,' Zinnia replied.

Mirella nodded. *Was it the faintest glimmer of relief deep in her eyes?* Zinnia wondered.

'I think it is a wise decision. You lamebren do not want to be embroiled in a legal battle for the rest of your lives,' Mirella agreed. 'I shall pass the message to the Governor.'

'But G11...'

'G11 will never be sent to Commander Burdock's house,' Mirella confirmed. 'You can be sure about that. Now can I have the holo-view please? I need to personally ensure that it is erased.'

Without a word, Zinnia handed her the padlet. She experienced a last twinge of defeat and guilt and desperation, but then she curbed it. What had Leo said? The universe meets out its own justice. She had to believe it.

Mirella's actions were swift as if she were in a great hurry to erase all proof once and for all. She handed the padlet back to Zinnia.

'Thanks. We presume that this subject is now closed for good. I need to highlight the importance of keeping it all very secret. Any leakage would mean flinging sludge on Commander Burdock without proof and you know where that would lead, don't you?'

Zinnia locked eyes with Mirella for a moment, the anger inside her seething. *She could've helped if she wanted to,* Zinnia thought. She could've convinced the Governor to take action against Burdock, but she didn't. Ultimately, all said and done, Mirella had let her down.

Crispin pressed a warning hand on Zinnia's shoulder.

'You may go now. I may not take class today, so you will probably be assigned duties.' She nodded her dismissal and the lamebren quit the Klugsage room.

'Will you feed Marquee his lunch?' Manda asked.

Zinnia nodded and accepted the plate from the Altklug. Five different coloured tablets were laid out on the plate.

'Make sure he eats it all. You know how fussy kids are—they just won't take in the right nutrition,' Manda said.

Zinnia had been assigned duty with Lady Manda who was finding it tough to look after her baby. Her husband Dicto had been away on duty for a few days and Manda had sent in a request to the Ret Cubicle for assistance. So here Zinnia was, once again in an Altklug house.

As the Altklug left Zinnia to her task, the lamebirl turned her attention to the six-month old kid. His face was puckered in concentration as he leaned against a tree and played with a padlet, solving puzzles.

'Okay time for lunch, Marquee,' Zinnia announced cheerfully.

Marquee, who was much shorter than her, displayed marvellous traits of an Altklug. He had the same air of snobbery, ignored her existence with a condescendence to rival an adult's and continued to play with his padlet. Zinnia approached him and stood patiently while he finished his riddle. She observed him as he solved puzzle after puzzle with the ease of a much older person.

'Marquee?'

'Can't you see I'm doing something?' his voice was sharp and rude.

'Yes, I can. But your mother has asked me to feed you your lunch,' Zinnia reminded him with a calmness she was fast losing.

'I'm not a baby to be fed lunch. I'll have it, just keep it on the table,' Marquee retorted.

Leo's words came ringing back into her mind. It was true that the Altklugs knew no childhood. Here was this six-month-old who was already on his way to being an adult. His tone and attitude—all spoke of his supreme confidence and growth. Would a six-month-old lamebroy speak or react in this manner? A six-month-old lamebroy would not even have begun his speech, leave alone respond in any manner. She remembered what Leo had said—if you want to change the Altklug world, you have to bring back their innocence. Bring back their childhood, bring back fear and insecurity...

On an impulse, Zinnia pushed past the little kid and jostled Marquee's hand so hard that he lost his balance and fell. Zinnia turned around, waiting expectantly. Surely he would cry and wail for his mother in fright?

Marquee, however, rose, brushed off the invisible dust and stared at Zinnia with venom in his eyes.

'What you did just now could send you to the Dissolution Crypt, you dirty lamebirl. But for now, you are fired!'

Zinnia stared at him in disbelief. This wasn't a six-month-old, innocent child who needed to be protected and fed his meals. This was a grown-up encapsulating the standards and teachings of the Altklug Ace-world. The hatred in his eyes shredded her belief in seconds. If this was how kids regarded the lamebren, there was no hope for any attitudinal change. Preceptor Amadeus could devote his entire life to transforming the Altklugs in favour of the lamebren, but it would only be a long and useless service. His efforts would remain completely unappreciated unless some fundamental things changed in the Altklugs. Only if the Altklugs really learnt to be children, only if their superiority was challenged by another supremacy, if their arrogance was shuttered with authority. Then, and only then, would Preceptor Amadeus's theories see the mark of success.

Manda appeared just then and regarded the scene with suspicion.

'Mama, she pushed me deliberately!' Marquee related what happened in a few concise words.

Anger flicked in her eyes. Without a word, she picked up the breakfast plate, and took Marquee by the hand.

'Wait! My padlet...the lamebirl will steal it!'

Unexpected laughter bubbled up inside Zinnia. Marquee had all the makings of a super, super Altklug. But she curbed the misplaced laughter and watched in silence as Manda snatched the padlet and led her kid into the house.

Perhaps she had acted rashly, Zinnia thought. Arousing suspicion about her intentions wasn't her goal. She merely wanted to experiment with what Leo had suggested. But trying to create a child out of an Altklug was certainly not as easy a task as she had thought.

'Manda was very angry. She has asked me to change her labourer,' Colonel Kripton informed.

Zinnia had been called to his office—the same room occupied previously by the earlier Supercustodian. Everything looked the same yet the sterile look of the office had somehow changed. What was the difference?

The flowers in the vase! Zinnia raised surprised eyes to study Colonel Kripton. He was pacing the room, a stern expression on his face.

'I have to warn you G23. You are careless and too spirited for a lamebirl.'

'I am sorry,' Zinnia mumbled.

'You have to curb your impulses which won't be regarded kindly in this world. Do you understand? What you did today, although unintentionally, accounts to accosting a kid, which is chargeable under Section 21 and can be interpreted as molesting a child. The consequences can be very lethal.' Colonel Kripton stopped pacing and stared at Zinnia. 'Do you follow what I am saying?'

'Yes, Sir.'

'Good because this is my last warning to you. You may go now.'

When Zinnia stepped out of the office, she expelled a slow sigh. A simple, harmless push amounted to accosting and molesting a kid. And the actual, deliberate molesting of a lamebirl amounted to nothing? It was only treated as a mere aberration on the part of the Altklug, a mistake... that too only because he was discovered. If he hadn't been discovered, it would have continued to be enjoyed as an Altklug right!

Anger whipped through her, as the unfairness of it all struck her. With every passing day the mask of perfection was slipping from the Super-Dome of this Altklug Ace-world.

16

'Am I glad to meet you all!' Cheska exclaimed. His face was flushed and riddled with anxiety. Reed and Maisie too looked a little disturbed.

'What is it? What has happened? Why did you send us the urgent message?' Crispin asked, concerned.

'Let's sit down, shall we? My legs are trembling even at the thought of it,' Cheska mumbled.

Camilla looked very worried as she glanced from her twin to Zinnia and Crispin. It was just after lunch when Cheska had sent a crisp message asking them to meet him at the lake as soon as possible. Zinnia, Camilla and Crispin had rushed down the Paramour Path and to the lake. Cheska, Reed and Maisie were already there waiting for them. One look at their uneasy faces and Zinnia knew that something was not right.

They sat down on the flat black stones by the lake. The afternoon sun lay lazily over the waters turning them into silvery blue. A soft wind had picked up and gentle music rose and dipped with it.

'For the last couple of days, we—all three of us—have been feeling these strange vibrations from the objects around the Cubicle. Everything that we touched, kind of discharged a current. It wasn't very strong—just like a little jitter of static electricity. We ignored it as something that sometimes happens during Snow Hour due to friction. But yesterday, we were at lunch and the Server had just delivered our plates. I was about to begin eating when the plate gave off such a sharp current that the food flew off my hand. The others experienced it too. Believe me it wasn't a nice sensation at all. In fact, the current began numbing my hand. I tried to rub some sensation in it, but it just got worse and worse. I was really frightened. I felt as if I was being paralysed hand upwards!' Cheska appeared so rattled, that he broke off to inhale deeply.

'I felt the same,' Maisie took up the narration. 'It was awful and the strong current hit each one of us. It was, in fact, quite crippling.'

'It does sound awful!' Camilla was horrified.

'But that isn't all. Cheska, tell them what happened last night,' Reed prompted.

'We were sitting up late, talking in our room, when suddenly a low wailing sound pierced the night. It was like a low, painful cry of a little lamebroy or lamebirl. More than the actual sound, it was the pain and grief in the wail which sent the shivers down our spine.'

'It was something like the Siren of Departure, only this one was definitely made by some human,' Reed added, almost in a whisper.

'We rushed downstairs because the sound seemed to be coming from below. The wailing was horrendous as if someone was in great pain and it seemed to be coming from one of the locked rooms. A security guard was standing outside the room but he seemed unconcerned with the sound. Either he was deaf or he was used to it. When he saw us, he just turned to us rather coldly and ordered us to leave. The sound stopped just then, so we returned to our dorm. But we couldn't sleep all night. The mournful screech kept ringing in my ears—it was the most terrible sound I have ever heard.'

'Goodness!' Zinnia exclaimed. 'What could it mean?'

'No clue but all I know is that I don't want to go back to that Ret Cabana again. Something weird is happening there behind those closed doors,' Maisie shuddered.

'Could it be the sound of an animal?' Crispin asked.

'If it was, it was in terrible pain. Until now the three of us managed to live away from all of you, in the hope that we could meet like this. We consoled ourselves that at least we were free to do as we please. But after last night, I am beginning to get frightened.' Reed sounded scared.

Zinnia's mind was working furiously. What could be happening at that Ret Cabana? What did the wailing sound mean? And more importantly, why were some of the lamebren transferred to that place?

'We've got to do something. We can't go on living there,' Maisie sounded desperate.

'Listen, we'll think up something. Give us a day or two,' Zinnia remarked.

'Be strong all of you,' Camilla spoke for the first time. 'At least the three of you are together.

That's a cheering thought, right? Just keep together and keep us updated.'

Although she put up a brave front, Zinnia knew that Camilla was torn with worry on the inside. Something had to be done and fast. She had this strange intuition that something terrible was about to happen.

'But where are we going?' Crispin asked for the umpteenth time, as the Fountain of Knowledge charabanc travelled speedily over the skyways.

'We've forgotten a very important thing that Leo told us. He said that lamebren have their rights and that if we wish to know them we can look them up at the Main KlugBiblio,' Zinnia replied, excited.

'How would that help us?' Crispin frowned.

'Think Crispin. We have *rights*! No one has ever told us this before. Possibly because no one *wants* us to know about them.' Zinnia's eyes gleamed.

'I see what you mean,' Crispin agreed. 'But even if we *do* have rights, will anyone allow us to use them? Will anyone pay heed to us?'

'Listen, until now, we weren't even aware we had rights, leave alone use them. So until we try, how would we know if the Altklugs would listen to us or not?' Zinnia argued patiently.

'You are right. In fact, now that I think of it, this may be just the solution that we're looking for.'

'Exactly!' Zinnia looked happy. 'So that's why we are going to the Main KlugBiblio.'

Crispin smiled at her. 'You really are something, Zinnia. You truly care for all the lamebren, don't you?'

Zinnia responded with a matching smile. 'When I was separated from my parents, I was only three years old but I could understand and remember everything—I still do. I was shattered when I had to go and live at the Ret Cabana. I missed them so badly. Then at the Ret Cabana I got close to Lily, Arry, Juju, Jinny and Peeta but again I was separated from them. That was so sudden and painful too. And finally when I arrived here, Iris was the first to befriend me and take me under her wings. Her... departure has shaken me up. I miss her so terribly, I can't even begin to describe the feeling. Now all I have left is the rest of my friends—all of you are my family. I don't want to lose any one of you, ever!'

Crispin observed the lamebirl as she spoke, her face earnest with the strength of her feelings.

'But right now, to tell you the truth, I am seriously worried about Cheska and the others. Something is not right at the new Ret Cabana. I feel that there's a reason why Cheska, Maisie and Reed have been transferred to that place. I fear for them. I think their lives may be in danger.'

'What!' Crispin was shocked. 'Are you serious?'

Zinnia nodded. 'It's just a gut instinct and my inherent distrust of the Altklugs. By now, we know that they don't do anything without a reason.'

Before Crispin could reply, the charabanc slowed down. A voice announced 'The Fountain of Knowledge'.

Zinnia and Crispin stared in admiration at the magnificent fountain with the jets of water sprouting out of the huge 'K', supported by the statues of Altklugs. The charabanc passed the fountain, and within minutes the vehicle halted and the side panel lifted, allowing the lamebren to descend. A tall, statuesque, monumental building stretched from one corner of the street to the other. It was so tall, that Zinnia could barely see the top. Everything about the Altklug Ace-world was so fantastic and magnificent. As they stepped through the huge doorway which vanished automatically and reappeared after they had entered, Zinnia was never more aware of how tiny and nondescript they were in this Ace-world. How much the Altklugs had achieved with their techno-advancements! The gap between the lamebren and the Altklugs was insurmountable.

The smooth, shiny floors and escalators criss-crossing overhead to form a network very much like the skyways, was like a whole new world in the building. Chips lined the walls and cupboards which moved forward on command and delivered the required chip. All sizes of chips were displayed on long tables, each display vying for attention—towers of chips, spiral displays and even tornado kinds, their tops seemed to vanish into ceiling-lined cupboards. Zinnia watched fascinated as Altklugs read from chips on their padlets. The atmosphere was one of overbearing reverence and only the brief commands of the Altklugs punctuated the silence.

'Look, that's the DNA section that Perceptor Amadeus mentioned where everything since the beginning of the earth is stored in DNAs—forever.'

Zinnia glanced in fascination at the room, which seemed more like a glass and metal octagonal structure in the middle of the KlugBiblio. The etched silver words on the Demarcator read 'Permanent Memory and History Storers—Entry Restricted'.

'Access only to Altklugs, I can see,' she observed, drily.

'What did you expect? Must be a world of fascinating truths in there,' Crispin whispered in awe. 'Where do we find the Lamebren Rights in this huge KlugBiblio?'

'I'm sure there's a Rights section or a lamebren section.'

'Yes, there must be an alphabetical order to it,' Crispin agreed.

He was right. Section R was on the fourth escalator. As they traversed the many floors, Zinnia felt transported to a fascinating planet of knowledge and information. They walked to the R section and were amazed at the hundred of chips that lined the walls.

'Lamebren!' Zinnia called.

Immediately a section of the wall glided ahead and an automated glass akin to a magnifying glass, moved over the chips, projecting the names: *Lamebren and their History, Taking Care of the Lamebren, Lamebren Psychology and Chaos, Lamebren Beliefs and Disbeliefs, A Comparative Study of Lamebren Behaviour, Behavioural Patterns and Disorders of Lamebren...*

'I can't believe this!' Crispin exclaimed. 'So much has already been written about us and I had no clue.'

'It is amazing, isn't it? These chips must contain authentic information gathered over years. Does it get automatically updated, do you think?'

'Seriously, it is beyond me. I'm dizzy even looking at these chips.' Crispin grinned.

'Look, Constitutional Rights of the Lamebren! Here it is,' Zinnia pointed, her voice shrill with excitement.

She extracted the chip and they sat down at the glistening, spotless glass tables with padlet sets. Zinnia inserted the chip into a padlet and instantly information scrolled rapidly.

'Goodness, this is all too much for us. There are so many details,' Zinnia blinked.

'Perhaps there's a summarised list of Rights?' Crispin suggested.

'Summarised list of Rights,' Zinnia repeated and once again the information scrolled.

Then, quite abruptly, it paused at a page. *Summary of Lamebren Rights.* Zinnia and Crispin glanced at each other triumphantly. Zinnia read it aloud:

'As per the Constitution, formed by Governor Seeya, the Lamebren have some basic Rights that the Altklugs cannot deny them:

1. *The right to feed themselves and to clothe themselves.*
2. *The right to education and good health.*
3. *The right to shelter, good living conditions and to choose their homes.*
4. *The right to information and knowledge.*
5. *The right to be heard, to opportunities and to excel.*
6. *The right to legal justice.'*

'Wow! I already feel empowered.' Crispin whistled.

'This is it Crispin. I have always puzzled why the Altklugs at all bother with us—now I know. We are protected by the Constitution of the Altklug Super-Dome. It is because of these Rights that we are taken care of at the Ret Cubicles and are being looked after. The Altklugs cannot ignore these Rights, so they have to abide by them. That is the reason why we have special classes...Governor Seeya was a good lady.'

'Yes, but it hasn't stopped them from putting Termination Dates on us,' Crispin reminded bitterly.

'That must have started much after Governor Seeya's time.'

'And I think it has more to do with their own Termination Dates. If they die at sixteen, then the lamebren die, too,' Crispin added.

'What a piece of good luck, isn't it? And look at this Right—the right to choose their homes. This is exactly what we need. Cheska, Reed and Maisie can now put forth their Right and demand that they be shifted back to our Cubicle.'

'You think the Commander would agree?' Crispin was doubtful.

'If the Commander is reminded of the lamebren Rights, then I think he would. Anyway it's worth a try. Do you see any other solution?'

He shook his head. 'Come on, let's go. And please, don't jump in excitement all the way out of the building. We don't want anyone to suspect that we've just been empowered.'

Zinnia grinned. 'Empowered we are. I am so pleased that I could hug you!'

Crispin looked alarmed. 'Please, spare me.'

Zinnia giggled. She felt elated with their discovery. As if no power in the Altklug Ace-world could dampen her spirits now. As they made their way down the escalators, a couple of Altklugs frowned at them in disapproval.

Zinnia could clearly read their minds. They were wondering, what were lamebren doing in the Main KlugBiblio? *You'll see, soon enough*, Zinnia thought, her mind jumping a happy skip.

They exited the grandeur of the KlugBiblio and waited by the pavement to cross over to the other side. Signals placed under the transparent road, automatically turned red, green and yellow. Spinners hovered about two feet above and automatically touched the road when they had to stop for the signal. Zinnia and Crispin waited for the signal to change. Just then a black vehicle paused at the red signal and a lady looked out of the window. Something about the way she held her head caught Zinnia's attention and the next moment their eyes locked. *Mama!* Shock and surprise reverberated through her body and spirit.

'Mama!' she cried spontaneously and waved.

The woman stared vacantly at Zinnia. Then the spinner moved and within seconds had shot forward and sped away. Zinnia stared after the spinner, instant tears welling up in her eyes. Her mother hadn't recognised her? She couldn't believe it. A tidal wave of misery coiled around her. *Oh Mama!* A silent wail rose inside her. She missed her mama terribly and here she was, face-to-face and her mother had ignored her. Zinnia burst into tears.

'That was my…my…mama…' she hiccupped, unable to control the gush of tears.

'Are you sure?' Crispin asked, looking confused.

Zinnia nodded. 'She was right there and I…I…couldn't speak to her.'

'Your parents are retired and old. They probably don't even recognise you.' Crispin's tone was cautious.

'No, that's not possible…they can't forget me…I want to meet them, I do. I have to go find my mama!'

Crispin stared helplessly at the lamebirl. He had no clue how to console her. He placed a hand hesitantly on her head and patted it awkwardly. Gradually, much to his relief, her sobs tapered off and she sniffed.

'I'm sorry…I…got carried away.' She brushed a hand across her eyes.

'Don't be, I understand. Look, if you feel so strongly about it, you *should* go meet them. We have the Constitutional Rights with us now, so we can have a meeting with Cheska, Reed and Maisie in a couple of days. That can wait. In the meanwhile, you can find your parents' Retirement Centre address from the K. Sensor, and go visit them,' Crispin suggested.

Zinnia raised hopeful eyes to her friend. 'You think that's the right thing to do, don't you?'

'I think it is.'

'Thank you.' Her tone was grateful, as a watery smile lit up her young face.

17

Sleep seemed to be trapped behind Zinnia's eyelids, refusing to be released. The image of her mother's blank gaze was glued in Zinnia's mind adding more distress to her already confused thoughts.

On reaching the Cubicle, Zinnia had rushed to the K. Sensor and had looked up the Retirement Centres. Crispin had told her that there were three types of housing systems in the Super-Dome: the classy Commander types, the adequately-equipped working class types and the basic Retirement Centres. All Altklugs transferred from home to home, as they transitioned from one phase of their lives to another. No private properties, just government quarters. Therefore, it was easier than she hoped to find the address.

House No. 54, Vera and Radley's home, was on the other side of the Water Vein, in the Fountain of Death, Southern Quarters where lamebren were not permitted to visit. But she didn't care. Tomorrow, she would take the charabanc and look for her parents' home. The thought sent a warm fuzzy feeling in her heart. She longed to meet her parents, talk to her mother at length and tell her *all* about her life at the Cubicle. They would be interested, wouldn't they? For the briefest moment, doubt hovered in her mind. After all, they had never bothered to visit her at the Cubicle but then none of the parents of *any* of the lamebren did so. The thought brought on a semblance of relief. Perhaps they had tried, but the Altklug rules prevented them from visiting. Well, *she* would go and visit them! Tomorrow, she would…

The charabanc zipped past the lanes and entered the Water Vein. Zinnia stared at the sparkling blue and green mass of water overhead. Sunshine filtered through the transparent roof, setting it aflame with gold. It was so amazingly awe-inspiring and just as beautiful as the rainbow in her dream. She glanced at the Altklugs in the charabanc. Did they notice what a sensational display of nature was exhibited all around them? Not a single Altklug was glancing up. Their heads were buried in their padlets, their uniforms pristine white, and their bodies stiff and unyielding. Zinnia almost felt sorry for them. Of what use was all their knowledge, super-intelligence and techno-advancement if they were incapable of admiring the magnificent fusion of their technology with nature? Their world may be perfect but it wasn't complete. Their time may be used with utmost efficiency all their lives, but if they didn't understand love and compassion, their lives were wasted!

Leo's words had had such an impact on Zinnia that with every passing minute, she had not only begun comparing the world of lamebren with the Ace-world of the Altklugs, but she had also begun to recognise the widening gap between them. For them, time was of paramount essence, for the lamebren it was emotions. For the Altklugs, efficiency of work mattered the most and everything hinged around their period of productivity but for the lamebren, everything revolved around relationships. The Altklugs believed that perfection was of the utmost importance, but for the lamebren imperfection was the way of life. Yes, Zinnia was beginning to really appreciate the difference of the two worlds.

The charabanc slowed down as it passed the Southern Quarter Fountain of Death and Zinnia stared at the 'D' in fascination. Black, grey and brown streams of water sprouted out of the silver metallic alphabet, while a purple jet of water slithered between the standing statues of the Altklugs like a snake. It was so evocative and released such a lingering feeling of unease that a shiver ran down Zinnia's spine.

The charabanc finally halted at the Retirement Quarters and Zinnia descended. Shaking off the brooding image of the fountain, she deliberately changed her mood. Very soon she would meet her parents, who would welcome her warmly. She would hug her mother and tell her how much she missed her. Her mother would hug her back and say it too. Zinnia's heart began to thud in anticipation. A small smile played on her lips, as she studied the house numbers. All the houses were box-like mini-bungalows with a surrounding garden. Shutters lined the windows, prohibiting inside view of the houses.

House No. 54 was a little different though. Instead of white shutters, the window shutters were black. A great deal of activity seemed to be going on in front of the house. A windowless vehicle was parked in the street. It looked very familiar, but Zinnia thrust the feeling to the back of her mind. What was happening here? Two Officers on duty were standing by the entrance of her parents' home. They looked unapproachable and similar to lifeless statues. Zinnia paused. She couldn't just barge in, could she? No, she would be stopped at once. On an impulse, she headed towards the back of the mini-bungalow. Surely there would be a back entrance?

She was right. A door stood ajar and Zinnia quietly slipped inside. The kitchen was cool and dark as Zinnia crossed it. She stepped into another dark room and halted. The room was bare with just two soft-cushioned chairs. On one sat her mother and bang opposite her, sat her father. Both were silent and were staring wordlessly at each other. The stillness in the room was disturbing and a little ominous. Zinnia frowned. *Something was not right...*

'Mama, Dad...' she whispered.

Startled, her parents turned around instantly. For moments, they stared at Zinnia, a vacant expression on their faces. Then, as understanding dawned, her mother's eyes widened and her mouth trembled.

'Oh my goodness, it's...you!' Vera exclaimed, shock and wonder written large on her face.

'Yes Mama, it's me!'

'Oh, my baby!' she cried and opened her arms.

With a rush of love and relief, Zinnia dashed into her mother's arms. Radley rose uncertainly to his feet and enveloped both of them in his arms. Tears of joy and gratitude streamed down Zinnia's cheeks. Her parents *loved* her! She had been right in her decision to come and visit her.

'Oh Mama! I've missed both of you so much!' she sobbed, giving vent to her pent-up emotions.

'I know, I know. Now hush, stop crying,' her mother comforted her in a gentle tone.

All three clung to each other, and it was a moment Zinnia was never going to forget. When she straightened, she smiled at her parents. They looked just the same, except a little frail.

'How did you find us?' her father asked in a low voice.

'It was easy, I looked up the K. Sensor. I was determined to find you and I'm so glad I did. Now I shall visit you as often as I please!' Zinnia declared.

Her mother shot a quick glance at Radley. Both studied her with deep compassion in their eyes.

'Listen to me baby, I don't have time to explain, but don't ever come to this house again. Take care of yourself—the best you can. And never—never let the Altklugs know what you're up to! You hear me, be very careful.'

Zinnia stared from her father to her mother, puzzled. Vera's hushed whispers made no sense and her gaze darted continuously to the door.

'What do you mean? I don't understand…'

'Here, take this.' Her mother thrust a small, black chip into her hands. 'Keep it somewhere safe. Treasure it and guard it well. One day, it will prove useful to you.'

'What is it, Mama?'

Her mother did not respond. She stared deep into Zinnia's eyes, as if trying to memorise the features of her face.

'Please, please forgive us…you will, won't you?' The pleading look in her eyes startled the lamebirl.

Zinnia's gaze flitted to her father and she witnessed the same emotion mirrored in his eyes. Confusion swamped her. Why were her parents behaving so strangely? Fearful and frantic…. But before she could utter another word, a knock resounded on the door. Vera threw a wild look at her husband. An imperceptible message passed between them. In a flash, her mother thrust her behind the long, thick, black curtain.

'Don't move,' she hissed and drew the curtain over her.

'Come in,' Radley called.

Within seconds, the door opened and two Officers marched in. Zinnia could see the activity through the curtains. Her heart began an erratic tattoo. What was happening?

'Time to leave Sir, Ma'am,' the Altklug Officer spoke respectfully.

Zinnia's parents rose. Their actions were slow and reluctant and for the first time Zinnia felt that they appeared old. Vera turned around and her gaze lingered across the room, to finally rest on the curtain. Zinnia stilled. The look in her mother's eyes froze the blood in her veins. It was a look of such longing and yearning that it travelled like a ray across the room and wound around her heart, squeezing it tight.

Then she blinked and her parents turned and followed the Officers mutely out of the room, shutting the door behind them. Puzzled, Zinnia peeped through the window, just in time to watch her parents climb into the black vehicle—a vehicle with no windows, no pictures and nothing written on it. And then she remembered where she had seen such a vehicle before. *On the night Iris was sent to the Dissolution Crypt!* Her breath caught in a gasp of comprehension. *Her parents were being driven to their death!* The shock of this realisation shot an electrifying bolt through her, and she almost blacked out, but steadied herself against the window sill. As the vehicle drove away, Zinnia watched helplessly. She felt as if her heart had been ripped away and a writhing hole had taken its place....

Spinners whizzed past her, their multiple honks jarring in her head while tears rolled incessantly down her cheeks. Her mother's last look burned through her brain—a look of naked desperation, of reconciliation, of acceptance of the inevitable death. Zinnia had found her parents, but she had arrived too late, meriting a wordless, final goodbye. Iris gone, her parents gone...Zinnia drifted on the skyway, her face a mottled display of tears. A numbing sensation had stolen over her entire body. It was the pain of growing up, of being flung into ruthless, adult emotions.

Some Altklugs passed her strange looks; others turned their nose when they realised that she was a lamebirl and some simply frowned but Zinnia was past caring. She felt as if her entire life had been shattered from the core. To witness her parents being sent to the Dissolution Crypt... she had to be the unluckiest lamebirl in the world.

A spinner speeded by her, almost touching her and snapped Zinnia out of the reverie. It took her a couple of seconds to tune in to her surroundings. The traffic sounds roared into her ears like a thundering wave. The numbing sensation receded gradually and the speeding world of the Altklugs came into focus. What was she doing here?

The spinner halted suddenly and reversed. The door opened automatically and an Altklug stepped out, 'G23!' bellowed Supercustodian Colonel Kripton.

Zinnia stared at him in a daze. Was he a vision? He couldn't be on this Skyway, could he? Colonel Kripton took one look at her white face and instantly drew her into the spinner.

'Get in,' he said briefly.

Zinnia became vaguely aware of the door shutting and the spinner speeding ahead. Silence filled the interiors of the spinner. At the back of her mind a thought niggled—she was in big time trouble, but did she care? Did she really care for the reprimands, the firing and the penalty that was sure to be her immediate fate?

But Colonel Kripton didn't utter a word. He drove on for a while, zipping through the Water Vein where the vibrant colours of the lake were vying for attention. Gradually, the spinner turned into a tree-lined lane and drew to a halt under a shady tree.

'Care to share what has happened?'

His voice was so surprisingly gentle that Zinnia raised startled eyes to him. He was searching her face and his kind concern touched a core.

'My mama…my parents…I just saw them being taken to the Dissolution Crypt…'

In an instant, her misery came pouring out and tears spilled again. Between hiccups and tangled emotions, she narrated her horrifying experience. Colonel Kripton was quiet, allowing her to release her pent-up sentiments. Finally, when she paused and her tears had tapered into an occasional hiccup, he turned to face her.

'G23...I am really sorry for your loss. It was unfortunate that you had to go through this...rather traumatic experience. But you have to understand—this is a routine practice of terminating old Altklugs who do not die a natural death. More importantly, you have to understand that you cannot wander around the Super-Dome in this manner. And especially not on this side of the Water Vein. It was lucky that I happened along. Actually I saw the red mark on my spinner screen alerting me that one of the lamebren from my Super-Dome was around. Otherwise you would've been picked up by the Patrollers and then anything could've happened.'

'Thank you,' Zinnia said, sniffing and rubbing her eyes.

'Also, such a blatant display of immature emotions could upset Governor Tisya and place you in the danger zone. I really have to advise you to control your emotions henceforth.'

'I'll try,' she mumbled.

For the first time, Colonel Kripton smiled. His Altklug face lit up and Zinnia stared. She had never really seen an Altklug smile in this manner—with honesty in his eyes.

'Now I'm going to take you back to the Ret Cubicle and you will try not to think of your parents. They were retired and every Altklug has to go to the Dissolution Crypt, if he doesn't die naturally. Death is regarded as a scientifically accepted phase, important for evolution. Your parents have led a complete life, fulfilled all their duties and I'm sure they departed with a content mind. The good thing is that you met them. Not many lamebren have the opportunity. So be happy about that.'

Zinnia nodded mutely. When Colonel Kripton turned the spinner in the direction of the Ret Cubicle, Zinnia stole a look at him. A confirmation surfaced and tinkered above her sad thoughts. Kripton was not a complete Altklug. She knew that for sure now. No Altklug would've treated her the way he had just now. No Altklug was capable of such an interaction. Kripton was certainly special.

Zinnia tossed and turned in her bed. Her mother's last look rose before her eyes and her final words continued to loop in her mind. *'Be careful…take this…treasure it and guard it…'* She sat up in bed quickly. The chip! In her grief, she had forgotten all about it. What had been so important about the chip? Why had her mother asked her to guard it and treasure it? She switched on her bed lamp and extracted the chip from her drawer. Affixing it to her padlet, she settled down on her bed to watch it.

The chip opened to reveal a young Vera holding a tiny baby in her arms. As the shots progressed, projecting her life as a child in an Altklug home, tears pooled in Zinnia's eyes. At least she had this memory of her parents, thanks to her mother and her foresight. She brushed away a tear and froze mid-action. Her eyes narrowed in incomprehension as she stared at the visuals on the padlet and her heart began a wild tattoo. *But…*she shook her head in confusion, 'Oh, my God!' she burst out spontaneously in shock. The truth finally sunk in with startling clarity. She now understood why her mother had given her the chip and asked to guard it well.

Zinnia shut the padlet and removed the chip. She had to keep it in a safe place. But there were no safe places in the Cubicle. She glanced around the room. Camilla was sound asleep, her gentle snores the only sound in the room. After a moment of thought, Zinnia slipped off Iris's band from her wrist. It was an adjustable thin metal, which could be increased into a hair band or a chain. Zinnia slipped one end of the band through the chip holder and hooked it around her neck. She touched the chip gently. It would be safe here.

18

'Constitutional Rights!' Cheska exclaimed. 'I had no idea we had any such rights.'

'Exactly! Zinnia feels that you should use your "Right to choose your home",' Crispin explained.

Camilla, Crispin and Zinnia had met the three lamebren from the Ret Cabana by the lake, which had now become their favourite meeting spot.

Zinnia glanced from Cheska to Maisie and Reed and anxiety pinched her unexpectedly. All three looked conspicuously thinner, with the beginnings of dark patches under their eyes. Maisie's hair was untidily braided and Cheska's close-cropped curls seemed to have flattened. His normally pink cheeks were shades lighter than his twin's. All three were a picture of careless boredom. As if these things didn't matter anymore. As if life was beginning to be just a chore.

'Right to choose where we live…And how do we go about executing our right?' Maisie asked, a little wearily.

'Why not go up to the Supercustodian and tell her directly that you wish to return to the Cubicle?' Zinnia suggested.

Cheska and Reed exchanged an incredulous look, as if she had just stated the worst course of action.

'Zinnia, you have no idea what you are talking about. It's just not that simple,' Reed stated, his voice revealing more a note of sadness, than exasperation.

'What do you mean?' Camilla asked.

'The atmosphere at the Ret Cabana is unhealthy. And Supercustodian is ten folds worse than what she was here,' Maisie replied, gloomily. 'Cheska can't play the floflute anymore. Yesterday, when he was playing a tune, Supercustodian snatched it from him. It was hours later that she finally returned the floflute with a stern warning. And there is very little reading material at the Ret Cabana. We have classes but it's mostly repetition and exercises, as if no one's really interested in teaching us anything.'

'And do you still hear those awful, mourning sounds and feel the shock vibrations?' Zinnia asked.

Cheska nodded, 'Yes, those too.'

He glanced at the other two, a question in his eyes. They all appeared tightly strung and looked like pale shadows of their earlier happy personalities.

'What is it, Cheska?' Camilla asked shrewdly.

'Actually, this morning we made a discovery which was kind of chilling. But we don't want to worry you unnecessarily…' Cheska's voice trailed.

'Now you *are* worrying me.' Crispin frowned.

'Tell them, they ought to know,' Maisie suggested and Reed nodded in agreement.

'Ok, I guess, you ought to know too.' Cheska sighed. 'This morning, I was assigned the duty of cleaning the windows of the Ret Cabana. I was given this tiny Cleaner and I quite enjoyed the task, till I came to the Forbidden Rooms' section. The shutters were drawn over the windows so I couldn't see much inside but just at the last window, at this one spot, the shutters had parted and the sun streamed into the dark room. And what I saw made my blood go cold…'

Zinnia leaned forward, 'What was it?' she asked, her voice a whisper.

'A lamebroy was strapped to a chair. His head was lolling on the side, as if he was asleep. As my eyes got accustomed to the dark in the room, I noticed another person right beside the boy, in a similar condition. Then I noticed that a lot of wires were attached to them, with lights flashing occasionally through the wires. It was when I saw the black uniform of the first boy that I realised he was a lamebroy. And the second...' Cheska swept his tongue over his dry lips, 'I recognised the second figure. His head was turned towards the window and his eyes were slightly open. But he was definitely unconscious. It was Preceptor Sven!'

Zinnia, Crispin and Camilla gaped at Cheska, stunned into silence for moments.

'Are you sure?' Zinnia asked, finally.

'Positive.'

'That is when we realised that Preceptor Sven and the lamebroy were being used in some kind of experiment,' Reed concluded.

'And the realisation is so frightening...' Maisie's voice trembled faintly.

'So those awful, mourning sounds belonged to these two?' Crispin confirmed. He flung a hand through his mop of hair, as if he needed to do something to drive away the sudden prick of anxiety.

'We think so. They are in horrible pain and we have no idea what the heck is happening at the Ret Cabana!' Cheska exclaimed.

'This is really shocking,' Zinnia murmured almost to herself.

'So, Iris was sent to the Dissolution Crypt and Preceptor Sven to the new Ret Cabana. This is his punishment. He was, after all, a Betrayer...and a Betrayer's fate is far worse than a person sentenced to the Dissolution Crypt,' Crispin remarked.

They all stared at him in silence.

'But the main question still remains—what are *we* doing in that Ret Cabana?' Reed asked.

He glanced at the rest of them through his glasses, his hollow checks like little dents on his thin face. And Zinnia read the unspoken words in his eyes—were they next on the list for the Altklug experiments?

Zinnia had wondered time and again if only Iris had been punished for her treacherous behaviour. She had been curious about what had happened to Preceptor Sven, but there had been no way of knowing. Well, now she knew. Preceptor Sven, an equal partner in their crime of love, had been sentenced to a lifetime of torture. And this, according to the Altklugs, was justice. A life packed with horror because he had dared to fall in love with a lamebirl.

Zinnia felt agitated. When Iris had been sent to her death, she had barely been able to bear the loss, feeling the injustice of it all. It was her parents' death which was a true eye-opener. Witnessing them being literally dragged to the Dissolution Crypt, had changed her life forever. If that was not all, Cheska had brought the news of the lamebroy and Preceptor Sven being subjected to horrendous experiments.

For the first time, she perceived it all clearly. Without a glimmer of doubt, the Altklugs were going about this all wrong. Their 'perfect' world was just an illusion that they wanted desperately to preserve and believe in. If they could send their own people—who had spent all their lives working diligently for the good of the Altklug Ace-world—without the slightest qualm to the Dissolution Crypts, then there *had* to be something wrong with the system. Or if they could subject Preceptor Sven to a life of pain and terror, without a hint of pity simply because he fell in love with a lamebirl, then they were more regressed than she thought. These could not be super-adults, these were just heartless machines in the guise of humans. And it was time that they faced the truth.

They had to realise that their perfect world was not ruled by human beings but by robots. Their flawed thinking lay not in their mantra of 'time and efficiency' but equating efficiency with an Altklug's existence, to use an Altklug as a continuous productive use of resource, and considering old age to be the end of a person's competence, was almost immoral. Treating the drained and exhausted old Altklug like a useless, depleted well of knowledge, meant that knowledge had turned into a curse for them. They may have proved that knowledge paved a path to progress, but ignorance was not the end of the world. Achievement did spell success, but failure to deliver, need not be a crime.

Zinnia sighed, logic clearing her thoughts. If living by your emotions meant that you were retarded, then she didn't mind being one. If going slow and steady meant being retarded, she didn't mind the pace. What mattered was not a life of peak efficiency, important because of your utility years, but the quality of the life as a whole. Life could not be a race against technology. Knowledge was important, but knowledge could not decide your existence. Because human beings were not made of knowledge, they were made of flesh and bones and feelings and emotions.

An inner determination fuelled Zinnia's mind. The constant debate and indignation in her mind had reached a head and she knew, with sudden clarity, what she had to do.

'G23 and B15, you have been assigned duty at the Governor's House this evening,' Colonel Kripton informed.

'It is short notice and a little out of character but Commander Hertz specially asked you two to be assigned.'

Zinnia and Crispin glanced at each other.

'There's a small dinner party at the Governor House and some important guests from the other Super-Domes are scheduled to arrive. G23 you will take charge of the holo-view coverage of the function, but be careful not to appear before the guests. Please record from a strategic point in the House. And B15 you will help out in the kitchens. There will be lamebren from other Cubicles too, but please do not interact with anyone else. Do you understand?'

'Yes Sir,' Crispin responded and Zinnia nodded.

Colonel Kripton extracted a flat, finger size unit from his pocket.

'This is the digi-eye. Excellent resolution and fantastic zoom with an automatic 360 degrees rotation.' He handed it to Zinnia. 'Apparently the Commander thinks you would be able to handle it well.'

Zinnia understood immediately why the Commander felt so. He was referring to the shots she had taken of Commander Burdock and Camilla. This was his style of reciprocating with sarcasm.

'The spinner is already outside. You should leave at once. Remember, talk to no one and just do your job.'

Zinnia and Crispin were led to the sleek, black spinner, waiting in the drive. The other lamebren, who were in the hall, were surprised as their two friends climbed into the vehicle. The spinner shot forward and as usual Zinnia and Crispin did not utter a single word. But Zinnia's mind was churning with thoughts—thoughts of her parents, of the Constitutional Rights and Preceptor Sven and she ached to get off this assignment. Contradictorily, she was also curious about Governor Tisya's house. How would it be? How did the Supremo of the Super-Dome live?

Her curiosity was satiated within minutes as the spinner zipped into the Fountain of Conscience Quarter. The Governor's House was unlike anything Zinnia had ever seen. In the midst of vast lawns, it was a stately monument in armour-like glass. As Crispin and she passed through the enormous doorway and into the hall, the colours of the glass walls changed from green on the outside to yellow on the inside. A central stairway led to the upper rooms which hinted at an orange and blue display. Zinnia was mystified. She would have never imagined Governor Tisya to reveal such a flamboyant taste in her house.

Bozo, the Humanoid appeared. 'About time. B15 to the kitchen at once and G23, you will stay upstairs and take the shots from above. No coming down until the meal is over, is that understood?' His voice was brisk and formal.

Crispin was whisked away and Zinnia barely had time to say good luck. She made her way past the glittering, sleek table laid out for ten guests. Then up the stairs which were carpeted in a velvet green material. If she hadn't known, Zinnia would've thought that they were made out of natural lawn. Once up the stairs, the scene was as grand as she could imagine. The colourful glass walls, lit from the inside with pale lights, gave the hall a feel of ethereal elegance. Zinnia extracted the small digi-eye and aimed it at the hall. Instantly, it began rolling. She took the embossed images of the four fountains on the hall glass walls, next she panned to her right. A beautiful, long corridor of orange glass led into several rooms.

Curiosity got the better of her, and she slowly ventured down the curtained corridor. It was just as she neared the end of the passage that she overheard the sobbing. It was loud and rusty almost as if the person was not used to crying. Zinnia peeped from behind the curtain, her digi-eye still rolling. Governor Tisya was seated on the bed, sobbing, as if her heart would break. She held a photo in her hand, which she kissed from time to time. 'My poor sister!' She muttered loudly and moaned as if in pain. Commander Hertz stood beside her. He bent and whispered something into her ear and she instantly turned and hugged him. Stunned, Zinnia stepped back and almost lost her footing. The scene was so unbelievable and mind-boggling that she whirled around and hastened down the corridor back to her position on the top of the stairs. But her heart was beating erratically and she willed herself to calm her nerves. What had she just witnessed? She wondered, her mind still reeling. The sobbing, the muttering and finally the hug—this was not just an obvious exhibition of emotions, this was a revelation. She opened her padlet, inserted the digi-eye into it and transferred the byte she had just shot. Then, carefully she erased it all from the digi-eye.

When finally the guests arrived and Governor Tisya emerged from her room to greet them, there were no telltale signs of her outburst. She was calm and collected and she swept down the stairs regally without affording a glance in Zinnia's direction. She shook hands with the Altklugs and spoke a few welcoming words to each one of them. Their different coloured uniforms represented the different Super-Domes but they were exact replicas of each other with shining intelligent faces and brief sentences. The dinner lasted for sixty minutes. Governor Tisya smiled formally and the discussion moved forward with apt promptings from the Commander. Everything was minutely organised and flawlessly implemented. Only Zinnia had been a witness to how close Governor Tisya had come to disrupting her evening.

19

'I've thought really hard about this. And I've decided what we need to do,' Zinnia announced. 'We will write out a petition, make an appointment with Governor Tisya and present it to her.'

The others stared at her incredulously. Their reaction was exactly as she had expected.

'Bad idea,' Azalea declared.

'Crazy, absolutely crazy,' Berk pitched in.

'Why is that?' Zinnia asked patiently, looking from one to the other.

'For one, Governor Tisya won't entertain any such petitions,' Crispin remarked.

'She won't even meet an insignificant lamebirl like you or anyone of us,' Ivy added, flicking her long braid behind her.

'As for agreeing to an appointment, well, they would instead parcel you off to the Isolation Chamber for even suggesting such a thing,' Berk predicted.

'Ok, I understand all your misgivings and apprehensions. But I've also given this a great deal of thought and I have come to the conclusion that the best way to approach our situation is the direct way. It is our only hope. Look, Crispin and I have been to Governor Tisya's house and have some idea of the kind of person she is. I want to give this a try. Is anyone going to support me in this venture?' Zinnia stared pointedly at each of the lamebren.

'How can we support something that spells doom?' Ivy asked.

'You are *assuming* that it spells doom. What if it is a success?'

'Zinnia,' Crispin began in a mature, adult one. 'You are young and hopeful and believe that some miracle will change the mindset of the Altklugs. But you have to understand that this is the way they are born and brought up. They are wired that way. Besides, where Preceptor Amadeus has not succeeded, how would you?'

'Because Preceptor Amadeus is not a lamebirl, *I* am. I know the life we lead, the problems we face. We *all* do. So a petition that comes from all of us is bound to be regarded with some seriousness. Even if it is discarded, it will awaken *some* thinking, don't you think?' Zinnia persisted. 'So, is anyone going to help me with it?'

They were gathered in the garden, during lunch break. Zinnia caught sight of Lorde in the hall, peeping out of the window from time to time. Bosco was working in the driveway, making some technical adjustments to the Fountain of the Pen. Zinnia had no doubt that his ears were trained on them. She glanced at the serious faces of the other lamebren. Her eyes rested on Camilla, who nodded.

'I will,' she replied, with a half-smile on her lips.

'I will too,' Crispin added, his chin-dimple showing.

'Good!' Zinnia was delighted.

'Okay, since you are so bent on it, I will too but don't say I didn't warn you it would be a failure.' Berk shrugged.

'Think positive.' Zinnia hugged the plump boy.

He looked embarrassed and shoved her away.

'Well, I guess we all are in,' Ivy grimaced and Cylia nodded.

Zinnia looked at Azalea for her confirmation. The frail-looking lamebirl sighed.

'Okay,' she remarked softly.

'Great!' Zinnia exclaimed. 'Thank you! We need to start work at once—do lots of research. Camilla you will find data on the number of lamebren living in all the four Cubicles. Ivy and Cylia, you will dig up the history on lamebren, how they came about, etc. Berk—you and Azalea will make a list of the lamebren in *this* Ret Cubicle and their qualities, their nature, their creative pursuits. All set?'

The lamebren nodded. A glint of amusement shone in Crispin's eyes. Zinnia was a natural at taking leadership.

'So we meet tonight and share notes. Crispin and I will now approach the Supercustodian and ask him to take an appointment with the Governor.'

'Good luck!' the others chorused and Zinnia smiled.

'We can't go in now. Commander Hertz is with him,' Crispin said.

They could clearly see the Commander in conversation with the Supercustodian through the glass Demarcator. It was indeed bad timing. Knowing by their previous experience, Commander Hertz would never permit them to meet the Governor.

'Come on, let's go before...' but Crispin's sentence was cut short by Colonel Kripton.

'Yes, come in G23 and B15,' the Supercustodian pressed a button and the Demarcator slid aside to allow them to enter.

The two lamebren inched into the office hesitantly. The Commander turned around and fixed a direct gaze on Zinnia. Instantly, she sensed his antagonism. *This guy hated her!* She moved a tongue over her dry lips, nervously.

'What is it?' Colonel Kripton asked, a hint of impatience in his voice.

'Sir, we...we want to present a Petition to Governor Tisya...and we...were hoping that you could get an appointment for us,' Zinnia stammered.

Colonel Kripton stared at her with such astonishment, that Zinnia almost giggled. It was an unheard of request to say the least. Suddenly, she began enjoying the situation.

'Impossible!' the Supercustodian exclaimed.

Commander Hertz continued to stare at Zinnia, in an unblinking gaze. His bald head shone as if it was polished with some latest discovery. The thought brought on another bubble of laughter inside her, dissipating the nervous knot completely.

'Did you say you want an appointment with the Governor?' the Commander asked, deliberately.

'Yes Sir.'

'Hmmm...I am indeed amazed at your audacity, lamebirl.' He looked amused.

Zinnia remained silent. Beside her, Crispin stood like a strong support, shifting from one foot to the other.

'And may I know why you want to meet the Governor?'

'I have been observing the manner in which the Altklug Ace-world is functioning and I would like to suggest some changes, especially with regard to us lamebren.' Zinnia's voice was calm and expressive.

Colonel Kripton inhaled sharply, but Commander Hertz burst into laughter.

'Guts, guts, guts...she's foolish but the lamebirl has guts,' he said to Colonel Kripton.

The Supercustodian was grave. Commander Hertz rose. He was as tall as Crispin, but his personality was imposing. He plunged his hands into his uniform pockets and closed his eyes reflectively for a moment. Then he turned to Zinnia again.

'As per the rules of the administration, transparency has been advocated in this Ace-world of ours. Your desire to make changes or whatever it is you want to present to the Governor will be taken into account. I shall give you every opportunity to express yourself lamebirl. I will personally take you to the Governor. Be ready the day after tomorrow at 1700 hours sharp.'

Zinnia couldn't believe her ears. A look of unconcealed astonishment crossed Colonel Kripton's face. Crispin frowned as he flashed Zinnia a quick glance.

'Come prepared for the appointment. You will be given precisely five minutes to present your ideas.'

'Yes Sir! We'll be there. Thank you!'Zinnia glanced from the amused Commander to Colonel Kripton, who looked completely taken aback.

She and Crispin stepped out of the office and the Demarcator slid shut. They hastened away and literally ran to the garden, the only place where they knew they would not be overheard.

'We did it!' Zinnia exclaimed thrilled.

'Yes we did,' Crispin was slower in expressing his joy. 'But it was unexpected, wasn't it?'

'Who cares? We have permission to present our petition. We shall be heard, think about it Crispin, we shall be heard!' Zinnia jumped around in joy and Crispin shook his head.

'I don't have the heart to tell you to be cautious.' He laughed. 'Enjoy the moment Zinnia while it lasts.'

'I know what you mean—about the Altklugs being tricky, etc. but I'm not going to let it affect this moment of glory,' Zinnia declared. She suddenly stopped dancing.

'My God, the day after tomorrow—such little time and so much to do! Come on, let's find the others.'

The lamebren worked hard throughout the day. Lorde peeped into rooms and sniggered. He was shooed away by Ivy every time he tried to steal a look at her padlet. At night, they all shared notes. Zinnia went through their day's efforts carefully.

'Berk and Azalea, good effort, but I want to know what is good about the lamebren, their qualities not just what they like and don't like. Camilla—you've got the exact number but you said that two lamebroys have gone missing this year and no one knows what happened to them, right? Well, try to find their names, will you? Ivy and Cylia, good job. Can you just summarise these pages of history into a paragraph? We have only five minutes to present our points.'

Zinnia was quick, precise and the others grasped her tone of authority without question. 'Crispin, you have our Constitutional Rights. Can you make a note on it?'

Crispin nodded.

Zinnia sensed the doubt underlying Crispin's acceptance. She knew what he was thinking. All this effort and what if the Governor refused to listen to them? What if she did listen but refused to do anything about it? It was a challenge and a risk. But at least they would've tried, wouldn't they?

'If I get the information by tomorrow evening, I'll sit down and compile it all into a presentation. Other than information gathered, if any one of you have personal opinions or questions, I'll put them down as well. Everyone okay with this?'

The other lamebren nodded.

Zinnia and Crispin worked through the evening and night, making the presentation. They made it as visual as possible, putting down points instead of long sentences.

'Everything revolves around time in this Ace-world—about using time efficiently. They won't want to waste a single moment more than what has been allotted to us. That is why, our presentation has to be on point, visual and self-explanatory,' Crispin said.

Zinnia agreed at once. They made a good team, she thought. Crispin was intelligent and sensitive, although too practical at times. She, on the other hand, had drive and courage, whose source, she could neither understand nor explain.

The presentation was previewed before the lamebren, during the Lunch hour, in their Cubicle. They watched fascinated as the captions and points rolled in, with visuals of the lamebren along with their quotes. When the presentation ended, the lamebren burst into applause.

'Fantastic!' Ivy exclaimed.

'Truly informative,' Camilla agreed.

'If this presentation doesn't change the minds of the Altklugs, nothing will.'

'It's useless!' Lorde shouted.

The lamebren turned to the door, startled. 'I saw it and it is useless. You think you are some group of clever people, making this smart presentation to the Altklugs, don't you? Well, you're wrong! You are nothing but a bunch of stupid lamebren and no one is ever going to listen to you, not now or ever,' Lorde declared, a sneer on his face.

'We'll see about that,' Zinnia responded calmly, but unease piqued her mind.

Lorde was a mischief-maker. She did not want him anywhere around their group to either belittle their efforts or to lower their morale. So far she had successfully kept him out of their plans. But apparently he had seen the presentation.

'We'll see about that—pompous Zinnia!' he imitated. 'But mark my words; you'll always only remain G23 for the Altklugs!'

'Ok enough!' Crispin rose. 'If you don't have anything constructive to say or do, you may as well leave. We have no time for negative energies within us lamebren—there are already too many out there in the Altklug Ace-world.'

'I'm leaving. Who wants to be with a bunch of dreamy idiots, anyway?' Lorde shouted as a parting shot, walked out and banged the door behind him.

Zinnia and Crispin were ready by 1630 hours. Their uniforms were creaseless and pressed. Crispin had taken special efforts to tidy up his ruffled mop and for a change, he projected the image of orderliness and efficacy. Zinnia too had restricted her wind-blown hair severely to a scarf.

'Good luck to both of you.' Camilla hugged them warmly.

'Zinnia, speak slowly and clearly. You tend to speak fast when you are excited,' Ivy admonished.

'And don't lose your temper,' Azalea added. 'You don't want to end up in the Isolation Chamber.'

'I'll remember your advices,' Zinnia assured.

'Don't worry, I'll remind her.' Crispin grinned.

'Commander Hertz's spinner is waiting in the porch for G23 and B15,' Bosco announced, from the door.

'Good luck, good luck! I do hope this petition helps in changing our lives and bringing Cheska and the others back to us,' Camilla prayed.

'I hope so too,' Zinnia replied.

She hugged them all again, then she and Crispin hastened downstairs. Colonel Kripton was at the entrance of the Cubicle, waiting.

'I'll be there too,' he said and looked directly at Zinnia. 'Be careful with what you say.'

She nodded, reading the warning in his tone and eyes. She knew that they were treading a dangerous path. A petition meant opening the doors to speculation. It meant revealing the lamebren's darkest fears to the Altklugs in the hope of remedy and wishing for a life that perhaps the Altklugs would never be set to give. And it also meant tempting the Altklugs with lesser morals, to use the knowledge against the lamebren. She read it all in his warning and realised that she had to be careful.

As Zinnia stepped into Commander Hertz's imposing spinner, she experienced a wave of excitement. This was the second time that she was visiting Governor Tisya's office. The first one had been a farce—an act put up for their benefit. It had led to nowhere. Would this initiative be treated in a similar manner?

Crispin was quiet in the spinner, as it dived into the maze of skyways and Zinnia did not prompt him to speak. She was tense and nervous, a continuous silent prayer on her lips. *Iris, Mama, Dad, help me,* she prayed. Governor Tisya had to hear them out, she had to listen! Not just listen with her ears, but listen with her *heart*. If the scene she had witnessed at the Governor's House meant anything at all, then she knew that Governor Tisya did respond with her heart occasionally. The question was—Would she do that this time?

The previous journey had been in the dark, but this time Zinnia saw their route through the amazing multi-dimensional pathways. Governor Tisya's office was in a stunning sky-scraper, surrounded by green hills and artificial trees laden with colourful fruits. Zinnia wondered idly if one could eat those fruits or were they just for decoration.

The spinner halted at the grand main entrance and the spinner door was opened by a Humanoid. The Elevator jogged her memory of the previous visit. She couldn't obtain justice for Camilla, but would she fare any better now? She glanced at Crispin. He was standing upright, his eyes reflective yet alert and his dimpled chin jutting out in a sign of determination. He smiled at her and nodded. Crispin was rock solid and a true friend. She was grateful to have him with her. Zinnia smiled back.

'You will have to wait. The Governor is busy with Preceptor Amadeus,' Hobo the Humanoid showed them the seats.

The lounge was one of the slickest she had seen. Twinkling stars shown through the transparent surface of the seating arrangement. It sunk as Crispin and Zinnia seated themselves, soft like a cushion and curving around their bodies in a solid grip. Zinnia glanced at the watch in her padlet. It was five minutes to 1700 hours but the time seemed to go slow. Zinnia's palms were cold with nervous anxiety. *It will all go fine,* she assured herself repeatedly. After all they had worked hard to produce an excellent presentation.

Exactly at 1700 hours, Hobo appeared. He led them through the Demarcator into the diamond-shaped, cage-like glass office which jutted out of the skyscraper, almost as if it was peering over the mesmerising view of the Super-Dome below.

'B15 and G23 from the Ret Cubicle,' Hobo announced and instantly receded.

The office was occupied by four people: Commander Hertz, Colonel Kripton, Governor Tisya in her ink-blue metallic seat and a fourth Altklug with a familiar face.

Preceptor Amadeus, Zinnia guessed. All eyes were fixed on the lamebren as Hobo announced their entry. Preceptor Amadeus, with his bald head, looked a lot like Commander Hertz. But that is where the similarity ended. He had light brown eyes and the glow of intelligence on his face was so strong that it seemed to create a halo around him. Zinnia remembered him from the holo-view Iris had shown them. He gazed at them with frank curiosity in his eyes. Colonel Kripton remained silent and grim.

Zinnia's eyes rested on Governor Tisya, a little fervently, with a deep yearning to establish contact with the Altklug. Her heart fluttered just a tiny bit as she searched the Governor's face keenly. But Governor Tisya appeared regal and uncompromising on her throne and studied the lamebren with an unwavering indifference. Zinnia's heart sank.

'Ah, the two lamebren with their petition.' Commander Hertz rubbed his podgy palms together in glee. He seemed to be enjoying the situation the most.

Governor Tisya stared at Zinnia and her gaze was so intense that it seemed to beam right through her brain.

'You are a foolishly courageous lamebirl,' she remarked. 'And you have exactly five minutes to say what you want to say.'

Zinnia nodded and opened her padlet. 'Thank you, Governor. We are both here today to present and request a different order of things. To suggest a different lifestyle for everyone—lamebren and Altklugs included. Can I please request all of you to take a look at this presentation?'

'No presentation. Just say your bit,' Governor Tisya brushed aside the suggestion in a curt manner.

Zinnia faltered. 'But Governor, the presentation says it all. We...'

'No presentations!' the Governor repeated in a tone that brooked no argument.

Crispin flashed a quick worried glance at his friend. Everything they had to say was in the presentation. How could Zinnia remember it all?

For a few precious seconds, Zinnia's mind went blank. They had worked night and day to get the presentation perfect, to ensure that every point was covered and given due importance. They had sweated to make a slide show that would create an impact! And now they *couldn't* show it? What in heavens could she do? Her heart beat fast and her throat stuck. She gulped her saliva and ran her tongue over her dry lips. *Leo Leroy…what had he said…Think, think…* Then she inhaled deeply and raised her head to confront the four faces gazing uncompromisingly at her.

'Okay, I'll be brief. We have two suggestions to make: One, give the lamebren their Constitutional Rights and two, allow them their right to live,' Zinnia began on a slow note.

Governor Tisya arched an eyebrow.

'The Altklugs have their lives chalked out to the last minute. You are super-intelligent, born with inherent knowledge and lead super-fast lives. But it is exactly the opposite with the lamebren.' With every word, Zinnia sensed an inner confidence slowly emerging within her. 'The lamebren come from a lifestyle that is centuries old, where life-spans were bigger and hence their physical growth and mental development was slower. These two opposites—Altklugs and the lamebren—need to co-exist in your Ace-world. The biggest problem today is not the *lamebren* as the Altklugs believe, but it is the Altklugs' *understanding* of the lamebren. Altklugs simply don't understand how the lamebren feel, behave or even think or act. Our needs are different and basic. We lamebren, as you call us, are harmless and we can serve the Altklug world better if we are left to lead our own lives and allowed to live longer, permitting us to die naturally.

We staunchly believe that since we are different beings, the approach to our "*death*" should also be different.'

Governor Tisya stared at Zinnia for a long moment with a mild interest in her eyes.

'Who taught you all this? Preceptor, did you?' She arched an eyebrow at the other Altklug.

'I've never seen this lamebirl before, but what she's saying makes sense to me,' Preceptor Amadeus responded, his gaze on Zinnia.

'Makes sense? Really?' Governor Tisya scorned, her eyes like tiny slits. She turned to Zinnia. 'What do *you* know about *our* world? Who are you to speak with such authority?'

Zinnia paused for an infinitesimal second, before she replied. 'I speak with such authority because I am *born* into your world. I *live* it every single minute of my life. I know about it because it's all around me—in the bed I sleep, in the classroom, in the kitchen, on the roads, in the trees and flowers—*everywhere*. I *know* about the Altklugs because I *interact* with them every single day. I agree that I may not be completely well-versed with your great achievements or your discoveries yet, but I am aware of the intellectual gap of knowledge between us. And because of that, I know that you consider us lamebren.'

Crispin stood like a statue beside her. Zinnia glanced at him briefly and his imperceptible, reassuring nod, gave her confidence.

'What I am trying to say is this: Co-existence is extremely important in the world. It will bring harmony, peace and goodwill. And that can only be attained if the Altklugs show some respect to the lifestyle of the lamebren and learn to accept us in your world. Acceptance will lead to lesser friction, better co-existence and more harmony. If you allow the lamebren to live their lives in peace and to their natural end, I promise you, this Altklug world would be a superior place for all to live.'

'A superior place? Well now!' Governor Tisya was sarcastic. 'Let me tell you that in reality, lamebren are of no use to us Altklugs and the sooner they are disposed off, the better. In fact, the lamebren are a sign of imperfection in our perfect world, where there is no crime, no disease, no ill-will and never will be. Life is straight, advanced and equal.'

'No crime and no ill-will?' Zinnia repeated, her eyes flashing the first hint of anger. 'As long as there is power, there will be inequality. As long as there are human beings, there will be crime and there will be ill-will. I don't need to spell out my experience with a certain Altklug, but it certainly assured me that ill-will and crime are two emotions which stem out of dissatisfaction. And I have already witnessed a result of that dissatisfaction in this advanced world of Altklugs, not only in the committing of the crime, but also in the dealing of it.'

For the first time, Governor Tisya flashed a quick uneasy glance at Commander Hertz but his gaze was fixed unblinkingly on Zinnia. Preceptor Amadeus leaned forward, curiosity now replaced with deep interest. Colonel Kripton sat motionless, his eyes on Zinnia but a flush on his face.

'Let me ask all of you something. Do you know the meaning—and I mean the non-dictionary meaning—of the words like "children", "love", "fear", "insecurity", "need", etc.? Do you know what it means to be a child—a *real* child longing for its mother's love, snuggling against her warmth, learning things from its father? Do you know what it means to play with a puppy or sing a song? Do you know what "old" means? Have you ever thought what it would be like to be old, I mean old as in being eighty years of age? Do you know what it means to be happy—really happy—where joy fills your heart and your life with sweet melody and the world is a combination of music and sunshine?' Zinnia asked, her eyes flitting from Altklug to Altklug.

The expressions on the faces of the Altklugs were stony and non-committal.

'As long as you don't know the non-dictionary meanings of these emotions, as long as you don't *experience* these emotions, the Altklug world will remain synthetic. This Ace-world of Altklugs is not perfect, it is lopsided, and the only chance it has of real happiness is if you allow the lamebren to live their full lives!'

Silence followed this speech, an edgy, thoughtful and angry silence. Governor Tisya turned to Commander Hertz and Colonel Kripton.

'I've heard enough. Take these lamebren away, this instant.' She turned her back on Zinnia without glancing at her.

Zinnia was taken aback at her abrupt manner. She wanted to protest but her words turned into a furious hammering in her head. Governor Tisya just didn't care! She never did. None of these Altklugs ever did. Sudden tears pricked at the back of her eyes. What had she expected? A fair hearing? An ovation? A pat on the back? Her eyes darted to Preceptor Amadeus who continued to stare at her. His nod was so slight that she almost missed it through her blurry vision. Crispin grasped Zinnia's hand and squeezed it. The petition was heard and discarded.

20

Hobo appeared at the door, so as to lead the lamebren out. They were at the Demarcator, when suddenly a couple of Altklug Officers in white uniform rushed rather unceremoniously into the office.

'There's bad news, Governor,' one of the Officer's informed in a clipped tone.

'What is it?' Commander Hertz asked.

'Sir, Commander Burdock has not been responding to our messages. We believe that he is missing'.

Zinnia barely heard the gasps and reactions, as she and Crispin were hustled down the corridor to the Elevator. Her eyes widened in shock and her gaze flew to Crispin. He shook his head warningly. He had heard them too! Commander Burdock was missing? A million thoughts flittered through Zinnia's mind—how, when, why? But she knew that she dare not utter a single word right now. The situation was too volatile to be careless.

All through the spinner ride, Zinnia felt dejected. She couldn't care less if Burdock was missing. All she could think of was the reaction to the petition, it had been so antagonistic that she had no doubt of its failure. She had failed the lamebren. The thought kept jabbing her in the heart and she felt profoundly depressed. But what if her petition had an adverse effect? Especially now that Commander Burdock was missing, Governor Tisya would be upset. Would she use the petition as an excuse to vent her anger on the lamebren?

It was only when she and Crispin were dropped off at the entrance of the Ret Cubicle, that Zinnia forced herself to be calm and centred.

Ivy, Camilla, Berk, Cylia and Azalea were awaiting their return by the sculpture of the Pen, their faces hopeful.

'How did it go?'Camilla asked, the moment the spinner zipped away.

'We can't talk here. Let's go for a walk,' Crispin suggested.

The lamebren looked at each other, at once sensing that something was wrong. The evening light was still bright and clear and they all trooped into the Paramour Path. The moment they reached the lake, eager questions bounced off the lamebren.

'Sit down and listen all of you!' Crispin said.

They settled down on flat stones obediently. Zinnia sat a little distance away, her head bent as she stared at the pebbled path, silenced by her own inner reprimands.

'We had all worked so hard on the presentation and the Altklugs didn't even see it!' Crispin began.

'What!' Camilla exclaimed.

'But, why not?' Ivy frowned.

'Because, they were not interested. I must say though that Zinnia made a fantastic oral presentation. She debated well and put her points across very clearly and succinctly.' Crispin glanced at the young lamebirl.

Zinnia raised her eyes to meet his in surprise. 'Did I really? I thought I was *awful*. I lost my temper, I questioned their rules and ways...'

'And that is exactly what they needed to hear,' Crispin cut in. 'You made us all proud by standing up to a team of intelligent Altklugs who were waiting to find fault with your logic. But they *couldn't* and whether they take it seriously or not, whether there is any change in the

Altklugs or not, they *know* deep in their hearts that what you said was the perfect truth and perfect solution. The possibility is that they will disregard what you said, because their ego and heightened sense of self-confidence will not permit them too. But they *do* know that you were right!'

Tears sprung up in Zinnia's eyes. 'Thank you Crispin, I wouldn't have known what to say if you weren't standing beside me fearless, giving me moral support.'

'Fearless? I was trembling at the knees!' He smiled. 'But listen to the whole story all of you.'

He plunged into a detailed narration of the entire episode and the lamebren listened with keen interest. When he described how Zinnia countered Governor Tisya's argument, Cylia and Azalea clapped hard in glee. Finally when he finished, a reflective silence ensued.

'I knew that it was a wasted exercise.' Berk was the first to react in a gloomy voice.

'Not really. For one, we know exactly where we stand with the Altklugs now. And two, they know that we aren't as dumb as they think us to be,' Crispin corrected.

'Whatever!' Berk kicked a stone into the lake.

'Cheer up, at least we tried,' Cylia said.

'So we are back to square one?' Azalea asked in a small voice.

'Hey all of you, come off it!' Camilla spoke up, a little angrily. 'We tried, ok? Zinnia *tried*. She showed courage and enterprise—which one of us would've done that? All our lives we've trembled before the Altklugs. Our tongues get entangled with our teeth when we face them. And Zinnia had the courage to stand up and be our voice. Let's appreciate it and celebrate it, what say?'

'Absolutely, I agree! Let's celebrate,' Ivy agreed, with a swing of her long thick braid.

Cylia began clapping again and one by one the others joined in. Zinnia smiled gratefully at Camilla.

'Besides, all is not lost. Preceptor Amadeus was very impressed with the oral presentation. He did say that he agreed with Zinnia,' Crispin added.

'Yes, that's true. In the future, we can seek his help,' Zinnia said.

'On that note, I'm going celebrate by distributing these patchwork pouches that I've made for each one of you,' Cylia declared. Her high pony tail, swung merrily as she extracted a bunch of colourful cloth pouches from her pocket. Names of the lamebren were artistically embroidered on each one of the pouch.

'Wow! They are exquisite!' the others exclaimed.

'Zinnia bought me some beautiful material with her Mudra and I thought I'd gift the pouches to you all today. It's our Petition Day remembrance.' Cylia grinned.

'Thank you Cylia, it really *is* lovely,' Zinnia accepted.

The mood had lightened and the lamebren had accepted their defeat. Only Zinnia was worried, as they returned to the Ret Cubicle. A feeling of unease was lodged in her. Had Commander Burdock been found?

It was just after dinner. The docunote on Altklugs was coming to an end when suddenly footsteps were heard clattering by the glass door and it was flung open.

'Cheska!' Camilla cried.

Cheska, Maisie and Reed walked in, lugging their bags and snowflakes clinging to their shoulders and heads. All three appeared thin and haggard.

Camilla ran to hug her twin. The other lamebren surrounded their former Cubicle mates eagerly.

'What's up? How come you three are here at this time of the night?' Crispin enquired, looking concerned.

'We've been sent back,' Reed replied. He seemed almost happy.

'Sent back? Just like that?' Zinnia asked, confused.

'Actually the atmosphere at the Cubicle was getting on our nerves. The screams at night and the currents which sent shocks up our body—we realised that it was impossible to stay there any longer. So we decided to just go and talk to the Supercustodian,' Cheska explained.

'That was brave of you,' Camilla chipped in.

'I don't know about that. We went prepared to listen to her sarcastic comments and punishments. But even the idea of the Isolation Chamber was more pleasant than staying on at that eerie Cubicle.'

'What did she say?' Ivy asked.

'She said we have a Constitutional Right to live where we please. So I said we would like to return to our previous Cubicle and she said, leave right this minute. We picked up our bags and literally ran, before she changed her mind.'

'Constitutional Right?' Zinnia's gaze darted to Crispin. 'What time did you talk to her?'

'About thirty minutes ago,' Cheska replied.

'Which means *after* we had presented our petition,' Zinnia concluded.

'What petition?' Maisie was curious.

Lorde hung at the edge of the crowd, listening intently. He was pretending to fiddle with his padlet, but Zinnia knew that his ears were trained on their conversation.

'Let's go up to the Cubicle and talk, shall we?' she suggested. 'You look tired. Have you had dinner?'

'No, we didn't want to wait a second longer than necessary. We just escaped from that horror Cubicle.' Reed shuddered.

'I'm going to go see if I can slip a plate off the Server,' Camilla declared.

'I'll come with you,' Ivy said.

As the two of them headed towards the Superkitchen, the others trooped up to their rooms. Cheska, Maisie and Reed looked so happy to be back in the old Cubicle, that Zinnia experienced a twinge of sadness. The poor lamebren looked as if they had shrunk—it was obvious that they had been under tremendous stress. But why had they been taken there in the first place? And why had they suddenly been released from that Cubicle? It was all a little confusing.

While the three friends relaxed on the beds, Zinnia and Crispin brought them up to date on the day's happenings. Cheska, Reed and Maisie listened intently, their eyes bulging when they heard how Zinnia had put up a strong front.

'Wow! I would have fled from the office,' Maisie admitted.

'The Altklugs have never mentioned our Constitutional Rights before. How come suddenly Supercustodian referred to them? It has something to do with the meeting today, don't you think?' Zinnia sounded hopeful.

'If it does, then that's one good result of the dreadful meeting,' Crispin agreed.

Camilla and Ivy returned with two plates of food. The three famished lamebren polished off the meal within minutes. They ate as if they hadn't eaten in days and Zinnia felt deeply sorry for them.

'We saw a lot of Government spinners zipping past, on our way here. There were sirens and announcements—does anyone know what's happening?' Cheska asked.

Before anyone could comment, a voice echoed through the Cubicle.

'This evening Commander Burdock was found dead by the edge of the Snarl, in unusual conditions. All efforts to revive him at the Clinics have unfortunately failed. This is to inform the lamebren not to step out of the Cubicle, until further instructions. Commander Burdock was a techno-expert and a much respected Altklug. May he be reborn as an Altklug again.'

Camilla's hand flew to her mouth in distress. Crispin too appeared startled. Commander Burdock dead? Zinnia couldn't believe it. She sensed a disturbing quiver of shock and alarm. Was it some kind of a trick the Altklugs were playing on them? But then why would they? Why would they waste time on pretending for the sake of the lamebren? No, this was for real. But then what exactly had happened? How had Burdock been killed and who had done it?

'Oh, poor Commander Burdock,' Camilla remarked, in a soft voice. 'I didn't like him much but he never really looked down on me and always treated me with respect, making sure that I didn't work too hard.'

'May his soul rest in peace,' her twin added.

Zinnia and Crispin stared, first at Camilla and then at Cheska. They looked so identical just then, in appearance and thought. Camilla's curly blonde head was bent in reverence and her cheeks were as pink as ever. Zinnia didn't know whether to be exasperated or amused. The poor innocent twins, if they only knew how the Commander had used Camilla they wouldn't be wishing the Altklug's soul good rest but would be wishing that it languished in some dirty trench! *Ignorance was certainly bliss,* Zinnia contemplated. It was true that sometimes the lack of knowledge protected you from the terrible truth and inevitable heartache. Camilla's heartfelt pity which, at the moment, stemmed from a pure conscience would most certainly be contaminated if reality intervened. She *needed* this protective armour of ignorance, which would shield her forever. *Yes, ignorance could sometimes lead to bliss…*

The night was unusually still. The snowflakes continued to fall silently, piling one on top of the other to make soft mounds. Zinnia stood by the window and watched the journey of the snowflakes from above the Cubicle to the ground. No noise, no fuss, just an exquisite display of spotless white. She remembered what Bamian had told them about snowflakes—snowflakes were six-sided delicate ice crystals, but no two snowflakes were similar by the time they reached the ground. Some melted partially in the warm atmosphere, then refroze in the cold atmosphere, some cracked apart but still remained connected to each other, some turned to sleet and some could die completely. Exactly like the lamebren. She and Iris were like the split crystals—split but still connected…

The Super-Dome was rife with the news of Commander Burdock's death. It was as if a dark sheet of mourning had shrouded the Super-Dome. The Rain Hour began early and extended into the evening merging with the Snow Hour. Gloom descended on the Ace-world. All the four Fountains were sprouting at half-throw, the markets were shut down for the day as well as the Altklug Knowledge Ports. The holo-view hoardings on the skyways carried a report on Commander Burdock's life and his journey from a kid to an esteemed Commander. The news in all forms—the audio streams, the visual streams through the multi-D screens in private and public spaces reported regular updates on the investigation. The Altklugs were determined to hunt out the culprit and declare him a Betrayer, Zinnia realised. Hadn't someone said that being a Betrayer was worse than being sent to the Dissolution Crypt? Wasn't Preceptor Sven living a nightmare right now?

The lamebren were given a day-off from classes by Bamian and Mirella. Zinnia, Crispin and the other lamebren watched the half-hourly reports with keen interest. Commander Burdock was glorified and raised to a pedestal by the Reporters, outlining his professional successes. Even Governor Tisya had something to say when she addressed her people.

'Commander Burdock was not only known for his achievements, but he was also known for his big heart. He was known to be a staunch supporter of the lamebren and made it a point to include them in his day-to-day activities, thus making the poor lamebren feel a part of this Ace-world of ours. What an exemplary attitude, such a commendable personality, such a loss to our Ace-world...'

'And yet someone did murder him,' Zinnia remarked, unable to hide the satisfaction in her voice.

Every single word of Governor Tisya's speech opened a gaping wound in Zinnia. Burdock—a supporter of the lamebren! More like an enemy of the lamebren, she thought bitterly. She glanced at Crispin who looked equally livid.

'This is the perfect adulation in this perfect Ace-world!' he replied, his voice layered with sarcasm. 'Covering up of soiled tracks and leaving no marks for the future.'

'Not that it will make an iota of difference to us. We know what kind of a man he was and nothing she says will change that,' Zinnia whispered.

Crispin nodded. But before he could respond, their attention was caught again by the screen.

'New developments are in. Investigators have thoroughly checked Commander Burdock's Memory Porter and come up with some interesting evidence. Commander Hertz is confident that this evidence will help crack the mystery of his death. Signing off for now, this is Kapel from Super-world News, All Fountains Network.'

The visuals then moved on to display the casket with Commander Burdock's body, making its one last journey through the Super-Dome. Soldiers marched before and after the casket as it glided down the streets. Altklugs from different pockets of the Super-Dome walked along with the procession, maintaining a respectful silence. The sound of the occasional saxophone announced their arrival in a particular sector, as a mark of respect for the departed Commander.

Zinnia and Crispin watched the livecast with mixed feelings. The twins paid heed for a while and then moved to the garden to read Camilla's poetry. The other lamebren had lost interest and were less concerned. They were only aware that a prominent personality of the Altklug Ace-world had passed away. They neither comprehended the gravity of the situation, nor did they care. Cylia was busy with her stitching, glad to find more time away from the studies. Azalea had nodded off in her seat. Reed and Berk were chatting, as were Ivy and Maisie. Only Lorde was deeply interested and his tiny eyes were glued to the screen.

It was sixty minutes later that Zinnia and Crispin were summoned to the Klugsage room. The summon itself was so extraordinary and unexpected that Zinnia wondered what the matter was. Mirella opened the Demarcator for Zinnia and Crispin to step into the Exector's room.

'G23 and B15, I need to talk to you about G11,' Mirella began without ceremony.

Zinnia and Crispin glanced at each other confused.

'You said G11 knew nothing about what Commander Burdock...did to her. Is that right?'

'Yes Exector. We didn't tell her anything at all,' Zinnia replied.

'And she gave no indication of having discovered it for herself? Did she mention anything?'

Zinnia was silent for a moment. She remembered the talk they had that night, when Camilla had first told her about Commander Burdock.

'No Exector. She was thankfully completely unaware of how the Commander was using her.'

'Well, I hope that's true. Because new evidence from Commander Burdock's Memory Porter is now available and there are some references to G11. I'm afraid she's in grave trouble.'

'What!' Zinnia's voice was a shocked whisper.

'What do you mean?' Crispin asked.

'There is some evidence pointing to G11. She could be in some way involved with his death.' Mirella's voice was calm and low.

'That's not true…' Crispin added, in an indignant tone.

'I'm afraid that's not for us to decide. All I am saying is that this doesn't look good, for any of you. This can grow to mammoth proportions and frankly, I am worried!'

Zinnia stared at her impassive, unlined face and her white robes. She suddenly reminded her of Iris—although very different in appearance, Mirella still carried that sense of peace amidst a storm, with her. Just like Iris did.

'We can vouch for G11's innocence,' Crispin spoke up.

'That won't be enough B15. I wish I could help, but honestly, the situation is out of hand now.'

'Out of hand! What situation?' Crispin burst out. 'Commander Burdock literally used Camilla and he got away scot-free. The Altklugs could do nothing about it. And now someone has gone and murdered him and the Altklugs conveniently need to find a scapegoat. And that scapegoat is poor, poor Camilla, who knows nothing—and

I mean absolutely *nothing*—about any of this! The Altklugs have created this situation, not the lamebren; so please stop blaming the lamebren for every mishap that happens in the Super-Dome.'

Mirella accepted Crispin's outburst without intervention. She stared at him without the slightest variation on her calm face.

'Are you done? If you are, you two may leave. I have nothing more to add.' She turned her back on them.

21

'How dare they accuse Camilla of something so horrible! How can they even *think* that a lamebirl is capable of such a horrendous act? Camilla is the sweetest, most innocent lamebirl ever!' Zinnia could barely control the steam of fury inside her. She kicked the well-maintained lawn and dug a hole in it.

'Scapegoat, they need a scapegoat,' Crispin repeated grimly. 'They want to put the blame on someone and the lamebren are the easiest targets. No one to defend them, easy to dominate...'

'But they can't get away with this, can they?' Zinnia looked at Crispin anxiously.

'They can get away with anything.' Crispin thrust his hand angrily though his tousled hair, there was a wild look in his eyes. 'Zinnia what should we do?'

For the first time, Zinnia realised that Crispin was afraid...afraid of what Governor Tisya was capable of, afraid for Camilla. She quickly took his hand and pressed it in assurance.

'We'll fight for her...we'll tell everyone what the truth is, we'll go to court if need be...but we won't let anything happen to Camilla. If they drag her into Commander Burdock's murder, they will have to prove it with evidence. It can't be that simple!'

'It can be simple. They can just pick her up and send her to the Dissolution Crypt, the way they did to Iris.' Crispin's voice was expressionless.

Zinnia was silent. Crispin was right. The Altklugs could do anything...*anything at all*.

'Lamebren, please report immediately in the hall!' The announcement was crisp and sounded urgent.

Breakfast had just been over and they were heading for Bamian's class. Zinnia and Crispin glanced at each other. It had to be something to do with Commander Burdock's death, Zinnia thought with a sudden acceleration of her heartbeats. She had agonised all night over it, aware that she couldn't do much other than worry. She awoke several times in the night to ensure that Camilla was still in bed and had not been smuggled away in the middle of the night like Iris. But the realisation that Camilla had not been approached by the Altklugs had aggravated her imagination and worry more than alleviating it. If Governor Tisya was silent, there had to be a deeper motive behind it and the early morning summons told her that her assessment of the situation was almost right.

They filed into the mirrored hall and took their positions in the two queues. Colonel Kripton strode out of his office with a thermionic paper in his hand. He looked as grim as ever. Losing Commander Burdock must have been a big shock to all the Altklugs, Zinnia thought. The Demarcator of his office slid open again and to Zinnia's great astonishment, Commander Hertz and Governor Tisya swept forward. Hobo followed at a respectable distance, but remained right behind the Governor. The lamebren stared at the latter. Governor Tisya had never visited the Ret Cubicle before. This had to be of the utmost importance. Poised and regal, she looked every bit the head of the Super-Dome, as her dark gaze swept over the lamebren in a haughty manner.

'I shall read out a list of numbers. Please step aside as I do,' Colonel Kripton said.

Zinnia's heart began thumping. Something was happening here—something that shouldn't. A ripple of alarm sparked through her body.

'Numbers G11 to B21, step aside please.'

Except for Zinnia and Lorde all the others moved away from the line. A low rumble of curiosity broke out amongst the lamebren.

'Quiet please!' Commander Hertz thundered and instantly a hushed silence hugged the hall. 'We have realised that certain circumstances beyond the control of the Altklugs have been set into motion—whether it is Commander Burdock's murder or a petition presented by you lamebren. The fact is, whatever the crime or situation, anyone who poses a threat to the peace and harmony of the Super-Dome, whether intentionally or unintentionally, will not be tolerated.'

Another murmur of confusion rose amidst the lamebren. Zinnia's heart pounded erratically.

'Two weeks from now is festival time, when two major festivals of this Super-Dome—Christmas and Diwali—are celebrated together. Immediately after the huge Community tree in the centre of the Square is lit, when the display of firecrackers is over and the gifts and sweetmeats are transferred to the six-month-olds, these lamebren will be executed, which means that they will be sent to the Dissolution Crypt,' the Commander announced.

The hall seemed to spin and Zinnia lost her balance momentarily. All the lamebren to be executed? She wheeled around and gaped at the others in horror. Their faces were pale with shock. The stunned expressions on their faces, as they stared at the Altklugs, sent a spasm of anger through her. Commander Hertz' and Governor Tisya's pleased smiles aggravated the fury inside her.

'Oh, there's one other thing to add,' Governor Tisya spoke up. 'Since its festival time and we do not want to disregard your Constitutional Rights, if you have a last wish, convey it to me through your Supercustodian.'

The emphasis on the word 'constitutional' did not go unnoticed by Zinnia. So this was it, this was the reaction to their petition, that was why Cheska, Maisie and Reed were allowed to return to the Cubicle so promptly, that was why Camilla was being roped into Commander Burdock's murder—not accused directly perhaps because of lack of evidence—but as a ready excuse of potential threat to the Altklugs, for the mass termination. And why were she and Lorde the only lamebren to live while others got the Dissolution Crypt, as a punishment for her audacity? This was the message they were sending to the lamebren across the Super-Dome—speak for your rights and you will be killed! Raise a complaining finger against an Altklug or try to reveal the truth and you will be penalised with the final sentence. This was how a perfect world reacted to a petition—dominant, autocratic and cruel.

Crispin raised a hand. His dimpled chin was jutting out in determination. The other lamebren stared at him aghast.

'Yes B15,' Colonel Kripton said.

'Would terminating us lift the potential threat to peace, from the Super-Dome?'

'Our committee thinks so,' Commander Hertz replied calmly.

'How's that Sir?'

'We don't have time to spell out our policies to you lamebroy.'

Zinnia also raised her hand. 'Harmless lamebren have now become a threat. Either this Ace-world of Altklugs is sliding in standard and supremacy, or the lamebren are growing more important in stature.'

'The Super-Dome sliding in standard!' Governor Tisya expostulated. 'You must be crazy!'

The twins glanced from Zinnia to Crispin, admiration in their eyes. Lorde cowered, trying to be invisible behind the bulky Berk and the tall Reed.

'Then you admit that you cannot control the growing stature of the lamebren, that you are incapable of countering their logic, their thinking. They are not a threat to the Super-Dome, they are threat to your autocracy, they are close to exposing the double standards in this Ace-world where a villain is projected as a hero. You cannot silence these truths with your heart and mind and that is why you are crushing them with your might.'

'Enough!' Commander Hertz's shout echoed off the walls.

His command boomed so loudly that Azalea and Cylia jumped, startled. Cheska moved closer to Camilla. Fear stamped on Berk's face and Reed shuffled his foot, his head lowered. Even Ivy and Maisie trembled.

The three Altklugs stared at the lamebren unblinkingly. Of the same height, with smooth, intelligent faces and eyes that could scour through their thoughts and read them, they appeared like identifiable copies of each other.

'I've heard enough of your nonsense. The order has been passed. No more discussions on this.' With that concluding bark, the three Altklugs marched out of the Cubicle and to the waiting spinner outside. Hobo shuffled after them.

A deathly silence filled the hall. The lamebren were too staggered to speak. Zinnia glanced from one face to another. They were still in their lines, immobile like statues. Tears welled up in her eyes.

'G23, *you* are responsible for what has happened!' Lorde cried out, appearing from his hiding place behind Berk and Reed. 'You thought you were someone great, taking that stupid petition to the Governor. You have led all these lamebren to their deaths, you understand? You will have their blood on your hands!'

Zinnia stared, pain gripping her heart and her throat constricting in shame. The other lamebren glanced up at her, solemn and wordless. Zinnia could read the accusation in their eyes and she felt as if her heart would burst with agony. She whipped around and rushed out of the door, her eyes blinded with tears.

'Zinnia wait...' Crispin called but she refused to stop.

It was as if her legs were caught on fire and her entire body burnt with guilt. For the first time Lorde was right! She was responsible for what was happening...*she* was the one who had gone to Mirella hoping for justice for Camilla, *she* was the one who had initiated the whole petition idea, wanting to change the Altklug world and hoping for a respectable position for the lamebren. Oh how naïve, ignorant and stupid she had been! She had now endangered the lives of her friends and because of her, two weeks from now, everyone would be sent to the Dissolution Crypt. And to top it all, she was sentenced to *live*, so that she could wallow in guilt for as long as the Altklugs deemed it fit. What a terrible fate for all the lamebren! She would never be able to forgive herself... never!

She ran till her legs refused to budge. Then she flopped down on the ground and her entire body racked in misery and despair. Her guilt refused to be swept away in the flood of tears. She had underestimated Governor Tisya. Somehow she had hoped...foolishly...She shook her head again, cursing her own immaturity and inexperience.

Finally, exhausted, she glanced up. She realised that she had automatically come to the Paramour Path, her one place of solace and peace. In her blind misery, she had ended up on the opposite side of the Lake, almost near the Diaphanous Seal. It was as her sobs tapered into hiccups that suddenly, a swift movement in the trees caught her eye. Someone was hiding behind the tree. A flash of white vanished behind another thick, leafy branch.

A little alarmed, Zinnia straightened, brushing away her tears for clearer vision. Was it an Altklug? The next instant, a figure stepped away from the tree and into the late afternoon hazy glow of the sun. Instantly, Zinnia's hand flew to her mouth to stifle a scream!

Walking towards her with slow, deliberate yet graceful steps was a beautiful apparition, with flowing long hair and a pristine white dress—*Iris!*

22

A soft smile played on her lips, as Iris moved towards the young lamebirl. The hazy backlight lent an ethereal quality to her white figure. Zinnia stared awestruck—A ghost! *Iris's ghost!*

'Iris...' she whispered hoarsely, rubbing her misty eyes again.

'Yes, it's me.'

Zinnia almost fainted. She stumbled and fell, but managed to hoist herself up with the help of a rock. Iris ran the last few steps towards her.

'Zinnia! It's me—I didn't mean to frighten you,' she exclaimed, but there was laughter in her voice.

'Iris! I can't believe it—it's really you and you are not dead? You are not *dead!*' Zinnia cried as reality gripped her like a penetrating ray.

She flung herself at the lamebirl unceremoniously and embraced her tightly. Tears gushed down Zinnia's cheeks and she sobbed hard, her head buried in Iris's coarse gown, relief mingled with joy and anguish.

'Hey, it's alright...' Iris hugged the young lamebirl back and stroked her head. 'Don't cry Zinnia...'

'You're alive...I can't tell you what I've been through... I've been so lonely...' Zinnia's voice was muffled and thick with tears.

'I know...I can understand...' Iris's voice was soft and comforting. 'Oh, hello Crispin!'

Zinnia turned to see Crispin. He was gawking at Iris in sheer disbelief. His face was white and he seemed overcome with a strong emotion he could barely control. Within seconds, he had rushed towards them and engulfed Iris in his arms. Zinnia couldn't suppress a fond smile.

Some minutes later, when the three lamebren were more composed, Iris said in a low and urgent voice, 'I can't stay here for long—anyone can spot me. I just came to tell you that Leo wants to meet you,'

'Leo! Are you staying with him? But first tell us what happened! We thought you were sent to the Dissolution Crypt.' Crispin appeared confused.

'I was, but my story can come later. First, let's go meet Leo.'

Crispin nodded and the three of them slipped through the gap in the Diaphanous Seal and entered the Snarl.

Leo was waiting for them on the same spot as last time. Doodle rushed to greet them, barking joyously and Zinnia bent down to pick up the bundle of energy.

'Ah, my dear friends, good to see you again!' Leo beamed and the wrinkles on his face seemed to double. 'Come and sit down. We need to talk.'

Zinnia released Doodle who immediately picked up a twig and began playing with his mother.

'Leo, something terrible has happened,' Zinnia remarked. 'Commander Burdock has been murdered and we have been sentenced to the Dissolution Crypt.'

She and Crispin narrated the happenings of the last couple of days, in quick breathless tones. Leo listened intently, frowning from time to time. Iris stood leaning against a tree, her attention on her two friends.

'Imagine putting the blame on Camilla for Commander Burdock's death!' Zinnia concluded anger flashing in her eyes. 'She didn't do it, you know.'

'Of course she didn't,' Leo said. 'Commander Burdock was murdered on the edge of the Snarl in strange circumstances. No lamebirl or lamebroy has the capacity to pull off such an intricate feat.'

He stared at Zinnia and Crispin, a curious glint in his piercing eyes. Something in the way he spoke, intrigued Zinnia.

'Do you know who killed him?' she asked, carefully.

'Let's just say that I'm glad he's gone,' Leo responded in a guarded tone.

Crispin and Zinnia exchanged quick glances. Leo sounded oddly secretive and Zinnia's mind began travelling long lengths of imagination. *What if...*

'But blaming Camilla for the murder is a clever strategy on the part of Governor Tisya. If they pin his murder on to some of the lamebren, they have a valid reason for terminating the lamebren,' Leo pondered aloud. 'After all, there are some good Altklugs who would wonder why, out of the blue, a bunch of relatively harmless lamebren were terminated a couple of years ahead of their scheduled dates of termination.'

'I believe you are right,' Crispin agreed.

'But it's because of *me* they had to look for this reason in the first place. I have failed my friends Leo, not once but twice! First, I tried to find justice for Camilla and then I had to mess things further with a petition which was barely heard. It is because of *me* that everyone is in this terrible mess,' Zinnia spoke, anguish in her voice.

'That's not true,' Crispin was quick to speak up.

'Crispin is right. Look at the way they treated Iris. Such a cowardly act on their part. They couldn't handle the situation with delicate expertise, so they were compelled to use force. The Altklugs solve every problem with one solution—the Dissolution Crypt. So no point blaming yourself, Zinnia. In fact, you did the right and legal thing. You tried your best and if the lamebren are wise, they will see it.' Leo smiled kindly.

'But what do we do now? We've got to stop this. We've got to save them all!' Zinnia exclaimed, in a frustrated tone.

Leo was reflective for a few minutes. 'It's difficult, I admit, but not impossible. And you have to understand that it is risky. You must also consider the danger factor to your life, Zinnia. You don't have to do anything or be a part of any of this. After all, you are not on the Dissolution Crypt list, so why should you endanger your life?'

'I don't care, Leo, whether I'm on the death list or not. It doesn't matter. What matters is the safety of my friends. I would do anything to save their lives. They are my family and I'd rather die than live in the Altklug Ace-world without my family!' Zinnia declared earnestly.

Leo and Iris exchanged quick looks of tacit understanding. A half smile touched Crispin's lips.

'Brave words, my dear, but then I did not expect anything less from you. Okay, then, I have a plan and before I explain it to you, you need to know how Iris escaped from the Dissolution Crypt.'

Zinnia glanced at Iris, who was listening in a composed manner, as if they weren't talking about her. Did she wonder at all about Preceptor Sven and what had happened to him? She had loved him dearly, surely she must think of him a lot? Should they inform her that the love of her life was being tortured by the Altklugs? For a moment indecision hovered in Zinnia's mind. No, it wouldn't do. Iris seemed to have adjusted to her life in the forest. No point digging up past memories and providing fodder for mental unrest.

'It's a rather long story, but I'll be brief. We have someone in the Super-Dome who provides us with information from time to time. That evening, we got the news that Iris was going to be picked up from the Ret Cubicle at two in the night and immediately executed. We had to act fast. I don't know if you are aware of how the Dissolution Crypt works. Once the person is strapped to a chair, a K. Sensor supervised system is activated. Everything is auto-programmed. The chair passes through a door and rays are infiltrated into the heart with a machine, killing the person instantly. Then the body is un-strapped and released into the Snarl! Yes, just hurled into a deep pit on the other side of the Diaphanous Seal—but the decay is rapid and odourless because of the special rays.'

'Sounds scary.' Crispin shuddered.

'So we had to act fast and smart. Once the person is strapped to the chair, the Altklugs don't wait because it's an automated system and nothing ever goes wrong. They press the start button and leave. Then thirty seconds later the process begins. It is clean and to give them credit quite painless.'

'So, this is what we did—once Iris was strapped to the chair and the button was pressed, the Altklugs left. Then we had precisely fifteen seconds to release her. I admit it was touch and go, but we did it.'

The lamebren listened keenly to Leo's explanation. The Dissolution Crypt seemed like some evil machine, smooth and ingenious, perfected to the last 't'. Trust the Altklugs to harness death with a resourceful discovery and treat it like a cold mechanical activity instead of a spine-chilling irreversible process. Zinnia shivered, and now, they themselves were this close to witnessing the Dissolution Crypt, if they didn't do something about it real fast.

'I was so frightened! And shocked when these strange people arrived and helped to release me,' Iris cut in. 'And so grateful…'

The old man nodded understandingly. 'We would have got you out of there, even if the automated process had begun,' he completed briefly.

'I'm so glad you could save Iris,' Zinnia remarked.

'Anyway, the long and short of it is that, since then Iris has been staying with me and the dogs. But Crispin and Zinnia—we have been following your progress minutely. While your efforts are laudable, the Altklugs will be Altklugs—mean, cruel and emotionless. So now, we come to our plan. Here's what I want you to do. You will go to your Supercustodian and make a last wish. Say that you want to put up a play for the festival. I'm sure they can't deny you that.'

'A play!' Crispin and Zinnia chorused in surprise.

Zinnia hadn't expected Leo to suggest something so unusual.

'That's right.'

'A play on what exactly?' Crispin enquired.

'On what you know best: The life of the lamebren in the Altklug world. And don't forget to put in guest appearances for Iris, me and Doodle!' Leo grinned. 'There's a film I saw long ago. There are at least fifty remakes of that film over centuries. You'll find stocks of the best films ever made in the world at the Main KlugBiblio. You'll find this film there. See the climax of the film and you'll understand the plan. It's been a while but I've always wondered if such a thing would succeed in real life. I guess, now's the time to find out. You have two weeks to plan the play and to get ready for the grand escape.'

'Grand escape?' Zinnia's eyes lit up.

'Yes, the grand escape after the play. But you'll know what I mean after you see the film.'

'We'll do that as soon as we return to the Cubicle,' Crispin said.

'Good. And it's paramount that you do not breathe a word of this plan to anyone.'

'Yes, we understand perfectly,' Zinnia assured and her face glowed with excitement.

'And you know how to contact me. Whenever you are ready, just play the code I taught you on this drum and I shall know that we are all set. I think it's time for you to leave now. We don't want your absence to be noticed. Good luck and as always, be strong!'

Iris hugged her two friends. 'Don't tell a soul about me, okay? We don't want anyone to know yet that I am alive. And I'll see you soon. Keep heart.'

Zinnia felt light-hearted as they trudged through the Snarl. Meeting Iris again had almost instantly removed the knot of irreparable loss from her heart and Leo had lifted the weight of her burdens. A light, sunny haze seemed to cloak the dense forest. As they made their way through the multi-hued green layers of the wild forest, Doodle accompanied them a short distance. It was surprising how the dreaded forest seemed a little less fearsome now. Instead it had almost begun to take the image of a refuge.

Suddenly the little puppy began to growl. His hackles rose and he rushed ahead into the forest.

'What's up, Doodle? Wait!' Zinnia called.

Crispin and Zinnia ran after the dog, following the sounds of his barking. They had barely gone a little distance when a strange sight met their eyes. Supercustodian Kripton was standing between the trees and Doodle was prancing around his legs, his tail wagging.

'Colonel Kripton!' Zinnia exclaimed.

The Supercustodian stared at the lamebren and at once turned to leave. But Doodle was insistent and whining, pawing him and tail wagging. To Zinnia's great surprise, he dropped to his knees and fondled the puppy behind the ears. Doodle instantly rolled on the ground and raised his paws allowing him to tickle him on the belly. Crispin and Zinnia stared at the activity.

'So, Colonel Kripton, you aren't a complete Altklug, are you?' Zinnia dared.

The Supercustodian did not respond. Instead, he turned and began retracing his steps to the Diaphanous Seal.

'I've suspected it for a while, but now I am certain.' Zinnia persisted, following him.

Colonel Kripton halted in his tracks. He looked directly at Zinnia.

'You're right,' he admitted. 'I do have traits of the lamebren in me. But, the Altklugs don't know it.'

'In that case, you've got to help us!' Zinnia exclaimed.

Colonel Kripton shook his head. 'No, I can't do anything.'

'Oh, but you must! You cannot allow innocent lamebren to die because of the whim of some Altklugs?' Crispin cajoled.

'I'm sorry.' Colonel Kripton turned abruptly and strode away without a backward glance.

Zinnia stared after him, suppressing a feeling of deep frustration.

The Main KlugBiblio carried the same aura of reverence as on their first trip. Zinnia couldn't help remembering how she had seen her Mama later. So much had transpired since their last visit to the KlugBiblio. Then she was learning to fight for their Constitutional Rights. Now, with the death sentence hanging on their heads among other things, she was fighting for their lives.

As Leo had said, the film section housed two whole walls of films dating from time immemorial. The collection was amazing as was the capacity of the Altklugs to garner knowledge in all forms.

Zinnia and Crispin settled in the seats and watched parts of the film. It was a story of a family's escape to freedom after their last show together. When the film ended, Zinnia glanced at Crispin.

'Wow! That was a happy end. Leo must have some memory to remember the film and suggest this plan to us,' Zinnia commented, removing the chip from the padlet.

'It's a good plan if it works,' Crispin conceded.

'For it to work, we need the support of the other lamebren. And after the fiasco of the petition, do you think, they will listen to us?' she asked, anxiety reflecting on her face.

'The petition was not a fiasco, Zinnia,' Crispin explained in a patient tone. 'In fact, it hit the mark so close that the Altklugs awoke out of their superior stupor with a jolt. They realised that you were a threat to them. Remember, the lamebren have never been a threat to their existence. We have always been left to our devices on the whole. But with the petition, they realised that you—we—are a force to reckon with, that we are aware of our rights. That things were changing and this fever of rights and existence could spread among the other Ret Cabanas and Cubicles, so the sooner they eliminate us the better.'

'But if that was the case, I would have been first on the list,' Zinnia reminded.

'By eliminating us, the Altklugs are ensuring that they eliminate the rebellious streak in you,' Crispin pointed out. 'What can a lone, eleven-year-old lamebirl do? How can she ever post a threat to the Altklugs if all her friends are gone?'

Zinnia nodded. 'I guess you are right. But we have to prove them wrong. We have to show them that despite death threats, the lamebren are still a force to reckon with.'

'That's the spirit.' Crispin smiled his approval.

'Now all that remains is passing on this spirit to our bunch of friends. Not a mean task, what say?'

Crispin chuckled in agreement.

All through dinner, Zinnia privately debated whether to involve Lorde in the Secret Society or not. After all they were now planning the 'grand escape' as Leo had called it. Could they trust Lorde? He was mean and spiteful, but he had hit the nail on the head when he had said that they could not sway the Altklugs from their opinions or stance, he knew them well. Perhaps there was a reason why he was always this mean—could it have something to do with his frustration and dread of the Altklugs and the Dissolution Crypt? After all, each of the lamebren could have a unique defence mechanism to cope with the idea of death. Azalea had taken to bed, feeling unwell again. Ivy and Maisie were sticking close, talking in whispers. Berk was silently following Reed—their earlier camaraderie now strained from Reed's side, although he was careful not to reveal it to Berk. Camilla and Cheska were together every minute of the day, but their earlier carefree abandon was missing. Cheska practiced his floflute and Camilla seemed to be writing something on her padlet, Cylia was in her own little world of clothes and stitching. Each one had their own way of dealing with impending death, why not Lorde? If they were all going to escape from the Super-Dome, they couldn't possibly leave Lorde behind. That would be unheard of! They would have to involve Lorde, however mean and unstable he was. But Zinnia was aware that it was the biggest risk the Secret Society would take.

After dinner that night, they all gathered in the Cubicle. It was obvious that the usual underlying streak of excitement at plotting and planning was missing. The lamebren were subdued and avoiding eye contact with each other. Zinnia had told Crispin to bring Lorde along and he sat in a corner, his small eyes flitting from one inmate to the other. Zinnia sensed an instinctive distrust for him, but they didn't have much of a choice.

'Crispin, will you explain why we are having this meeting to-night?' She still felt a little uneasy about the reaction of the lamebren although, except for Lorde, not one of them had pointed an accusatory finger at her.

Crispin nodded, understanding her need to take a backseat. The light in the room was dim and the shadowy faces of the lamebren were solemn and grave. Not a single person appeared eager or enthusiastic. It was as if each one of them had reconciled to the idea of their final fate—the Dissolution Crypt. Outside, the Snow Hour had begun and the snowflakes were falling gently to the ground.

'Two weeks from now we have a date with death,' Crispin began. His voice was low and clear. 'We made a petition to the Governor and you all know what happened to it. They discarded it without a glance at it. Zinnia did do her best, but we have to understand that Altklugs have only one goal in life—eliminate the lamebren, because we are "useless" to them. As we all know that's not true. In the nature of things, in the Universe, nothing is useless. But the Altklugs don't have the time to step back and think about life. They are in a constant race against time...'

Crispin paused. He had managed to garner a glimmer of interest. Ivy had sat up straight. Cylia who was stitching even in the low light had paused in her activity. Cheska was staring at Crispin and Camilla had stopped fidgeting with her curls.

'Coming back to the date with death—we can either accept it calmly or we can put up a fight!'

'You mean a real fight?' Berk asked.

'A real fight yes, but not a physical one.'

'I vote for the first option—go calmly, this is our fate, there is no escaping death now…' Azalea spoke up, her voice weak.

For a moment, everyone stared at her, as if she had spoken in a foreign language. She had actually voiced her opinion without the slightest pretence at heroism. She had also voiced their deepest thought and their reconciled state of mind.

'I don't agree,' Ivy refuted harshly. 'Just because the Altklugs think we have no more right to live, why should we accept their verdict as final?'

'We second that,' the twins added.

'I say we put up a fight,' Reed added. 'I still shudder to imagine what is happening at the new Ret Cabana. Something horrible…the Altklugs are capable of doing anything under the pretext of science and technology. And one way or the other, we will always remain connected to their activities. Not one of us is immune to their actions. If it's the Dissolution Crypt for us today, tomorrow Zinnia and Lorde will face the same fate.'

'Reed is right. I vote for a fight,' Maisie added.

Crispin glanced at Zinnia. A smile lit up his face.

'I am so glad that we all think the same,' he beamed. 'So, all those in favour of this final fight for freedom, please raise your hands.'

Ten pairs of hands shot up. Only Lorde remained in the corner, his hands by his side.

'B22?' Crispin asked.

'Not in favour,' Lorde commented. 'Waste of time. I still have three more years to live, why should I take part in such a foolhardy activity and hasten my trip to the Dissolution Crypt? You lamebren are stupid and are committing the same mistake again. Fight for freedom! You still haven't got it into your thick skulls that there is *no* freedom, either from the Altklugs or from death.'

'In that case, you may kindly leave the room,' Zinnia remarked. She was secretly relieved that he would not be a part of the planning.

'Who wants to stay anyway!' Lorde scoffed. He rose and left the Cubicle, without a backward glance.

Crispin waited till the door closed and then turned to the other lamebren. 'So then it's decided. Zinnia will now explain the plan for our secret mission: The Grand Escape!'

23

'A play?' Colonel Kripton repeated in surprise. 'But such things are now extinct. No one has the time to sit and watch lengthy plays and films. All come in compact capsules for leisure periods. Live shows are a rarity and only entertained for not more than ten to fifteen minutes.'

'Governor Tisya said that we could express our last dying wish. And this is it. We want to put up a short play for the festival,' Crispin remarked. 'Something to remember us by.'

'It's a strange dying wish, but I shall talk to my seniors.' Colonel Kripton shrugged. He glanced at Zinnia who was standing silently beside Crispin. 'And will you also help him put up the play?'

Zinnia nodded. 'Yes, I shall do everything in my power to assist them in fulfilling their last wish,' she replied quietly.

The Supercustodian nodded. 'Wait outside in the hall.'

Crispin and Zinnia exited the office. Neither spoke a word. They knew Colonel Kripton was talking to Commander Hertz and Governor Tisya that very instant. Zinnia closed her eyes and prayed to the Universe. Everything depended on what the Governor said. If permission was granted then their plan could be executed. If not, that would be the end of any chance of escape.

A few minutes later, the Demarcator slid open and the Supercustodian strode out.

'Right, my Superiors were equally surprised that you want to engage in such a frivolous activity minutes before the Dissolution Crypt. But I've managed to convince them. Ten minutes is all you shall get to perform—not a minute more—immediately after the gifts have been distributed. Ten minutes only, is that understood?'

'Thank you!' Crispin and Zinnia exclaimed, delighted.

'As soon as your performance is over, the charabanc would take the lamebren to the Dissolution Crypt.'

'Can we begin preparations at once? We'll need stuff for the play, so can we go to the Dome Piazzar—costumes and other stuff?' Zinnia asked.

'I don't see why not. Bamian has anyway opted out of the teachings till the next batch of lamebren arrives. So you have plenty of free time to prepare for the play.'

Bamian has opted out because there was no point teaching a group of lamebren who was anyway going to be killed, Zinnia thought bitterly. Neither the Exectors, Bamian and Mirella, nor Kripton had intervened or thought it right to object to this mass massacre—Yes, mass massacre was exactly what this was of innocent lamebren! They were all just mute spectators, indifferent to the evils practiced under the name of power. But Zinnia didn't dare voice her thoughts. She gulped them down and sealed her lips. Nothing would make her jeopardise their last chance at freedom.

'Camilla and I will write the play. Cheska, you will compose the music for the play with your floflute, which you and Crispin will record later. Cylia, we'll buy some material and you can make us some nice tops to go with these trousers. Crispin, Reed, Berk and Maisie—you will make a list of things we shall need.'

'Need?'

They were sitting by the lake in the Paramour Path and not a single Altklug was around, but still Zinnia lowered her voice.

'Yes, things we shall need. We are going to escape into the Snarl. Although we know that Leo is there to take care of us, we have to go prepared.'

'That's right,' Crispin agreed. 'Small food items which can last us for a while, a blanket or two, other emergency stuff. We have to remember that we shall quit the high-tech comfortable Altklug Ace-world for good and move to a rather ferocious forest. We have no clue what survival there means, so we must go prepared.'

'I'm frightened,' Azalea said. 'I'd much rather stay here.'

'You would hate to be here without us, even for a day,' Ivy scoffed. 'Buckle up Azalea, we don't have a choice.'

Azalea did not respond. She looked pale and tiny and Zinnia felt sorry for her.

'We'll manage,' she assured her. 'Leo managed for sixty years!'

That seemed to cheer up the frail lamebirl and she smiled. 'I guess you're right.'

'I've been thinking. Why can't we just walk out into the Snarl right now? What will happen?' Maisie asked.

'You will be hunted down and killed on the spot. Don't forget that there are Scanners in the sky which pick up every activity in the Super-Dome. Besides, if one of us disappears the others would instantly be punished. So it will have to be all or none,' Crispin explained.

'But you've gone into the Snarl and nothing happened to you,' Reed pointed out.

'That's because we returned. Had we gone missing, hell would've broken loose.'

'But if the Altklugs don't want us, why can't they just let us go?' Berk wondered.

'It's not just that they don't want us. They want to *eliminate* us forever, so that more will not be born, so that all the super development that they have achieved will not go into regression. They fear that intermingling of the lamebren with the Altklugs would lead to a polluted race, and their efficiency would suffer. If they eliminate all the lamebren, they would ensure that their race would continue pure and unadulterated,' Crispin clarified.

'Which means it's either the "grand escape" or "death",' Zinnia said, her gaze cruising over the reflective faces.

They were all silent for a few moments. Zinnia was aware that their minds were churning with questions and fear seemed to gyrate between emotions of anger and hope.

'I know what I'm going to do,' Cylia said, breaking the tense pause. 'I'll stitch up our three sets of clothes one on top of the other, so that we don't have to carry anything on hand.'

'Splendid idea,' Crispin agreed. 'And you can add secret pockets to the insides, where we can stuff the small items.'

'So you boys make a list and in the afternoon, we'll all go to the Dome Piazzar. Please don't forget to get your Mudra added. We'll need all the money we have,' Zinnia said.

Cheska glanced at Zinnia. 'You are confident that we'll make it to the Snarl , aren't you?'

Zinnia nodded. 'Yes I am. I am also excited and a little worried because if our plan fails, that's the end. But somehow, deep inside I feel that some power in the Universe will look after us. All we have to do is to try to execute this plan with all our heart and soul.'

The others looked at her with hope in their eyes.

'Between the Dissolution Crypt and the Snarl, I choose the Snarl. So let's send this message out to the Universe: I choose to live in the Snarl,' Zinnia emphasised the last words.

'I choose to live in the Snarl.' One by one the lamebren repeated the sentence.

'And every night before you sleep, repeat this affirmation at least once,' the young lamebirl added and the others nodded obediently.

Crispin glanced at Zinnia and smiled.

The last and only time Zinnia had been to the Dome Piazzar, had been with Iris, when they had met Preceptor Sven. Now when Zinnia thought back, she wondered if they had met him by chance or perhaps it had been a premeditated appointment. Perhaps Iris had planned the market trip in the first place, just so that she could meet Sven there? In hindsight, Zinnia realised how naive she had been. She hadn't fathomed the intricate workings of Iris's mind at all.

The lamebren stood in the centre of the huge Square, the surrounding towers rising high into the sky.

'We shall have to split. Ivy and Maisie can take charge of the food items. Crispin and Cheska can get the props for the play. Reed and Berk can buy us some ring-lights, with the longest range and sharpest light. And Camilla, Cylia and I shall see about the clothes. All set everybody?'

'Yes, we'll meet at this central tower in sixty minutes,' Crispin agreed.

They all dispersed in different directions. Zinnia, Camilla and Cylia had to hardly wait for a few minutes, before the internal charabanc glided along and they hopped into it. A few Altklugs were seated in the front and the three lamebirls took the back seats. They passed Store No. 55 where Iris had bought her scarf and Zinnia almost smiled at the memory of the older girl's excitement. What a blessing it was that she could smile at the memory now and not grieve at the thought of Iris.

The clothes store was amazing. The materials were of the softest variety—the ones that breathed the best, the ones that absorbed sweat, the ones that cooled the body and the ones that warmed the body. The variety stretched as per the weather hours, a different choice for each hour. Zinnia's head swan with the options. Finally, Cylia picked an all-purpose variety in yellow and white. They fed the cloth into the machine, wrote the number of metres they needed and pressed the green button. The automated system measured the exact cloth and cut it smooth and straight. Zinnia fed in her padlet number and the Mudra from her account were balanced against the amount. The supervising Altklug kept a sharp eye on them but did not interfere. The lamebren took their parcel and walked out of the shop.

'Wow! I feel as if I have achieved a feat,' Camilla exclaimed.

'It is really a strain on the nerves—the precision, the automation and yet for the Altklugs, life is so much simpler,' Zinnia remarked.

'I enjoyed it all.' Cylia giggled. 'And I'm going to enjoy using up all this material.'

'We'll need a couple of blankets too. You have some Mudra in your accounts, don't you girls?' Zinnia asked.

'I do—I've never used it. Anyway, all the Mudra would go waste if we don't use it now. So, may as well empty the account, what say?' Camilla said.

Sixty minutes later, everyone met at the Central tower, armed with their shopping bags.

'That was kind of fun, wasn't it?' Cheska asked his twin.

'I thoroughly enjoyed it,' Camilla agreed.

'Shopping for the food was a little unnerving,' Ivy remarked. 'The sheer choice is mind-boggling!'

Maisie giggled. 'Finally, we just turned off our thoughts and chose every alternate packet.'

'And we've bought the best ring-lights of the Ret Cubicle,' Berk declared proudly.

'That's right. A bit expensive but well worth the money,' Reed supplied.

'So then, we are now all set. We return to the Cubicle and begin work on the play immediately,' Crispin announced.

'Yay!' The twins grinned, showing their crooked teeth and a general wave of excitement and anticipation passed through each one of them.

The lamebren threw themselves into the preparations of the drama. Zinnia and Camilla wrote and rewrote the script. Cheska practiced several tunes for the background score. When Camilla gave him the song, he tried to compose a nice catchy number. Crispin and he tried to record the tracks on a chip. The timing had to be perfect. Cylia and Azalea stitched hard, making deep, stretchable pockets that could hide small articles, like pocket lights. Zinnia realised that Cylia was a miracle with her needle; she could convert a harmless-looking piece of cloth into something amazing. Reed, Ivy, Maisie and Berk collected and organised the props for the play. They slit open the blankets and filled them out with more clothes and another blanket. But they were careful not to overload or make it bulky. Cylia then stitched it up again and it looked as good as new.

The lamebren began rehearsals with Zinnia directing the play. Their excitement was laced with anxiety at first, but gradually as they began to get engrossed in the performance, their nervous energy was converted into positive activity. The play had diverted their attention from the impending death appointment, and for some precious hours during the day, they almost forgot the goal behind the performance. Even Azalea seemed to be roused from her pessimistic frame of mind to actually display some enthusiasm. She seemed weaker than ever and Zinnia was careful to keep her away from any stressful conversation.

Not for long however. A momentary lapse and reality came rushing back to them. Zinnia did her best to keep those moments at bay. She prodded them into thinking, charged them with affirmative thoughts and filled them with funny, joyful emotions. She was grateful for the play—it served perfectly in alleviating the pain and grief that inevitably accompanied the countdown to their death. Or countdown to *freedom*—whatever transpired.

Crispin noticed that a couple of Humanoids were appointed at the Ret Cubicle and warned his friends. Under Bosco's instructions they seemed to be patrolling the Cubicle at odd hours. Lorde kept a safe distance from all of them, but his hawk-like mean eyes missed nothing. His presence made Zinnia nervous, even more than the Humanoids.

With a week left to go for the festival, Zinnia and Crispin slipped into the Snarl. The clearing where they usually met Leo was deserted. Crispin picked up the stick and played the rhythm code that Leo had taught them. Dhun, dhun, dhun-dhuna-dhun—the sound of the drum reverberated through the trees, lifting with the wind like an echo deep into the forest. Crispin and Zinnia waited for a few minutes then repeated the code. Fifteen minutes later, Doodle came prancing up to them, woofing happily. Leo appeared in the clearing.

'Hello there!' the old man greeted cheerfully.

'Wow, this actually works,' Crispin said, amazed.

'What did you think, young boy? Communicating non-verbally and with whatever tools available—that is the real meaning of survival,' Leo remarked.

'Right Sir,' the lamebroy accepted, with respect in his voice.

'So are you all set? How are the children holding up?' Leo asked.

'Better than we thought,' Crispin replied. 'The play is fun and everyone is involved, so it takes their mind off the real thing.'

'You suggested this play on purpose didn't you?' Zinnia asked with sudden insight. 'So that all of us would be too involved to sit and brood over the death penalty?'

Leo chuckled. 'Sort of…it helped, didn't it?'

'It certainly did. Now we are all geared up for the play and the grand escape.' Crispin grinned.

Leo nodded. 'On our part, we are all set too.'

'You mean you and Iris?'

'We—there are some others involved too,' Leo said briefly. 'But you don't have to know who. The less you know the better, in case something goes wrong. Good luck! And keep up the great work. We'll be there at the appointed time, so fear not. Just believe that you will succeed…'

He embraced the two lamebren, patted them a little awkwardly on the head and smiled warmly at them. 'See you on this side of the world soon.'

There was one thing that Zinnia knew she had to do, before the big day of the festival. One morning, three days before the play, she caught the early morning charabanc. All through the ten minute ride through the skyways, her mind was filled with trepidation. Would she find all of them there? The little lamebren, Peeta, Aerobut…it had been almost a year since she was transferred to the Ret Cubicle. A year was a long time in Altklug years. Would Peeta still be there?

The Ret Cabana looked just the same—square boxes and cold. Hesitantly, she entered the small hall and approached the kitchen. Four little heads were bent in silent concentration over their breakfast. Jinny, Arry, Lily and Juju—their solemn, innocent faces brought on a rush of affection in Zinnia.

'Hello!' she greeted cheerfully.

Their heads shot up and for a moment they stared.

'Zinnia!' Arry cried out in recognition and all at once, four little bodies flung themselves at her and clung to her in joy.

The next few minutes passed with such a criss-cross train of excited questions that it sounded garbled. Zinnia had a hard time understanding and calming down the excited lamebren. She was a good deal taller than them now. She recalled how immature and innocent she had been at the Ret Cabana. So confused and puzzled. So much had changed since then. Here she was, a completely new person, perhaps meeting these little lamebren for the last time.

'Zinnia, you look so pretty now!' Lily admired.

'And your hair's grown long and lovely,' Jinny added.

Zinnia laughed. 'Thank you, sweethearts. Look, I've got some gifts for you…'

She passed them the pic-chips that she had picked up at the Piazzar—little stories which came alive around you and the characters took you along in the story.

'Thank you!' they chorused in delight.

'Oh I love these, thank you.' Juju looked happy.

'But how have you been?' Arry enquired.

'Where do you live now? Can we come visit you?' Lily stared at the older lamebirl.

Zinnia tried to respond to the best of her ability. She didn't want to reveal too much, nor keep them totally in the dark. After all, very soon, it would be their turn to be transferred to the Ret Cubicle. The thought sent a chill down her spine and she shuddered...

'Where's Peeta? I want to meet her,' Zinnia said.

The lamebren flashed quick looks at each other.

'Last month, she said goodbye to us...said that her time had come and that she was not returning to the Ret Cabana. On her last day here, she specially prepared a delicious meal for us and said that she wished she could've met you one final time. We told her that we could call you...but she refused. Said she did not want to disturb you in your new life...but there were tears in her eyes when she left us. After that we never saw her again...' Juju replied.

Never saw her again because she must've been dispatched to the Dissolution Crypt, Zinnia realised with a bitter jolt. Since the life of every single individual hinged on efficiency, was it at all surprising that Peeta had reached the end of her road?

'We miss her...' Lily added. 'The new Cook is not at all nice. She says it's a waste of time feeding us...'

Zinnia stared at the naive faces before her—clueless of what life held for them, isolated in their solitude, unloved and treated like disposable items. A padlet-sized lump rose in her throat and she couldn't speak. *These poor lamebren... Peeta no more...*the thought stabbed her in the heart and a tide of grief overcame her but the tears refused to fall. They had congealed into the Snow Hour by now.

'All lamebren in the hall, at once!' The amplified voice was stern and cold.

Now what? Zinnia wondered. It was the evening before the festival. Tomorrow at 2345 hours they would perform and set the plan of the grand escape into motion. Even the thought made the hairs on her arm rise. If all went well, the day after, at this time in the morning, they would be free birds, with no looming shadow of the Altklugs over their lives.

Zinnia stepped into the hall where the other lamebren had already gathered. The mirrors on the wall, multiplied the lamebren into double and Zinnia was glad that it was just a reflection.

Colonel Kripton strode in, followed by Bosco. He looked grimmer than usual. He was holding a thermionic paper in his hand. For a moment, his intense gaze flicked over their faces.

'I have orders to inform you that the scheduled play has been cancelled. Governor Tisya and Commander Hertz have cancelled the play. As per the old schedule, the lamebren will now be sent to the Dissolution Crypt as soon as the gifts have been distributed,' Colonel Kripton announced, a stony expression on his face. 'Till then you are all forbidden to leave the Cubicle. Disobedience of any kind will not be tolerated and will be treated with the utmost harshness.'

He shot the lamebren a final, undecipherable look and strode back to his Office. Bosco remained standing, his hands on his lips and his legs planted firmly on the ground.

24

Immediately the lamebren broke into shocked exclamations and comments. The confusion, combined with a wave of anger, spilled into the hall. Zinnia was stunned. Everything had depended on the successful culmination of the play and now their last route of escape was inadvertently blocked. What could've happened? Why had the play been cancelled? Their plans were made in utmost secrecy…*Lorde?* Her gaze sailed across the hall in search of the lamebroy. He was standing against the wall, listening quietly to the whispered murmurs. Surprisingly, there was no triumphant gleam in his eyes. He stared at the groups formed in the hall, a look of enigmatic indifference on his face.

They trooped up to the Cubicle and huddled on the beds. The spontaneous outpouring of shock was now subdued, into a thick silence.

'Just like them to cancel the play at the last minute—no explanations, no apologies, just outright cancellation. Why do you think they did it?'Maisie spoke aloud what was up most in everyone's mind.

'I believe Governor Tisya never meant us to perform. She was just having some fun at our expense. It's her wicked sense of humour I think,' Reed figured.

'You could be right. There *is* no way our plans could've been leaked to them, could they?' Zinnia wondered.

'Colonel Kripton would've said so, wouldn't he?'

'The guards have been doubled outside the Cubicle,' Cheska announced gloomily, looking out of the window into the porch.

'More Humanoids?' Crispin asked.

'No, Officers in uniform.'

'They are worried about something…' Ivy suggested. 'Perhaps they have somehow *learned* about our plan for escape?'

'I knew it. It was all a waste of time and energy.' Azalea sighed. 'To be honest, I am relieved. At least the pretence and the farce is over and we can go to the Dissolution Crypt peacefully.'

Zinnia shot Camilla and Maisie a worried glance. Azalea was back in her pessimistic mood and could anyone blame her?

'You were right all along, Azalea, I knew it too,' Berk added. 'It's funny that we really thought we could outwit the great Altklugs and escape from the Super-Dome. We are stupid and pitiable and we are doomed to death after all.'

'Stop it you two!' Crispin exclaimed. 'All is not lost yet.'

'Really? Is there anything left?' Reed couldn't help asking.

'Tomorrow is the festival. Tomorrow night we will be executed. What do you see changing from today to tomorrow?' Ivy asked patiently, a note of annoyance underlying her tone.

'Listen, everyone. I know that now that the play has been cancelled, our only chance of escape seems to have dissolved. But let's not give up hope,' Zinnia said.

'It's easy for you to say—you are not the one being sent to the Dissolution Crypt tomorrow!' Ivy blurted.

Instantaneously, an awkward silence dropped into the room. Zinnia experienced a stab of hurt, but she did not retaliate. The twins glanced at each other, their pink faces pinker. Cylia stopped fiddling with her pony and Berk shot an anxious glance at Reed. Crispin closed his eyes, shook his head and pursed his lips.

'You're right, she isn't going to be sent to the Dissolution Crypt like the rest of us,' Camilla spoke up with a hint of temper. 'Which is why, like Lorde, she should've opted to keep away from the bunch of us and leave us to our fate. But she didn't. She unselfishly put her life on line and insisted on finding a way to save us all. She must be crazy I think, because only a crazy person would waste her time on a bunch of ungrateful lamebren!'

Ivy had the grace to look ashamed. 'I'm sorry…'

'No, don't be…it's alright, really,' Zinnia cut in quickly. 'I understand perfectly what each one of you is going through this moment. It may not be my turn for the Dissolution Crypt just yet, but a big part of me *will* die if all of you have to ultimately leave tomorrow.'

Zinnia spoke with such sincerity and feeling that Camilla hugged her and Cylia followed her example.

'But I firmly believe in Miracles. We must all believe in them…' she said.

Her gaze met Crispin's and he nodded.

'Yes, we should believe in miracles. It's our only hope…'

The lamebren stayed in the Cubicle, talking in low voices. As night fell and Snow Hour began, it became cooler. No one wanted to eat, so they huddled together in the room. The door burst open and Crispin walked in, dragging Lorde after him.

'Here's the culprit! The reason why Governor Tisya cancelled our play!' he announced.

Zinnia stared at Lorde.

'He didn't…'

'Yes he did! I caught him laughing, loud and alone in our room and I knew at once. He squealed to Colonel Kripton about our plans. Tell them yourself, you scoundrel.'

Lorde had lost his usual swaggering confidence. 'I thought if I told them about your idea, I would never be sent to the Dissolution Crypt. So I reported to Colonel Kripton that you have planned to put up some kind of a fight. He wanted to know how you planned to escape and when, but I swear I didn't tell them anything more.'

'That's because you didn't *know* anything more,' Zinnia remarked, her voice thick with sarcasm. 'Seriously, you are worse than I imagined, Lorde.'

The other lamebren stared at the lamebroy with such unconcealed revulsion in their eyes that for the first time Lorde revealed fear. He cowered in a corner in fright, a shock of untidy hair falling over his mean face.

Sleep seemed to have escaped from the thick walls of the Cubicle, replaced by a dark veil of sorrow. Outside, the Officers patrolled around the Super-Dome, snow covering their small footprints in minutes. Even Colonel Kripton did not retire for the night. The snow continued to fall and as Zinnia stared out of the window, she realised with a little start that perhaps this would be the last time she would see the snow from her window. The soft snowflakes—beautiful, white creations of nature which provided the perfect and magical relief to her disturbed mind. The snowflakes, which in her deepest reflections she had associated with the lamebren. If something happened to the lamebren tomorrow, she would never be able to enjoy this image ever again.

'Cheska, why don't you play some songs on your floflute?' Camilla suggested.

'Yes, do play something. It will feel so good...' Azalea agreed.

Zinnia glanced at the lamebirl worriedly. Since the announcement that evening, Azalea seemed to have given up on life entirely. It was as if she was shrinking of her own volition. She seemed frailer than usual and her eyes were lustreless.

Cheska extracted his floflute from his pocket and within seconds, the room echoed with the music from the instrument. The notes were so sweet and enchanting, that the room filled with a soothing balm for the sad, aching hearts. Camilla began singing with the tune and one by one the others joined in. Zinnia wrapped a blanket around Azalea and thrust the window open. A cold, gentle breeze swept into the room and a smattering of snow travelled to the windowsill. Very soon the resonating sounds of the floflute and the accompanying chorus travelled through the open window into Colonel Kripton's room. He shivered as the singing seemed to clutch at his heart.

The night carried the sweet songs and notes far and wide, past closed doors, closed K. Ports and offices and into the homes of the Altklugs. The musical hum throughout the dark night sent ripples of unrest amidst them. This was worse than the mourning of the Siren of Departure. That they could understand and identify with, but they couldn't understand the melodious, touching music of love and life.

At dawn, when the sky was stained with pink and orange, one by one, the lamebren fell asleep out of sheer fatigue. Only Zinnia stayed awake by the window and stared at the glory of nature. The snow had melted leaving the roads wet and clean. But the frequencies of their heartrending songs seemed to linger for a while and were gradually absorbed by the natural ambience of the Super-Dome.

Breakfast was grand and instead of the Server serving it, it was laid out in the form of a buffet on a long table. Titillating aromas lifted from the array of exotic dishes but Zinnia could barely touch anything. Her stomach growled with hunger but the food tasted like dust. *A special goodbye breakfast before they slaughtered the lamebren.*

Would lunch be even bigger and better than this meal? She glanced at the others and they too were fiddling with their food. How could one possibly eat when death was round the corner, looming low and ready to strike? Did they really deserve this trauma? And did the Altklugs really enjoy inflicting this pain or were they so far gone that they did not even feel the pleasure? Zinnia shook her head, perplexed. And she had thought she was beginning to understand the Altklugs...

'Officers still outside,' Crispin reported. 'I wonder what exactly it is that they fear. That a bunch of harmless lamebren would rebel? Threaten them? Or point a weapon at them?'

Zinnia couldn't help smiling. 'I believe that they fear we may appeal to their heart.'

'Unlikely. Heartless people like Altklugs need never fear that,' Cheska added.

They returned to their room and once again settled on their beds. Azalea's hands were cold, so Ivy and Maisie took turns rubbing her palms. Cheska had no wish to play the floflute and he and Camilla sat holding hands. Crispin looked as if he had just cleaned out his room. He hadn't bothered to comb his hair and he sat pinching his dimpled chin. Reed suddenly rose and began pacing the floor. For once, Berk's attention was not on his friend. He kept rubbing his clammy hands against his trousers.

With a heavy heart, Zinnia observed her friends struggling to remain composed. The smell and presence of death seemed to pervade each corner of the room. And it was beginning to touch the brave spirit of her friends.

Waiting seem to be their only chore now. *Waiting for the final call,* Zinnia thought, counting the hours which were only too fast dissolving into minutes and seconds before they hug each other, weep and say goodbye. Then each one would be strapped to the chair and the automation process would begin. A machine ray would stop the heart and the bodies would be disposed off in the pit behind the Diaphanous Seal and within hours the body would vanish without a trace...the lamebren would exist as mere faceless numbers in the padlets, a page of history that no one would be interested in opening. Instead, the Altklugs would be fanatically inclined towards sweeping the remnant memories into oblivion. Zinnia instantly closed her eyes to her own disturbing thoughts.

'Dear Universe as Leo calls you...please help us...this is unfair, all *wrong*! If there are miracles in this world, let there be one now, *please* help us...' she prayed fervently. Her passionate plea seemed to emerge from the bottom of her heart, touched with humility, yearning and desperation.

It was ten minutes later that Bosco came trudging into the room.

'There's a visitor for all of you. Supercustodian has called you downstairs,' he remarked in his gruff voice.

A visitor! Was it Leo? Zinnia wondered in surprise. Would Leo dare to enter the Super-Dome in broad daylight? Wouldn't he be recognised and caught?

But it wasn't Leo. Zinnia was taken aback to see the short figure, his bald head shining with the glow of knowledge. *Preceptor Amadeus!* He turned to them as they trooped into the mirrored hall. His gaze rested on Zinnia and his brilliant, intelligent face broke into a kind smile.

'G23, if I remember right,' he remarked and his voice was soft and gentle.

'Yes, Sir, but I like to call myself Zinnia,' she replied.

'Zinnia is a better name, I agree. I have a bit of news for all of you.'

A spark of hope lit up inside Zinnia. The Preceptor's mild gaze moved around the lamebren, assessing and gauging before returning to the thermionic paper he was holding in his hand.

'Good morning everyone,' he greeted pleasantly. 'Your play got cancelled because the Governor heard that you had a plan to escape your death. That is why security was tightened. No one, absolutely no one can escape death. However, I believe that your last wish should be granted and that is why I have got special orders for you to perform tonight. I had to convince the Governor that you lamebren were incapable and ill-equipped to plan an escape and that she need not worry. She finally agreed and although security has been beefed up, you will be able to perform tonight.'

Zinnia could not believe their luck! She shot a happy glance at Crispin and the twins. Some of the lamebren let out a spontaneous gasp of joy. Preceptor Amadeus turned a stern face on them, but his eyes were twinkling.

'Thank you, Sir!' Zinnia was so relieved and happy that she sounded breathless.

'Thank you, Sir!' the others chorused.

The Preceptor looked directly at Zinnia and the twinkle in his eyes vanished. 'Ten minutes, you understand? You have only ten minutes to fulfil your last wish tonight.'

Then he strode away—a rather stout and jaunty figure with a glistening bald head. But for Zinnia, he was the most compassionate and impressive guardian angel that the Universe had sent.

Back in the Cubicle, the lamebren fell into a frenzy of activity. Everyone wanted to speak at once. Gone was the depression and a new optimism had replaced the negativity. Even Berk was smiling, the permanent anxiety on his face replaced by a touch of hope.

'We have to work fast now,' Zinnia said to the group. 'Ivy, Maisie and Camilla, gather all the props together. Crispin and Reed—we'll need to have a quick rehearsal and time everything perfectly.'

The excitement spiralled through the room, like a physical wave.

'I don't think I shall have the strength to go with you,' Azalea said quietly.

Zinnia turned sharply to the fragile lamebirl. The animated babble suddenly stopped and a thick silence filled the room.

'What do you mean?' Zinnia asked, alarmed.

'I can't, Zinnia. I have no strength left. I shall only be a nuisance and a hindrance to you all. I'll just stay back after the play and...and...go peacefully to the Dissolution Crypt. It is best for me...'

'Nonsense!' Crispin objected fiercely.

'You don't understand. I feel so weak, I can barely stand...'

'You've got to be mentally strong, Azalea. Remember, it's now or never! So just pull yourself together. We *are* going to do it!' Camilla encouraged.

Azalea sighed but she looked pale and thin. Zinnia observed that her straight, chin-length hair looked lacklustre and the dark circles under her eyes were prominent.

'We are not going without you,' she said quietly. 'Some super power has sent us this second chance, so we cannot fail either him or ourselves. So it's up to you Azalea—do you want to use this chance and save all your friends or do you wish to condemn them to death? It's your choice.'

Momentary silence followed this dare. The lamebren paused in their activities and stared at Azalea, awaiting her response. A faint colour brushed her face.

'Alright. I want all my friends to be safe, of course!'

'Yay!' the chorus of approval brought a strained smile to Azalea's lips.

25

'The charabanc has arrived. Lamebren, kindly report immediately to the entrance of the Cubicle.' The announcement which boomed from all corners of the Cubicle was brief.

Zinnia turned to study each one of her friends. They were all dressed for the play, layered with clothes, and articles tucked away into hidden pockets. They would've appeared funny and shapeless if it was not for the expressions on their faces—eager yet guarded, controlled yet apprehensive. She experienced a wave of affection for all of them.

'I want you all to know, that whatever happens tonight, I love you all. If all goes well, we'll be together. We are going to put in our best effort, right everyone?' Her gaze moved from face to face.

'Absolutely right. It's not a do or die situation for us. It's do and *live* situation for us,' Crispin remarked and the others murmured in agreement.

Zinnia quickly hugged each of the lamebren and kissed the lamebirls on the cheeks. Cheska and Camilla were holding hands, looking very identical with their short cropped hair, crooked teeth and similar clothes. Berk hung around Reed, looking rather plump in his triple garments. Reed towered over them all, lanky and baggy. Ivy had her arm over Maisie's shoulder and Cylia supported Azalea who was enveloped in a thick blanket. As they all trooped downstairs to the waiting charabanc, Zinnia threw one last look at the Ret Cubicle. Her home for a year now, it was time to say goodbye.

Lorde hung back, sulking and detached. Not a single lamebirl or lamebroy turned around and said goodbye to him. Not a single person had a thought for him.

The fountain in the shape of the pen looked like a frozen piece of blue ice, as they trudged past it. The hood of the charabanc arched open and they all climbed in and took their seats. The glass doors to the entrance of the Cubicle glinted in the moonlight and Zinnia glanced up at the bedroom window through which she had observed the snowflakes daily. Her lips moved in a silent goodbye to the Cubicle. The Snow Hour had been delayed till after the function, so the lawns were a sparkling green. Bosco climbed in and the charabanc took off, leaving the Ret Cubicle in the past.

The Super-Dome Square was like a natural island in the centre, where the four Water Veins met at a crossroad under the lake. Beautiful, ornate arch-bridges led to the Square from each Quarter of the Super-Dome. Below the Square, the calm waters of the blue-green lake were like a smooth length of a velvet cloth.

The Super-Dome Square was large and crowded as the lamebren descended from the charabanc. Zinnia had never before seen such a wide range of Altklugs assembled on one spot. A muted excitement prevailed like a tangible wave in the atmosphere. An elaborate stage with a huge backdrop stood imposingly at one end of the square. Thick curtains which seemed to bounce-off brilliant shades of light, enveloped the stage. The seating arrangement opposite the stage began with six-month olds and one-year olds, in the front row, to fifteen-year olds in the last row.

Bosco ushered them to the last row. Zinnia stared fascinated at the beautiful Christmas tree which rose gracefully into the sky, from the left side of the stage and was so lavishly decorated that it dazzled the eyes. The branches were aptly laden with gifts and snow clung to the gorgeous green arms. On either side of the seating, the ground was lit with hundreds of lamps, their artificial flames ejecting a sprinkling of colourful twinkling dust, every few seconds.

The lamebren took their places just as Governor Tisya appeared on the stage. On either side of her stood Commander Hertz and Hobo, their eyes cruising the crowds in a sharp and alert manner. The Governor's face was taut and the expression on her face was stilted and wooden. Her gown was so pure white and she looked so much like the statue of Governor Seeya, that Zinnia couldn't take her eyes off the Altklug. *Such a resplendent personality but such little warmth,* she thought. As she stood on the stage, the Altklugs broke into a welcoming applause. The stiff expression curved into a smile, as she raised a hand to silence the applause.

'I would like to wish every kid and Altklug here a very happy festival time. Merry Christmas and Happy Diwali! May your lives be filled with the wealth of knowledge and joy of efficiency.' Her gaze swept over the audience. 'I just have a small announcement to make. Beginning form tomorrow the Time Travel sport will now be permitted to the younger kids as long as they are accompanied by their parents.'

A cheer broke out amongst the one-year olds and Tisya's smiled widened.

'We shall now see the splendid Diwali fireworks display after which the lamebren from the Northern Quarter Red Cubicle will perform a ten-minute play. This is their last wish before they are sent to the Dissolution Crypt.'

Another murmur broke out as Governor Tisya waved to the audience and quit the stage.

Immediately the sky was filled with soundless but magnificent fireworks. They formed patterns and names against the inky darkness of the landscape and the Altklugs read out the names in chorus. But Zinnia and Crispin were not admiring the display. Their eyes were on the Soldiers which were appointed at every exit of the Square. Their slim guns looked ominous and dangerous. A shiver ran down Zinnia's spine. She shouldn't allow herself to dwell on the danger now…after all, danger lurked in every corner, path and heart of the Altklug Ace-world. It was an inevitable routine for existence. These guns were just a blatant physical representation of that ever prevalent peril. So why fear danger now?

'Northern Quarter Lamebren, kindly come up on the stage, to fulfil your last wish,' the announcement interrupted Zinnia's thoughts.

The lamebren rose at once. For a moment, they all held hands in a chain. A silent prayer passed from one physical touch to the other, lodging the power of strength, fortitude and luck into their hearts. Then Crispin nodded and without a word, the lamebren stepped out of their line and walked towards the stage, carrying their props. Some kids sniggered, while other Altklugs turned an arrogant gaze on them. Zinnia caught sight of Mirella and Bamian in a row. Mirella met Zinnia's gaze with a solemn nod.

The lights were dimmed and the play began. Crispin and Cheska operated the recorded chip. Reed took control of the lights while Zinnia took the stage with trepidation. *This was the moment, this was the place, the first step to freedom…*

'Today we bring to you the tale of a lamebirl born into the Ace-world of Altklugs,' the voice-over began as the curtains parted to reveal Zinnia.

Zinnia flung herself into the performance as she enacted a lamebrain, her confusion, her fumbling and mistakes. Humour was woven into the dialogues with a backdrop of songs. The Altklugs watched fascinated as the play unfolded. Ivy, Maisie and Camilla came on stage acting as Altklugs, expressing surprise and disgust as the lamebirl found simple math difficult, when she cried for her mother, and at her desire to sing, laugh and cry.

The Altklugs were completely engrossed when suddenly a woof was heard and Doodle ran on stage. Startled, some six-month-olds shrieked but Zinnia instantly lifted the pup and cuddled it, demonstrating what a playful pup it was and such fun.

Then the stage went dim again and the lamebren moved backstage. In the centre beam of light, an ethereal-looking lamebirl in white made an appearance. She looked so beautiful that the audience gasped. She smiled at the Altklugs as she began singing.

'I watch helplessly as they come and go,
Touching my life with a special glow.
With a hungry mind and a hungry heart;
They enrich my life, as they depart.

I watch as they disappear into a haze
Touching my heart in oh, so many ways.
Teaching me love and the art of giving,
And making me a better being.

I'm not an Altklug, just a lamebirl in the Super-Dome
This isn't my world, nor my home
Soon, I will have to say goodbye,
Without asking how, when and why...'

She looked so sad and the song was so poignant that some of the Altklugs moved restlessly in their seats.

Finally, the lamebirl stared at each one of audience members. Her voice was soft as she said, 'Today, I'm a ghost. And only *I* know what it means to be put to death. Yes, I died some time ago and it hurt, not because I was executed at the will of the Altklugs but because had I lived, I would've lived to be hundred!' Her voice echoed and her white gown swirled around her.

A ghost! Taken aback, a disturbed gasp escaped from the Altklugs. Some of the six-month-olds began to whimper. Commander Hertz frowned. He stared at the beautiful lamebirl on the stage and bent forward and whispered something to Governor Tisya. She inclined her head in an affirmation. In the background, the lamebren continued to sing their song. And then the stage went dark again and the lamebirl disappeared and the strangest creature appeared on stage. He was huge and his face was wrinkled and ugly and he looked frightening in the eerie light.

'It's a monster!' someone screamed.

'Monster, help!'

Sudden commotion broke out amidst the Altklugs. The six-month and one-year olds shrieked and left their seats, running helter-skelter. Their parents ran to catch them and all hell broke loose. The soldiers clutched their guns, ready to spring into action. The lamebren continued to sing their chorus in the background, their sweet voices in unison with the rhythm and undisturbed by the chaos off-stage.

The stage went completely dark for the second time and for some moments, darkness prevailed, obstructing vision. Confusion reigned as the Altklug kids were cajoled back into their seats. It took a while for some semblance of order to return. The song continued in the background, as the voices of the lamebren repeated their chorus.

'Something's wrong,' Governor Tisya remarked suddenly, with a frown. 'Commander Hertz, check at once!'

Commander Hertz obeyed without wasting a second. He hastened backstage and stopped short. Not a single lamebirl or lamebroy was in sight. Neither the ghost in white nor the wrinkled, ugly monster. Only a recorded chip continued to sing merrily.

'Guards! High alert in the Super-Dome. The lamebren have escaped,' Commander Hertz roared into his audiocrone.

Fury clouded his eyes and his brain. How dare they attempt to hoodwink him! As if escaping the Super-Dome, right under the smart noses of the Altklugs was a lamebirl's play. Let him just lay his hands on them, he would instil such fear in their hearts that no lamebirl or lamebroy would ever think of going against an Altklug again. Commander Hertz's eyes flashed with venom and he ground his teeth in fury.

26

'Please lie low till you are told to do so,' the driver spoke on the PA system.

He was wearing a black mask and Zinnia could only spot his eyes and his lips. The lamebren were huddled in the charabanc, lying flat on the clean, smooth floor. Zinnia's heart was still palpitating. Leo had met them backstage, with Doodle in his arms. He had quickly instructed them that an Altklug charabanc was waiting for them, a little distance away from the stage. The lamebren were shocked to meet Iris. The twins had clung to the smiling older lamebirl and Azalaea and Cylia had burst into tears of joy. As soon Iris had made her entry on the stage, Leo had quickly and quietly bundled them on to the waiting vehicle. The name 'Fountain of Life' sparkled flamboyantly across the charabanc. *A message from the Universe?* Zinnia had wondered in muted delight.

'You will be dropped off at a safe spot from where we can enter the Snarl,' he had whispered. 'Just trust the driver.'

'What about you, Iris and Doodle?' Crispin had asked.

'Don't worry about us. We are separating only as a precautionary measure. We'll meet you at the Dissolution Crypt. You just co-operate with the driver. Let's just hope that you can manage to pass across the Super-Dome, before you are found missing. Now go!'

Soundlessly, they had driven out of the Square from a back route. The charabanc had picked up speed once out of the Square but the lamebren were still lying on the floor of the charabanc. Zinnia was worried about Leo, Iris and Doodle. They would be able to escape too, wouldn't they?

'Don't worry, they'll be alright,' Crispin voiced her thoughts. 'They managed to enter the Super-Dome undetected so they must have an escape route planned too. Just concentrate on us right now, okay?'

Zinnia nodded. Crispin was right. They needed to be very alert with their wits around them. The danger was far from over. By now, Governor Tisya must've discovered that the lamebren had vanished. Hell must've broken loose...

'Oh no! Looks like the alert has gone off earlier than we thought. Soldiers have barricaded the road ahead. The red signals under the road are all lit up,' the driver spoke in the PA system. 'Hold on now!'

Zinnia raised herself a bit and peeped out of the window. The street lights illuminated several Officers standing by a barricade ahead on the road, their slim guns in position. She had been right. Apparently the alarm *had* gone off and they *had* been discovered to be missing. Zinnia's heart began to race. Would the driver stop? Because if he did, that would be the end of their plan...

The charabanc lost a little speed and Zinnia frowned. *Don't stop, don't stop.* The other lamebren were tense too and Crispin dragged himself closer to Zinnia to take a look out of the window.

'Lie low all of you. Not a sound!' Crispin whispered to the others.

The driver slowed down the charabanc and for a moment Zinnia thought that the game was over. But the next moment, the charabanc picked up tremendous speed, breaking through the barricades. The lamebren clutched whatever part of the seats they could hold on to as the charabanc literally flew off the skyway. Azalea began to sob softly and Ivy hugged her and whispered encouragement into her ears. The twins held hands tightly as did Reed and Berk. Maisie began muttering a prayer and Cylia closed her eyes tight. All around them flashes of red signals began popping up. Insistent sharp and squeaky alarms screamed from all across the skyways. The entire Super-Dome flashed with red alerts, as the charabanc dodged spinners and blocked streets. Behind them, other vehicles seemed to be catching speed, the distance closing between them.

'We are being chased by officers and soldiers, so I can't take you where I am supposed to. There's only one thing to do. I am going to plunge into the Paramour Lane adjacent to your Cubicle. I'll stop for exactly five seconds. Please get off like lightning. There's a short cut, so head back to the Cubicle via the Forest Door. I've left it open. Hide in the basement, till you hear from me again. Do *not* go into the forest. You will be hunted out and killed within seconds.'

Zinnia listened, stunned. 'Colonel Kripton!' she exclaimed.

'Not now, Zinnia. No time to talk. Just get ready to embark,' Colonel Kripton's tone was urgent.

The lamebren rose, stumbling with the speed of the vehicle and holding on to each other. Their heavy clothes loaded with food and small articles, made movement difficult.

'Okay, get set everyone. Five seconds…' Colonel Kripton repeated.

The next moment, the charabanc jerked to a halt and the door of the charabanc rose like a hood. The lamebren tumbled out, clutching to their props and blankets. Ivy and Maisie supported Azalea between them. The next instant the hood slid into place and the charabanc took a sharp U-turn and vanished into the dark.

A small path seemed to cut between the tall, shadowy trees. Crispin took the lead and the others followed him under the cover of darkness. The path curved and looped around the trees, finally joining the Diaphanous Seal. The Snow Hour had begun and the snowflakes settled on the ground in white sheets, making the ground slippery. The cold was biting and hard. Sharp sounds punctuated the silence of the night, like a string of short sirens and the sounds became alarmingly louder.

Crispin led the way along the shining Diaphanous Seal and the lamebren trooped after him.

'The forest door's open, like he said,' Crispin sounded relieved. 'Remove your shoes all of you and carry them in your hands. We don't want to leave tell-tale footprints.'

Zinnia admired his presence of mind. Just like Crispin to think clearly and practically in a moment of crisis. The black metallic forest door was open and they slipped off their shoes.

Crispin peeped in through the door. The hall appeared empty and dark.

'All clear,' he whispered.

One by one the lamebren slipped into the hall. The silence was eerie as they crossed the mirrored hall, their reflections like shadowy duplicates as they slid down the corridor and headed to the basement. Taking the small flight of stairs, Crispin slid open the basement door and stood back as everyone slipped into the cool, dark interiors. Then he stepped in and shut the basement door softly. Only then did Zinnia expel a slow, easy breath.

'No talking anyone. We have to maintain complete silence,' Crispin cautioned.

It was freezing in the basement as gusts of wind and snow made their way into the gloomy room through a tiny window. Berk slid the window shut and the sound bounced loudly off the walls.

'Shh...!' Ivy put a warning finger to her lips.

Berk looked abashed. Azalea began shivering, so Zinnia tucked a blanket around her to keep her warm. Maisie and Cylia shared the other blanket. Crispin paced the floor. The twins clung to each other and Ivy stood on guard by the door with Reed.

The darkness was oppressive and breathing was laboured. Zinnia inhaled deeply, concentrating on the little snow-reflected light which filtered through the glass window. She stared at it, willing herself to keep calm. This would all be over soon. The red alert would be called off in a while, then they could slip out of the Cubicle. Like Colonel Kripton had said—right now, the forest was sure to be searched by top scanners, for the lamebren. Their only chance of survival was to wait out the emergency...but when would that happen? And what if it didn't? Zinnia could imagine a dead end—how were they ever going to get out of this Cubicle alive? The ambience in the basement was thick in the grip of anxiety and fear.

Suddenly, hurried footsteps approached the Basement and the lamebren sat up. Shouts and commands carried easily though the door. Zinnia's heart beat at breakneck speed. There was someone right outside the door. She held her breath.

'I have checked the entire building, Officer. There's no one around,' a calm voice reported. *Preceptor Amadeus!'* Perhaps you should check all the Paramour Paths. It is easier to hide there.'

'You're right, Preceptor! We shall scout the Paramour Paths at once,' a grating voice agreed. 'Soldiers, head out at once! Comb through every Paramour Path.'

'Wait!' a young voice shouted. 'They are in there—the basement! I saw them!'

Lorde, Zinnia realised, with horror.

'Are you sure lamebroy?' Preceptor Amadeus confirmed. 'Don't waste our precious minutes playing tricks. This isn't the time.'

'No Sir, I saw them,' Lorde insisted.

Oh, the little rat, Zinnia muttered under her breath.

Running feet once more approached the basement door.

'If you will excuse me, Preceptor?'

'Of course! I must've missed the basement...'

The lamebren waited with bated breath, as the basement door slid open. A soldier stepped in and stared at the frightened faces of the huddled group. Zinnia's heart sank. In that second, the young and innocent faces of all the lamebren swam before her eyes. All routes to their grand escape were now cut off for good.

'I've found the lamebren!' the soldier exclaimed.

Within seconds, two more soldiers trooped in. They were of the same height as Zinnia and in the dark of the basement looked like duplicates. Their faces were stony as they thrust the lamebren out of the basement like a batch of dirty dogs. Lorde had parked himself unobtrusively in a corner, but Crispin and the others threw him such looks of loathing that he sunk back further. Preceptor Amadeus carried a look of mild interest on his face.

Governor Tisya was pacing in the hall, her gown trailing behind her. Commander Hertz was perched on the edge of a seat. Colonel Kripton stood a little distance away. One look at their hard, expressionless faces and Zinnia knew, without the shadow of a doubt that the game was over. There was no way they could leave this Ace-world alive now. Colonel Kripton flashed a quick glance at Zinnia and Crispin, then withdrew his gaze to the floor.

Zinnia's hand trembled to her throat and involuntarily touched the chip she wore around her neck. *Her treasure...*

her other hand dipped and felt another chip that she carried in her pocket. For the briefest moment, indecision hovered in her mind and then her hand closed over the chip in the pocket. All routes to escape were blocked... *unless*...she tried to calm her accelerated breathing. *Unless, she took matters in her hand...*

The soldiers pushed the lamebren roughly towards the centre of the hall and Azalea tripped. The twins instantly supported her and glared at the soldiers.

'Hey, be careful. You don't have to handle them like they are made of metal,' Colonel Kripton spoke, his tone angry. 'You better treat the inmates of my Cubicle with dignity. And if you've finished your task, kindly step outside and wait for us.'

The three soldiers passed Commander Hertz questioning looks and he nodded.

'Come on, let me escort you out,' Preceptor Amadeus said cheerfully and led the soldiers into the garden.

'I've had just about enough of these lamebren. I order that they be taken without further delay to the Dissolution Crypt,' Governor Tisya commanded. Her normally cool countenance was ruffled and her face was red with fury.

Colonel Kripton had moved and was standing right next to Zinnia. *It was now or never*, she decided. She pulled out the chip from her pocket. Surreptitiously, she slid it into Colonel Kripton's hand. He glanced at Zinnia startled and she angled towards him with a beseeching look. He nodded briefly. Zinnia inhaled deeply and turned to Governor Tisya.

'Commander Hertz, please take charge,' the Governor retorted.

'With pleasure!' Commander Hertz responded. 'Time to teach these brats a lesson.'

'Please wait. I have something to say,' Zinnia interrupted.

Crispin turned to Zinnia in surprise. Now what was she up to? The other lamebren too gaped at the young lamebirl.

'You utter another syllable and you will be the first to go!' Governor Tisya thundered.

'Enough, lamebirl! You've done quite enough damage already. Don't say another word,' Commander Hertz warned. There was glint of hate in his eyes.

'I didn't want it to come to this.' Zinnia's voice was calm and controlled, almost as if she hadn't heard a word they had spoken. 'But it is now time to reveal a terrible secret.'

Crispin stared at Zinnia. Governor Tisya faltered, a frown dented her forehead. Her eyes collided with Zinnia's, drilling into her head. Commander Hertz expelled a short, sarcastic laugh.

'The lamebirl is up to her stupid tricks again. Nothing is going to work. You will not walk out of this Super-Dome alive and that's an Altklug promise,' the Commander spat out his declaration.

'I'd like to speak to Governor Tisya alone,' Zinnia persisted quietly.

'Come on, take them away, she's just buying time,' Governor Tisya ordered impatiently.

Zinnia signalled to Kripton to insert the chip into the K. Sensor. The big screen in the hall flickered and a heartrending sobbing filled the room. All heads jerked towards the screen, their attention riveted. Governor Tisya and Commander Hertz snapped around to face the projection.

'What the...' Commander Hertz began infuriated... then he paled.

The images of Governor Tisya and Commander Hertz filled the large screen, as the Supremo of the Super-Dome wept, mourning for her sister. The lamebren stared, too bewildered to react. Even Crispin appeared shocked.

Commander Hertz gasped. Governor Tisya went pale and clutched the Commander's hand in a tight grip.

'Stop the chip at once!' Commander Hertz marched to the screen, jabbed at the playback ruthlessly and confiscated the chip.

Governor Tisya collapsed in a chair, staring vacantly at the ground. Gone was her haughty demeanour and arrogance. Gone was the proud tilt of the head. Her shoulders drooped and her face contorted into a frustrated ball of emotions.

'This is fabricated…trick photography…I shall…' the Commander growled angrily.

'This is neither fabricated, nor trick photography Commander,' Zinnia piped in. 'This is the *real* Governor Tisya. Mourning the death of her sister, understanding the pain of loss. This is the real image of the hardcore ruler of the Altklug Ace-world.'

'It was just one moment of weakness,' Governor Tisya hissed.

'One moment of weakness is enough to upset a lifetime of work. Specially in a world where emotions are considered a waste of time and where bonding is considered a hindrance. If such a chip were to go public, can you imagine the reactions of the Altklugs? Imagine their shock when they realise that their leader is an emotional and sensitive human being, capable of loving her sister and mourning her death. And what a shame that would be, wouldn't it? What a letdown for them! How can they ever trust the reigns of this Ace-world, in the hands of an Altklug who can sob her heart out like a lamebirl over the death of a sibling?'

'Stop it!' Commander Hertz pinned her with an enraged look.

'One moment of weakness...just one...' the Governor muttered again, distraught.

'Not *one* moment of weakness, but *two* moments...' Zinnia emphasised, softly.

The Governor glanced up at the lamebirl, a look of candid perplexity crossing her face. Zinnia wished she could remove that look of confusion and instil some comprehension in her. She wished she could show her the contents of the chip that she wore round her neck. She wished she could reveal all. But most importantly, she wished she could instil some compassion for the lamebren and remove that icy clutch over her heart. But she knew that she couldn't. It was up to Governor Tisya to surface the drowning, frozen logic of her hard heart and her Ace-world, all by herself.

With a deep sigh, the lamebirl turned to the Commander.

'For your information, I have several copies inserted into K. Sensors all over the Super-Dome and on the network too in the Main KlugBiblio. It would take you a couple of days to hunt them out and destroy them.'

'You think this stupid game of yours will destroy the Governor? A brave and brilliant Supremo who is the hope of generations of Altkugs?' Commander Hertz scorned.

'No, it may not destroy her but doubts can create rifts and rifts can crumble an empire,' Zinnia retorted softly.

Commander Hertz swallowed hard.

'What do you want?' Governor Tisya's voice was cold.

'You *know* what I want. I want the safety of the lamebren.'

'This is blackmail!' the Governor protested.

'Blackmail? No, *bargain* is the word I would choose. Some time back, I wanted justice for my friend. But you played an unfair game, *denying* justice despite an Altklug indulging in an unforgiving crime. *You* are the one who *blackmailed* us into backing off. Next, I approached you with a petition and you did not even deem it fit to give me an unbiased hearing. Not only that, you concocted evidence of a murder, linking it with the lamebren and used that concoction to decide our termination dates. *That* was worse than blackmail. Now, it's my turn to drive a bargain. I want the safety of the lamebren. This secret will remain a secret if the lamebren are permitted to leave the Cubicle, go wherever they wish to go, without hindrance or violence. You will not hunt them out and you will allow them to live their life in peace,'

Zinnia gazed at the still, bent profile of the Governor. Despite her resplendent gown, she appeared like a lifeless robot. The Commander was silent as he glanced at Tisya. A look of defeat crossed his face. He knew what she would say.

'Governor Tisya?' Zinnia prompted.

Startled, the older Altklug glanced up and for a moment their eyes collided. The Governor's eyes were glazed and uncertain while Zinnia's were moist.

'Let them go,' Governor Tisya whispered. 'But not a word of this must leak out of this room, ever!'

Zinnia expelled a slow breath. Her gaze flew across the hall to Crispin and her friends.

'Thank you...Governor Tisya,' Zinnia said softly. 'Would you like to formally announce the good news to our Supercustodian?'

'Colonel Kripton, please accompany the lamebren to wherever they wish to go. They will depart in peace and will not be followed by the Altklugs,' Commander Hertz remarked, his voice low and sullen.

Colonel Kripton stared at the Commander in disbelief and then at Zinnia. For the first time, a happy smile lit up his entire countenance. Zinnia responded with a matching smile.

The lamebren too looked stunned. A wild look of joy crossed Crispin's face and he could barely control his elation. The twins hugged each other in wonder and Azalea almost fainted with incredulity.

Outside, a golden light was streaking across the sky. The tender rays of dawn were turning the Dome into an orange landscape. The lamebren were quiet and tired as they walked down the Paramour Path. Colonel Kripton led the way, as multiple hues illuminated the path by the lake. The flowers were in full bloom and a smooth breeze created gentle ripples over the turquoise blue water of the lake. As they approached the gap in the Diaphanous Seal, Zinnia hung back and halted.

'So, this is it. Goodbye everyone and good luck!' she said.

Crispin and the twins turned to her in surprise.

'What do you mean?' the twins chorused, confused.

'You aren't coming with us?' Crispin asked, a small frown creasing his forehead.

Zinnia shook her head. 'I can't. My task isn't over yet. In fact, it has just begun. I have to stay back and protect the other lamebren. I have friends from the Ret Cabana whom I consider as my little brothers and sisters.

They will soon be transferred to the Cubicle. I don't want any one of them to face the same fate as we were going to face.'

'Oh no!' Azalea wailed. 'You can't...you mustn't...'

'How will we manage without you?' Cylia asked in a wondering tone.

'It's a new life, a tough life—we need you to be with us,' Ivy agreed quietly.

'I *shall* be with you, in spirit. You have each other, so you don't have to worry. Besides, life in the forest, how much ever difficult, would still be a pleasure, because *you* will be *free*. Camilla can write to her heart's content and Cheska can play his floflute for the birds. Cylia can stitch baskets out of the leaves and Berk and Reed can collect fruits. Yes, life will be difficult but oh, so much better than in the Altklug Ace-world. It will be yours to do as you please.'

The lamebren gaped at her, a mixture of awe, unease and comprehension on their faces. Crispin's eyes rested on Zinnia's flushed face and long, wind-blown hair and a half-smile of understanding touched his lips.

'And Iris and Crispin will be there to help you and guide you. And most importantly, Leo will teach you how to stay healthy, grow old and lead a normal life. He will teach you to be happy.'

'And what about you?' Cheska asked, his tone a little challenging.

'I shall visit, of course,' Zinnia replied. 'And learn how to live a normal life from all of you. But as of now, I must return to the Altklug Ace-world.'

Zinnia's eyes met Crispin's gaze over the heads of the lamebren. She read the question in his eyes.

'If you've made up your mind to stay back, I shall do the same,' he remarked calmly.

'You will?' Zinnia asked, with a sudden spark of hope. The idea of living all alone at the Ret Cubicle with only the mean and treacherous Lorde for company was daunting. Then realisation jabbed her logic. 'But you can't, Crispin. You have a termination date on you. Governor Tisya would not permit you to stay on at the Super-Dome.'

'I don't care about the termination date. I can't allow you to stay all alone in that weird Ace-world.'

'She won't be alone. I'll be there with her,' Colonel Kripton spoke for the first time.

Crispin glanced from the Altklug to Zinnia, a trifle hesitantly.

'You go on with the others, Crispin. We'll all be in touch, so don't worry,' Colonel Kripton assured.

Crispin nodded. A warm smile defined the dimple in his chin. 'Okay, but I'll be around,' he said.

'I know,' Zinnia said simply.

She ruffled up Camilla and Cheska's hair and planted a firm kiss on Azalea's cheek. She hugged Ivy and Maisie and shook hands with Reed and Berk.

'Thank you, Zinnia,' Camilla remarked. Tears glinted in her eyes.

'Take care, all of you. We'll meet again…' Zinnia said and her voice choked a little.

'Goodbye, Zinnia!' the others chorused.

'I'll be back soon,' Crispin promised.

Zinnia watched as Crispin led the lamebren through the gap in the Diaphanous Seal. They trudged into the dark depths of the forest, where orange rays of the sun struggled to slip through the tangled branches. The twins turned around and waved once, just before the trees swallowed them within the dense foliage. A melancholy ache throbbed in her heart.

'It hurts deep inside when you are really alone, doesn't it?' she grimaced, her eyes moist with unshed tears.

'But you *aren't* alone. I am with you and so is Crispin…'

Colonel Kripton smiled kindly and Zinnia realised that she had found a new, genuine friend.

The lake shimmered as a cool breeze touched the crystal clear blue-green waters. Soothing music played in the background and mingled with the soft breeze murmuring through the tree tops. Zinnia and Colonel Kripton strolled down the Paramour Path, as luminescent shades of marigold light dispelled the shadows from the trees and enveloped the Ace-world in a resplendent glow.

Epilogue

As I sit here in the forest, trying to pen down my thoughts, I experience a sense of achievement. Cheska is playing his floflute and the notes are weaving magic through the forest. Reed and Berk are swinging on the trees, the natural elasticity of the wild branches springing them high. Maisie and Cylia are playing with Doodle, who is now growing tall and strong. Ivy is collecting berries and Camilla is relaxing under the tree, enjoying her dreams for the first time in broad daylight. Azalea is gaining strength, with every passing day the fresh outdoors is doing wonders to her health. Crispin has gone off to explore the snarl, venturing deeper into the forest with every passing day. And Leo is watching over all of us, like a fond, grand, old father. Life is different in the forest—demanding and hectic and certainly not easy, but we're free. We are no more Slaves of the Altklugs and that is what makes it all the more worthwhile.

I may not have been physically present at all moments in Zinnia's struggle for justice and freedom, but I *was* with her in spirit. She does acknowledge that I taught her a lot, but strangely she's the one who changed my life. She taught me to see the world through the eyes of other people. She taught me to be responsible. She taught me that life is love but love is unconditional and not necessarily only Sven…

Zinnia is back at the Super-Dome. She said that we were like the split crystals of a snowflake—split yet connected. Although that can be largely true, we are not equal. Her love is greater than mine, her spirit stronger than mine. And her vision grows bigger not by the day, but by the second and with every emotion. To my great satisfaction, she has Colonel Kripton to share that vision and spirit with her. Because, although she isn't aware of it yet, Zinnia has set out on an epic mission and she will need all the support she can get to conquer the most complex purpose of her life…the Ace-world of the Altklugs.

Altklug Age Vs Normal Age and Pattern of Lifestyle

Altklug Age	Equivalent Normal Age	Life Activity
1 year	6.25 years	Begin education
2 years	12.5 years	Education continues
3 years	18.75 years	Education complete, knowledge of sciences, coding programmes, etc.
4 years	25 years	Courtship, government service, move out of parent's house
5 years	31.25 years	job, marriage, kids
6 years	37.5 years	Productive year
7 years	43.75 years	Move to private service under govt. accepted companies,
8 years	50 years	Work, kids move out
9 years	56.25 years	Work
10 years	62.5 years	Work
11years	68.75 years	Work
12 years	75 years	Retirement from active job, volunteering for the Government in experimentation, teaching, research
13 years	81.25 years	Same as above
14 years	87.5 years	Enjoy retirement
15 years	93.75 years	Natural death
16 years	100 years	Failing natural death are sent to Dissolution Crypts

Acknowledgements

This book is a result of my crazy love for animals, especially dogs. A dog whose one year is equivalent to seven human years. Who lives in a world where some people think that they own the world and who consider street dogs a hindrance. In a world where co-existence should be a norm for peace and harmony, but where people use all their intelligence to abuse, harm or kill man's best friend. This story is completely inspired by this relationship between such people and dogs.

I have often wondered—what if we were treated the way dogs are treated, in some world where some super beings felt that we were a nuisance and that they deserved to live more than we did? What would happen then? Well, what happened was the *Revolt of the Lamebren*—the first book in *The Super Dome Chronicles*. And I am indebted to each and every dog who has entered my life and touched my soul and core in myriad ways.

Most important are my daughters Tuggy, Sheena, and Miku; my son Brownie, and my grandchildren Lakhan and Funtoosh who made my life meaningful and taught me unconditional love and acceptance. Others, also beloved, include Kaalu, my two Rajas, Rani, Sandy, Benji, Blue Cross, Chinu, Bruno, Julie, Reshma and many more…I am filled with gratitude for each one of them, forever…

A book like the *Revolt of the Lamebren* can only be conceived with a lot of help from experts on the future. And for me this expert was the internet. I am grateful for all the resources that I gathered from umpteen articles and essays and sites which I cannot individually mention here.

I would like to offer a deep-felt thank you to my sister Leena for ironing out the manuscript and being the perfect editor that she always is and also for being an important part of my writing journey.

Thanks to Bipinchandra Chaugule, my husband, for his technological and futuristic inputs in making the premise of the novel authentic.

A very hearty thank you to my agent and friend Suhail Mathur and The Book Bakers for believing in this book and finding the perfect publisher for it.

A huge thank you to Dipankar Mukherjee and Readomania for publishing the book. And thanks to Indrani Ganguly, Rima Kar Ghosh and the entire hardworking team for all the love they have showered on this very special effort of mine.

Heartfelt thanks to my family—sisters Purnima and Sonia—and specially my mother Shobha, for her immense faith in this book and her continued encouragement since its idea stage. Love you all...

An earnest thank you to all my readers...without you I wouldn't have existed as a writer...Thank you for your support, for reading my novels, for your feedback and for continued your encouragement.

Finally, tremendous gratitude to the Universe and God for choosing me as a channel for the relentless flow of ideas and imagination...and for the joyous experience of creation.

MANJIRI PRABHU
2018

About the Author

Dr. Manjiri Prabhu holds a doctorate in Communication Science and is an independent filmmaker for television, a writer/novelist in English and also the Founder/Director of a Literary Festival. She has directed over 200 children's TV programmes, more than 50 short fiction and travel films and has authored 11 books. Her unpublished psychological thriller novel was adapted into a Hindi feature film by NFDC, titled *Kuchh Dil Ne Kaha*. Her thesis, converted into a book, titled *Roles: Reel and Real*, has become a rare reference book for students of Hindi cinema. Prabhu has been acknowledged as a pioneer in India among women writers of mystery fiction, and she has a diverse global fan following. She is also the first female mystery author to be published outside India and has been labelled as the 'Desi Agatha Christie'. And much recently, Prabhu has been acknowledged to be a 'match for Dan Brown' by Dr. Shashi Tharoor. She has been invited to reputed International Literature Festivals like the Agatha Christie Festival, UK and International Women Fiction Writers, Matera, Italy. One of her novels, *The Cosmic Clues*, was selected as a 'Killer Book' by Independent Mystery Booksellers of America and another, *The Astral Alibi*, was honoured as a 'Notable Book' in the Kiriyama Prize. Her books have been published by varied reputed publishers like Penguin, Bloomsbury, Random House USA, Jaico Books, Rupa Publications and Times Group Books. As the Founder/Director of Pune International Literary Festival, Prabhu has brought Pune city on the international map of Literature and Arts festivals. She believes that literature heals and is a prerequisite to a peaceful society.

She has been awarded with the 'Inspirational Women of Maharashtra—Excellence in the Field of Writing' (2017) and 'Most Admired Leader of Maharashtra' by ERTC Global Herald (2017). Prabhu was also awarded the Rex Karmaveer Gold Medal Award (2016) instituted by iCONGO and the UN.

She is also an animal welfare activist promoting caring and adoption of street dogs.

More details on her can be found at: www.manjiriprabhu.com

About the Author